Murder
in Starry Cove

A Poppy Lewis Mystery

Book 1

Lucinda Harrison

Murder in Starry Cove

Copyright © 2021 by Lucinda Harrison

ISBN: 978-1-7367596-0-8

*This book is dedicated with love to my
mother, Elizabeth*

One

THAT, I THOUGHT, *is a very purple house*. I slumped, exhausted, in the seat of my car on the gravel driveway that ran along the side of the property and stared up at the two-story spectacle. The Queen Anne Victorian loomed like a giant plum shining in the midmorning light. I'd seen pictures, of course, but they didn't tell the complete story. This was a beast, a stately monster, all scrollwork and sunbursts.

An intricately carved porch wrapped around the front half of the first floor, and soft pink and green gingerbread motifs filled every fussy corner. A trail of violet clematis grew along the porch railing, and another grew wild and unkempt along a quaint arched trellis that adorned the entry walkway from the street. The house rested near the edge of a cliff overlooking the vast Pacific Ocean, and with the car windows down, I heard waves crashing on the rocks far below. The horizon was sea and clouds as far as the eye could see. If the view from the driveway was this spectacular, the view from the house must be magnificent.

The ocean bordered the back of the property, but the front faced a quaint roundabout. The main roundabout. The *only* roundabout in the small coastal village of Starry Cove.

I grabbed my coffee from the cup holder and emerged into the cool coastal air from the warmth of my Prius, which served me well on my long drive from Past Life, U.S.A. to this new adventure. Wisps of black hair escaped from my ponytail, knotted and messy from hours of driving with the windows down. My pink coveralls sported numerous wrinkles and creases from so long in the car.

I had taken a leap of faith, moving up here from the city to this strange house in a strange town I didn't know with people whom I probably shared nothing in common. Stepping away from my old life—away from my ex-husband, away from the hotel business we'd grown together—was terrifying. I was thirty-six years old and starting new. It was madness. *But it's the right time*, I thought, taking a deep breath. *You can do this*.

As I set my coffee mug on the porch and grabbed a single box from the car, a stout little woman rushed up the walkway in a flutter of short curls—dyed blonde to hide the gray, I noticed. Her mouth flashed an extravagance of red lipstick.

"I wanted to be the first to greet our new resident, so I came right over when I saw you drive up," the woman said. Her appearance surprised me since I hadn't noticed anyone lingering nearby when I parked and, despite the long drive, it was still fairly early in the day. Definitely too early for red lipstick.

"Arthur didn't mention any children, though," the woman said, eyes gauging me as though I may be an imposter, a fraud who'd gone to all the trouble of packing up and driving to a small town hoping to find an abandoned house I could just move into with no one noticing.

"He didn't have children. I'm his niece, Poppy Lewis. Nice to meet you."

"Pardon my manners, I'm Kelly Newman. But you can call me Lovie. Everyone else does." She smiled and offered her hand, but her gaze was on the house.

"Pleased to meet you, Lovie."

"Nice of Arthur to leave you his house. Big thing, very old." She dragged out the last word as though I hadn't noticed the house was built long before either of us was born. "I don't believe you've visited much."

Arthur was my uncle, but I hardly knew him. Lovie must have noticed she'd hit an awkward chord because she quickly added, "Well, I mean I haven't ever seen you in town."

"We weren't close, but my sister and I were his only remaining family."

"Were you now…" Lovie leaned in closer. "Just the two of you? Arthur lived here for so long, and I had no idea."

"It was a bit of a shock when I heard he'd left the house to me, but the timing couldn't have been better. I've decided to fix it up. Maybe open a B-and-B."

"Are you now…" Lovie trailed off, staring at the house looming behind us. "I can't say our little town has need for that type of business."

"Why's that?"

"Gosh, we're so small. There's not much to Starry

Cove past this roundabout." She gestured toward the street. "Just our little Main Street here, and past that we've got an itty-bitty sandy cove. It's beautiful, don't get me wrong. The cove's got two high bluffs on either side. We even get a few young folk trying to cliff dive every year. But other than that, we get few tourists. Not much to see, I'm afraid."

"Oh. That's too bad, but maybe my bed-and-breakfast will bring them in?"

"Maybe," she said with a plastic smile.

"Well, it was nice to meet you," I said, hoping to get moving as I still needed to unpack the rest of the car. "I should really get going—all these boxes." I lifted the heavy box I'd been holding since Lovie appeared, hoping she'd take the hint.

"Oh right, right. I'd help you, but my back is not what it used to be." She clutched a hand to her back and frowned. "Nice to meet you, Poppy. Hope to see you down at Shelby's Diner soon. You can meet almost everyone there any time of day."

"Thank you." I turned away and carried the box up the broad steps to the porch. At the top I turned back, but Lovie had already disappeared down the path and onto the street where I could no longer see her.

The enormous front door in the same pink accent color used elsewhere on the house towered in front of me. Two full-length sidelights framed the door and a stained-glass transom window in an elaborate petal pattern sat at its crown, allowing a fragment of colorful light to filter into the foyer as I entered and shut the door behind me. I found a light switch not far off above a narrow and dusty entry table, but when I flicked it up, no lights came on. I tried a few times—nothing. Maybe a bulb was out. I tried the next room, which I thought must be the kitchen, but no light flickered on when I toggled the switch in there either. I tried the gas stove—no gas either. I'd done my preparation and expected the electricity and gas to be on by the time I arrived. I tugged my phone from my back pocket and dialed the number for the handyman. After many unanswered rings, I hung up. I'd try again later. For now, I needed to finish unpacking the car.

After spending almost an hour unloading boxes, I'd finally emptied the car and at least stowed everything inside the house, albeit in a haphazard pile in the foyer. My stomach rumbled a long low growl, which was code for food-now-or-else, so I strolled down Main Street to find lunch. I passed the usual village retailers meant for the community and the quaint shops tailored to the day-trippers who may have lost their way and accidentally passed through the town on their way to and from the public beach a few miles up the coastal highway. Shelby's Diner occupied one of these establishments, past the barbershop and the bakery. A small-town diner serving small-town diner food. *Perfect*, I thought, and strode in.

A bell above the door jingled as I walked in, and the cacophony of indistinct chatter came to an abrupt halt. A sea of faces turned my way, and I instantly regretted not wrangling the fly-aways in my hair at least a little before venturing out.

"You must be Arthur's niece, Poppy." An elderly gentleman with wispy white hair and a twinkle in his blue eyes turned from the closest counter service swivel chair and held out a knobby hand. "Fixin' up the old place, I hear. Going to open a bed-and-breakfast."

"I see word travels fast." My eyes searched that sea of faces for Lovie as I shook his hand.

"Walter Dogger. I do cars. Or, I used to before I retired a few years back after the dealership closed down. Still love cars. What kind of car have you got?"

"Um," I stumbled. An odd question to start off with. "I have a Prius."

He nodded. "One of those fancy hybrid cars. I used to sell them, too. Very popular." His white whiskers twitched along with each word. "You here for the food? Best in the county here at Shelby's."

"I stopped in for some lunch. The electricity and gas line aren't turned on at the house. I planned ahead to have someone get them turned on, but looks like he didn't show. I don't really have any food to cook there anyway, so it's takeout for me."

"Shouldn't be too hard to get someone out there to get it straightened out. Most folks around here would jump at the chance to work on that old house, no doubt." His eyes met mine, knowingly, and a faint smile peeked out beneath his mustache before another older gentleman swooped in from behind.

"Poppy, did you say it was? Nice to meet you," he said, holding out an even knobbier hand. "I see you've met Walter. I'm his older and much wiser brother, Vernon."

"Yeah, but I'm better looking," Walter said, winking at me.

"Old Dogs of Starry Cove. Maybe you've heard of us?" Vernon asked.

"Sorry, no."

"No matter. They call us that because they say we

run in a pack, ever since we were young. Just don't let this one give you any trouble or he'll answer to me." He waved a hand at Walter, a crooked grin spread across his face. "I own the Treasures of the Coast salvage shop just up the Coastal Road."

"Junk yard."

"Hush, Walter." Vernon turned back to me. "It's a cornucopia of gently used and unique treasures, ripe for the picking. You might find something you need if you're going to spruce up that old house. Arthur was a good friend to all of us, and we're just happy to see his legacy continue."

"Thank you, I—"

A loud thwack startled them as a plump, rosy-cheeked woman swiveled through the kitchen doors. Her hair rose in a towering silver beehive, and a scattering of hot pink barrettes, like little bees, kept the hive in place. When she noticed me at the counter, she hustled over in a tizzy.

"Step back, Vernon, you old dog. Give her some room," she snapped. "Hi dearie, I'm Shelby Shepard. You must be Poppy."

"I suppose everyone knows who I am already."

"Don't mind us. We're harmless. Lovie's just shared that you'd finally arrived, and well, we're tickled pink to greet the newest resident of Starry Cove. You know Arthur was a regular here in my diner. We miss him dearly, don't we boys?"

Walter and Vernon both nodded.

"I'm really just here to restore the house. I haven't decided if I'm staying in town permanently." I tried to keep my voice low, but the diner was dead silent, all

7

interest hung conspicuously on my every word.

"Restoration is expensive business, especially with that old house," said Vernon. "I hope you've got some good people lined up to do the work. I can help you with that if you need."

"Thanks, but I plan to find a local company to take on the work. I have money saved up from my mom's estate and from Arthur's, so I'm ready to go full steam."

"Sounds like you have a good head on your shoulders."

"Sure does," said Shelby. "Now, what can I get for you, dearie?"

"I'll have a burger, small fries, and a very, very large coffee." Everyone in the diner continued to watch—it was like being the new girl at school as all the other classmates stared, sizing you up as a potential friend or foe. A nice quiet place to eat alone was all I wanted. "To go, please," I added.

***

I slouched on the front steps of the house, enjoying the breeze after inhaling my lunch. Just a few fries remained. The mist felt gritty on my face and smelled like seaweed, or whatever that salty smell was when you knew you were close to the ocean. I rested my eyes and sipped on my coffee, enjoying the silence. All the unpacking and the whirlwind meet-and-greets of the morning left me exhausted, and a quick rest and refuel was just what I needed.

A rustling noise caught my attention as a tall figure sauntered up the walkway like a model on the runways of Paris. Except this model wore a mail carrier's uniform.

Well, mostly a mail carrier's uniform. The gap between where her rainbow socks ended and her regulation uniform shorts started revealed a set of gangly mocha legs. Her brown curly hair bobbed in time to her step and her mailbag, perched on her hip, bounced in rhythm.

"Good afternoon," I said as the young woman approached.

An enormous toothy smile lit up her face. "Hello there," she replied, a few loose letters clutched in her hands. "I'm Harper. I do the mail, as you can see." She stopped to pose in her uniform then twirled in a circle on her toes. "Pleased to meet you."

"Poppy Lewis. But you probably know that already."

"I suppose I do," she said, smiling. "But not because Lovie Newman's already shared your life story with half the town. I have some letters for you."

This took me by surprise. I wiped my salty, greasy hands on my overalls before taking the letters from Harper. "I didn't expect mail here so soon."

"Looks official. I see you've made it to Shelby's already. That must have been fun."

"Yes, I've run the gauntlet of nosy residents."

Harper replied, "Oh don't worry, there'll be many more before you're granted legitimate residency in Starry Cove. We're mostly harmless, though. And only some of us bite."

I chuckled. "You seem to have your finger on the pulse of this town, Harper."

She shrugged. "Hard not to when I'm in their business every day." She looked up at the house and added, "It's a relief knowing someone will take care of this old place. I've lived in town my whole life and this house has always been such a wonderful memory. I'd hate to see it rundown. Or worse, torn down."

"Did you know my uncle?"

"Arthur? I sure did. He'd always greet me the same way. 'Good day to you, Miss Harper,'" she said in a low, rough tenor. "I was always 'Miss Harper,' even as a kid, but he greeted everyone that way. He ran the pharmacy in town, so everyone knew him."

"I didn't know him at all. We lived so far apart most of my life. I was surprised to learn that he'd left the property to me."

"Were you disappointed?"

"Confused, but excited now. The more I think about it, the more ideas I have about making this place really shine. I have plans to turn it into a bed-and-breakfast."

"That's what Lovie said, although her voice was much more doom and gloom." Harper rolled her eyes. "Like your beautiful B-and-B is going to turn the town into a slum or something."

"I'm still working out the details. First, I need to get my electricity and gas turned on. It was supposed to be on when I arrived, but I guess Mr. Teach didn't make it."

"Bobby Teach?"

"Yeah, that's right. I hired him to have it all turned on by today. I even sent him a key and instructions. That was over two weeks ago, so I'm not sure what may have held him up. I tried calling him, but I got no answer."

"Let me try. He doesn't really like strangers, so if he doesn't recognize your number he probably wouldn't answer right off."

Harper whipped out her phone, which was shaped like a blue cartoon teddy bear, and plopped herself down cross-legged on the step next to me. She searched for Bobby's number in her phone and dialed, but after a moment she put the phone down. "That's weird."

"What happened?"

"He didn't answer. And it didn't go to voicemail either, which is *super* weird."

Just then, a sturdy little woman waddled up the walk, her short legs moving as fast as she could, looking frantic.

"Harper," the woman gasped, breathless. "Have you seen Deputy Todd?"

"I haven't, Angie. What's wrong?"

The woman wiped a patch of dark honey hair away from her brow, blue eyes wide. "They found..." she gasped. "They found a..." another breath. "They found a body below the bluff. It's Bobby Teach."

Two

THE CROWD MILLED around the flagpole at the center of the roundabout. It was not quite dusk, but they began arriving an hour or so previously. At first it was just Lovie and a few women I hadn't met yet, but soon more and more flocked to the flagpole, like a mass of birds making their short migration, led by an unseen force to this location which, according to Harper, was the unofficial meeting spot for all things important in Starry Cove. Quiet murmurs of "awful" and "can't believe it" floated through the clusters of two-to-three people before they broke away to form new clusters with different people, murmuring the same words of disbelief before doing it all again.

The roundabout was located at the entrance to Starry Cove off the freeway and it served as the intersection of Main Street and Second Street, which split off like spokes on a wheel. The shadow of Arthur's Victorian sat just off the center. I stood alongside Harper, who joined me as the crowd gathered, under the arched trellis that marked the entry to Arthur's property off the roundabout.

"I hate to repeat myself, but it's really awful. I can't believe it," said Harper.

I didn't know what to say. I hadn't known the man, but his sudden death honestly shook me. I groaned a little inside, remembering how I'd complained about my gas and electricity all while this man was already dead. Having lived in a large city, death wasn't new to me, but this town seemed so innocent, and this event clearly shattered that delicate facade.

The crowd suddenly hushed and parted as a tall man in a pale blue polo shirt, jeans, and pristine leather cowboy boots lumbered up the path to the center flagpole. "All right, everyone," the man shouted. "By now I'm sure you've all heard that one of our own was found dead this afternoon." The crowd was silent. "I'm sure you're all curious, but this is a law enforcement matter so we will not be sharing details. Go about your lives. Go on," he urged, shooing the crowd with his hands.

"What do you mean 'law enforcement matter,'" someone shouted. "Are you saying this wasn't an accident?"

"Did someone kill him?" another asked from the middle of crowd. A collective gasp rose all around, faces turned to others in disbelief.

Then I spotted a large-brimmed hat bobbing its way along the parted crowd. I couldn't see who wore it over the heads of those gathered, but it bobbed along at a leisurely pace. Faces turned to follow the hat until it reached the flagpole where a wiry man emerged, wearing what appeared to me to be a deputy's uniform, except it hung loose on his skinny frame like a teenager wearing his father's suit. The man sported a bushy mustache above his lip, and the hat seemed to me too large for his head. It must have added half a foot to his height.

He cleared his throat a few times before addressing the crowd. "It means," the man looked around before continuing, "the circumstances lend themselves to *professional investigation*." He lingered on the last few words, dragging them out, nice and slow. "Now, I'm going to have to ask this unauthorized gathering to disperse before it creates a hazard."

The crowd grumbled but reluctantly gave way and slowly scattered back whence they came. The two men stayed behind, deep in conversation.

"Who are they?" I asked Harper.

"Mayor Jim Thornen. A.K.A. Mayor Thorn-in-my-side. The other one is Deputy Todd Newman, Lovie's husband, and the assigned deputy for Starry Cove. He's the reason no one has any fun around here. Those two are always jockeying for town title of Most Effective Kill-joy."

As people meandered away, I saw the woman Harper had called Angie coming our way.

"Hey, Angie," said Harper, her voice consoling. "How are you doing with all this?"

"You know me, I get upset at the sight of roadkill, poor creatures." She wrung her hands. "But this was *Bobby*. We went to school together." She shook her head in disbelief, tears welling in her eyes, which already looked like they'd been working overtime.

Harper wrapped her arms around Angie, engulfing her with her long limbs. Angie buried her face in Harper's armpit. Angie was short even by conventional standards, while Harper towered at close to six feet, even before considering her abundance of gravity-defying hair.

"I'm so sorry," said Angie, breaking away and extending a hand to me. "I guess we didn't get to meet properly. I'm Angie Owens. I saw you walk by my bakery earlier, but Roy burned my buns and I couldn't get away to say hello. And now this..." Angie's face wilted.

"Nice to meet you, Angie. I'm sorry about Bobby. It seems like he was well liked, judging by the turnout."

"This old town, bah." Angie's face grew stern. "All these people knew him, but not half truly cared a whit. They're just here for the spectacle. And those two..." Angie turned and stared at the mayor and the deputy, still in hushed conversation. "I'm sure they don't want the bad publicity for the town, but I'm also sure they love the authority they get to lord over everyone now."

"So then, business as usual," Harper said.

I studied the two men who seemed to be in an awfully heated discussion. Although I couldn't hear what they were saying, the deputy—Deputy Todd, Harper had called him—gesticulated in curt motions. His lips moved wildly, clearly agitated by something the mayor said.

"Oh crap, I gotta go," said Harper, bringing my attention back to our little group. "I still have to finish my route. Neither rain nor sleet nor the death of poor Bobby Teach shall stay this courier from completing her rounds." And with a flourish, Harper strode off, but turned and said, "I'll catch up with you tomorrow, Poppy. What a dismal welcome we've shown you."

"Bye, Harper," Angie and I said together.

"Gosh." Angie stared back to the big Victorian. "Are you really going to turn this into a bed-and-breakfast? That sounds like so much work."

"I'm up to giving it a try, but right now I've still got some unpacking to do. The big moving truck doesn't come until next week with all my furniture."

"So, it's totally empty? Do you even have a place to sleep?"

"It has my uncle's furniture still, but it's all covered and I wouldn't feel comfortable sleeping on his old bed. I brought an inflatable mattress, but without electricity I can't blow it up, and without my gas turned on I won't have any heat tonight."

"It gets really cold here on the coast, Poppy. You should come stay with me and Roy. We have a guest bedroom that's already made up. It's small but you'll be nice and toasty."

"I couldn't put you out like that."

"It's really no trouble. You just pack what you need before it gets dark and come straight over. We're the green cottage just down that street there." Angie pointed toward the other side of the roundabout, where Second Street spoked off and meandered away from the coast before turning sharply to the left. "Can't miss it."

I was reluctant to accept the offer. After all, I'd just met this woman and, although she seemed nice enough, I really didn't want to intrude during what could be an awkward night of grieving.

"I'll make a big pot of my special occasion Kona coffee—I have decaf too, if that's your thing—and you can tell me all about your plans for the house. Plus," she added, "I could really use the company." That sealed it for me. I could never turn down a cup of coffee, or a new friend.

Three

I'D RETURNED TO the house early the next morning, eager to finish unpacking the last of my boxes. While Roy left to open the bakery, Angie and I shared more coffee over her homemade muffins, and I was pleased that I'd found a friend with such good taste and skill in baking. Angie also shared information of a man in town named Nick who could get the electricity and gas turned on. I'd called him up straight away and he was due to the house at nine o'clock.

Old leaded glass windows stretched from counter height to nearly the top of the twelve-foot ceiling, allowing light to fill the space that Arthur used as a kitchen. Many of these old Victorian mansions were previously renovated to include modern convenience kitchens, and I was sure this kitchen proved quite an upgrade in the 1970s when, based on the styling, Arthur or someone had the renovations done. Now it was an antique of its own with avocado appliances and faded laminate countertops.

Sunlight streamed in across the sill as I set out my

ceramic bird collection. While preparing to leave my old life behind, I had lovingly wrapped each bird in an abundance of bubble wrap and now cursed myself for not thinking about the annoyance of *unpacking* my overcautious packing. The tiny art pieces were an indulgence, something I spent real money on when I had none to spare, knowing better than to opt for art rather than food while making my way through college. But these colorful sculptures with their fat rotund bodies and puckered beaked faces brought a smile to my face. And sometimes, a smile is what you need more than a slice of pizza.

"Hello," came a man's voice in the entryway. "Door was open, so I came in. Hope you don't mind."

I turned from the birds to find a tall man standing in the kitchen doorway. His white cotton shirt clung tightly and betrayed a chiseled form underneath. Messy blonde hair crowned his head, as though he'd just stepped out from the wind, and his eyes were a soft blue, their color enhanced by the light shining through the window. He could be thirty, or maybe forty. I wasn't sure.

"Hello?" he repeated, cocking his head a bit to the side.

"Sorry." I composed myself and wiped my hands on my overalls before extending a hand. "You must be Nick. Thank you for, uh, coming on such short notice. I'm Poppy."

"Nice to meet you, Poppy, and it's no problem at all. Usually, Bobby did these types of jobs, but I suppose it's just me now."

"I'm so sorry. Did you know him well?"

Nick wiped his arm across his brow, swiping his sweaty hair, leaving the front even more disheveled.

"Yeah. We worked together, taking the odd jobs around town or contracting out with the utilities, like for you."

"Well, I appreciate your time. Just, um, call out if you need anything."

"Will do," he replied and headed back out of the house.

Nick was gorgeous and I let my mind wander for a moment before catching myself. *Snap out of it. That's the last thing you need right now.*

I got back to work on unpacking the spoons, forks, knives, a few pans, my super jumbo sixteen-cup coffee pot, and other kitchen paraphernalia I'd be needing in the interim between now and when the moving truck arrived. My favorite apron spilled out of one box, and I unfurled it with a flourish. I spied a hook on the back of the door to the basement and I hung the apron proudly on display before closing the door to give the apron a more prominent spot. After my divorce, I needed an outlet and I fostered grand plans on becoming an accomplished home cook at some point. My ex-husband wasn't one for exotic foods—steak and potatoes only—and now that I'd broken free, I wanted to explore all the cuisines I never got to enjoy while married. I couldn't wait to get the kitchen in working order so I could continue to experiment, which meant the kitchen renovation absolutely had to come first.

I only needed to unpack one more box I'd set on the little table up against the wall before I'd finish with the kitchen. As I reached for it, I found a large ginger tomcat poised on the edge of the table, staring at me with unblinking yellow eyes.

"Well, hello there," I said. The cat blinked once or twice and carried on observing me silently as though sizing me up for some purpose, probably trying to determine if I had any food.

"Sorry buddy, I haven't made it to the store yet. Do you have a name?" I saw no collar, but the cat appeared to be well-fed and cared for. It must have come in through the front door like Nick. I'd left it open and the cool ocean breeze felt nice flowing through the house. It was definitely a big change from where I'd come from—the stench of the city gladly left far behind.

The cat seemed familiar enough with these surroundings, dare I say comfortable. I wasn't aware that Arthur owned a cat, and I guess it could be anyone's. Cats wander, and this one probably has a food dish on every porch in town. He—I thought it was a he—let me scratch him behind the ears, even turned into it to get a better angle. After a moment he put his paw up as if to tell me to stop, then jumped from the table with a little trill and wandered toward the foyer and out the front door. I'd have to ask Harper or Angie about him. My past life didn't accommodate pets—no dogs, no cats, not even a fish—and if it was Arthur's, then it may become my responsibility now, as unprepared as I was to take on the care of a living breathing soul.

After I'd unpacked the last box, I headed up the switchback stairway in the foyer where the four bedrooms were situated off a main landing upstairs. Uncle Arthur's room was the closest door on the left and offered a breathtaking view of the ocean. Although larger, I felt it better left to him and his memory for now. Besides, I didn't need all that space. Arthur's room was twice as big as the other bedrooms and featured a private bath and balcony. All his furniture throughout the house remained untouched, and the smaller items—books, clothing, pictures—remained where they lay the day he died.

I stopped short as I stepped onto the landing. *Was that door open yesterday*, I thought. *I'm sure I closed up everything before I left last night.* The door eased partway open, just enough for me to peek my head inside. Everything seemed fine. Nothing was out of place that I saw, although, admittedly, I wasn't exactly familiar with the room's layout or contents to begin with. It was probably just a drafty house. I made a mental note to have the windows resealed during the renovation. It wouldn't do to have a breeze opening all the doors and windows on my future guests in their most private moments.

Before I could begin removing the cloth drapery over the furniture in one of the other three bedrooms, I heard footsteps on the stairs. Two sets of footsteps.

"Hello?" I projected my voice out to the landing.

"Hello there," came a man's voice. It wasn't Nick, and I wasn't expecting anyone else.

I met two men on the landing. It was the mayor, whom I'd seen at the roundabout the night before. And with him was Deputy Todd.

"Jim and Todd, right?"

"*Mayor* Jim Thornen, yes. And this is *Deputy* Todd Newman." The deputy simply nodded his giant hat.

"What can I do for you, *Mayor*?"

"Thought we'd come meet our new neighbor. We heard you're turning this place into a bed-and-breakfast. Looking to bring more tourists into town then?"

"Probably couldn't hurt. I'm sure the local businesses wouldn't mind."

"Yes," he drawled. "But it also brings noise and

other… troubles."

"Crime," said Deputy Todd. "It brings crime."

"I highly doubt anyone staying at a purple Victorian bed-and-breakfast on the coast would be the criminal sort, Deputy."

"In case you hadn't heard, Miss Lewis, we recorded a suspicious death yesterday. Locals will tell you this is a quiet little village, but it's been getting worse and worse as more strangers come into town."

"I hope you don't mean me?" I was genuinely shocked. This was not the type of greeting I expected from anyone, let alone the mayor and the deputy.

Deputy Todd held up his hands. "Of course not, Miss Lewis, but it is my job to investigate these things. Now, we heard at the diner that you may have had business dealings with Bobby before his, uh, untimely death."

I wouldn't have categorized a single phone call so dramatically. "He was supposed to turn on the gas and electricity before I arrived in town. I spoke with him maybe two weeks ago." *Barely two weeks*, I thought. *And now he's dead.* I couldn't shake it.

"I see." Deputy Todd pulled out a ringed pad of paper and turned to the first sheet. He scribbled some notes before he asked, "Now, was this over the phone or in person?"

"The phone. I've never been to Starry Cove before yesterday."

"I see." More scribbles. "Now, how did he sound when you two spoke?"

"Fine, I guess. I didn't notice anything strange, if that's what you're asking. We arranged for me to send the house key and some basic information about the house by mail, which I did that same day. It should have arrived a few days later."

Deputy Todd repeated the words as he wrote them down in a rushed scrawl.

"Thank you, Miss Lewis," Mayor Jim said in a syrupy tone. "Did you ever speak to Mr. Teach after that?"

"No, I didn't. But when I tried calling him yesterday morning after I arrived, he didn't answer his phone. Now I know why. The house was locked when I got here."

Deputy Todd exchanged glances with Mayor Jim. "Thank you, Miss Lewis. Mind if we take a quick look around the property? For my report, of course." He motioned to the half page of indecipherable notes on his writing pad.

I didn't have any qualms, and if it could put their minds at ease or help with the investigation, then I was glad to help. "No, of course not. I've barely unpacked, so you may see my boxes lying around. Otherwise, the place is exactly as I found it yesterday."

"Thank you, Miss Lewis. Hope to see you later at church."

As the two men turned to head downstairs, I remembered my other visitor. "Oh, and there's a guy here now turning on my gas and electrical. Nick is his name."

The two looked askance at one another. "Thank you, Miss Lewis," said Mayor Jim, and they continued downstairs without another word.

I returned to the room I'd been inspecting, ready to dive back in to settling in, but as I pulled the cloth coverings off the furniture, my mouth fell open. Fully expecting to see the same musty modern comforts I'd uncovered downstairs, imagine my surprise when the first cloth unmasked an elaborately gilded dressing chair with a delicate violet damask seat and back cushions. I gasped as I let the dusty white sheet fall to the floor. Beneath the rest of the coverings I discovered more treasures of stately furniture, all true to the Victorian period, with vibrant velvets and silks and ornate carvings of mahogany and walnut. Each piece proved more elaborate than the next.

My heart leaped at each reveal—a dresser, the chaise under the window, another matching dressing chair. With just one piece left to expose, I knew it would be the *pièce de résistance* and I was not disappointed. Under the last sheet, the largest of them all, I discovered an enormous fourposter bed with an eight-foot rosewood headboard of carved leaves, vines, and cherubs. A shimmering tufted cream silk duvet spread across the mattress. This was no ordinary bedroom; it was a time capsule. Arthur must have spent his life accumulating these pieces. A collection fit for a museum.

"Wow," came a voice behind me. "This is *so* cool. Can I take some pictures?" Harper, straddling two drinks in one arm, tried to pull out her teddy bear phone. "Where did you get this stuff?"

"It was here. It's Arthur's. I just found it like this. And none of the rest of the house has anything like it, at least that I've found so far."

"Are you telling me that Arthur, that sneaky old devil, hid this the whole time? I mean, I'd heard rumors that Arthur had some cool stuff, but this is beyond anything I could have imagined."

"Yeah, he'd probably been collecting it for a long time."

"I wonder what else he was hiding?" Harper mused.

"Here, take this." She handed me one of the drinks. "I just came from Angie's bakery and she said you liked coffee. I believe her exact words were that you 'exhibited a nose for exceptional beans.'"

"Thanks." This was my first coffee since leaving Angie's that morning and I was already feeling the effects of withdrawal.

"I hope you don't mind I came in without knocking. The door was open."

"That's okay. It feels like Grand Central in here today. First Nick, then the mayor and deputy."

"Nick, huh?" Harper raised an eyebrow like I was already guilty of some salacious crime.

"What?" I asked, trying to sound innocent, because I was, of course. "He's here to get my gas and electrical going."

"Uh-huh. I'm sure he's here to get *something* going." Harper tried to stifle a laugh.

"He is certainly nice to look at," I admitted. "What's your story with Nick?"

"Uh, no story. Definitely one hundred percent not my type. So, what did the mayor and Deputy Todd want?"

"I'm surprised you didn't see them when you came up. They were nice enough to stop by to tell me I'm going to rain crime and destruction down upon the town."

Harper shook her head. "What? How?"

"By opening this house as a bed-and-breakfast. The deputy seems to think it will bring crime, as if every honeymooning couple who might visit are Bonny and Clyde, barely wasting time between signing the guestbook and robbing the diner."

"I warned you those two would give you grief. At

25

least you got to stare at Nick." Harper grinned. "I'd be careful of that one, though. He's uh, how do I say this… known around town, if you catch my meaning."

"Gotcha." I nodded, catching on quickly. I'd known many Nicks in my day and they were all nothing but trouble. "Good thing I'm not looking for romance then. I just want to live my life in peace and quiet."

From downstairs the slam of the front door made me and Harper both jump in our skins.

"What was that?" I asked, as we both headed out of the room and down the stairs.

But when I reached the landing, I stopped sharply. *No,* I thought. *It can't be. Please, no.*

Lingering in the foyer below stood the most callous and narcissistic person I knew, and the last person on earth I wanted to see—my very own sister, Lillian Lewis.

Four

WE LOCKED EYES. "The door was open, so I closed it for you," she said. "Smells like seaweed and there was a dingy stray cat outside, probably riddled with fleas." Her sneer was almost imperceptible as the words slithered from her mouth. She wore a large-print floral day dress, puffed out at the hem and espadrille wedged heels. Not a black hair was out of place under the large-brimmed hat on her head, and rosy lips perfectly matched the floral on her dress, as usual.

"What are you doing here?" I demanded.

"Nice to see you too, Sister." She did not seem surprised at the greeting. "What a charming house. Too bad about the garish color." She ran her eyes across the details in the foyer before placing a hand on the newel post at the base of the stairwell. "Though, I wouldn't bother unpacking any further." Her fingers tickled along the smooth wood banister.

"And why is that, Lily?"

"Because I'm contesting the estate."

"You're what?" My mouth dropped open in complete shock. "The probate has been closed for over a month. You can't be serious." I crossed my arms defiantly.

A grin tugged at her lips. "I assure you I am. I've been in Europe for the past six months working on a collaboration with Beau Chapeau of Paris. I wasn't notified of poor Uncle Arthur's will and it seems you've swooped in and claimed the estate all for yourself."

"I didn't *claim* the estate—he left it to me. They notified all interested parties and relatives by mail. You didn't bother to show up to the reading."

"Alas, I was in Europe," was all she replied, spreading her hands in front of her, an entirely counterfeit expression of concern on her face, as though that simple explanation could wipe the last few months of my hard work off the calendar. "Odd, from the sound of your voice it's as though you hadn't received a letter from my attorneys just yesterday."

I seethed, red with anger. "What letter?"

"Maybe she means the official-looking letter you got in the mail yesterday," Harper said quietly, trying her best to stay out of what was clearly a contentious conversation.

"I believe your friend is correct." Lily turned her attention to Harper. "Please excuse my sister's rudeness. I'm Lillian Lewis, Poppy's sister, as doubtlessly you are now aware."

"Harper Tillman. Pleased to meet you," was all Harper managed in response.

"Well, it was lovely catching up with you, Sis, but I've got to get back to the hotel in Vista for a call with my production manager. I'm sure we'll be seeing more of each other very soon." Lily turned back before opening the front door. "It was nice meeting you... Harlow, was it? Goodbye."

And just like that she was gone. In like a tornado and out like a hurricane. I balled my fist, too mad to cry and took one angry swig of my coffee then stomped down the stairs into the kitchen. I grabbed the letters off the counter where I'd left them yesterday and flipped through them one by one. One from the County Recorder's Office and, frustratingly, one from Johnson, Esterbrook, Rowan, and Knowles, Attorneys at Law.

I boiled inside. "That monster."

"I guess that was your sister, huh?"

"Yes, my sister, if you can call her that." I leaned against the counter, looking up at the ceiling and let out a heavy sigh. "I didn't even look at these letters yesterday after Angie ran over. And then we went to the town meeting. I guess I just forgot to look. She's always one step ahead of me."

"Sounds like she's a bit behind, actually. I thought Arthur left this house to you in his will?"

"He did. He left me everything here."

"What's the problem then? What does she mean she's going to contest the estate? Can she even do that?" Harper peppered the questions one after another.

"I don't know. I'll have to call my lawyer."

Heavy boots plodded into the kitchen. "Hey there, Harper," said Nick. "I saw Mayor Dewey out back."

"And how is my handsome boy?"

"Wait, what?" I asked, thoroughly confused. "I thought the mayor's name was Jim, and now I have some serious questions about your taste in men."

"Not *that* mayor. Mayor Dewey is the town cat. We gave him the title of Mayor to piss off ol' Jim Thorn-in-my-side." A satisfied grin spread wide across her face.

I suspected Harper coined the cat's name herself. "That must be the orange cat I've seen wandering around the property. I thought it might have been Arthur's."

"No, no. He's more of a town mascot, a real wandering soul. He doesn't settle in one place for too long. Too independent. But he's my handsome boy because I always see him stalking me while I'm on my route."

"Yeah," said Nick. "Mayor Dewey's always on the prowl. You'll see him around a lot. So, um, Poppy, I've got some good news and some bad news."

My shoulders slumped. "What's the good news?"

"Good news is that your electricity and gas are working."

"Great. And the bad?"

"Bad news is that you're probably going to need to replace the circuit box on the outer wall—they don't last too long in this climate."

I placed a hand on the counter, bracing myself for the inevitable. "And what is that going to cost me?"

"Unfortunately, it runs about fifteen hundred bucks."

"Ouch," Harper said, glancing at me woefully. "I guess the renovation costs start now."

Five

"SHE SAID *WHAT*?" Angie leaned over the pastry case at me and Harper. After Lily's visit, Harper suggested we get some free pastries to lighten the mood, so we'd walked down to the bakery to kibitz with Angie.

"And then she just walked out, cool as a cucumber," said Harper. "That lady is ice cold."

The bakery door swung open, announcing Lovie Newman whose face searched around before finally honing in on me.

"Poppy, so nice to see you again. After the nasty events last night, I was worried we may have scared you off."

"I'm not that easily deterred. Plus, I needed to give this bakery a try. Angie's cinnamon rolls are a thing of magic and just what I need right now."

Angie's face split into a wide grin.

"Er, yes, they are quite good." Lovie's mouth twisted at the words, as though compliments did not come naturally. "I couldn't help but notice—"

"Here we go," said Harper, rolling her eyes. "Don't pretend you weren't spying on Poppy's house this morning."

Lovie's eyes flattened at Harper before continuing. "I couldn't help but notice that you received several visitors this morning, including a very smartly dressed woman. Was she, perhaps, an investor in your bed-and-breakfast?"

"She was my sister, Lillian."

"Sister? Well, my, my," said Lovie, breathless. "She wouldn't perhaps be Lillian Lewis, the hat designer?"

"The one and only."

My words were curt, but Lovie continued, "Oh, I absolutely love her hats. Todd, er, the deputy got one for my birthday a few years ago and I just *know* it cost too much but it *was* my birthday, after all. I don't wear it often, of course. I only bring it out for special occasions—church events, that sort of thing."

My lips were iron. "Of course."

Lovie's mouth opened to continue talking, but Harper snatched me by the arm. "Time to go, Poppy. Gotta head back to the house for that thing we have to do. Bye, Angie." We spun past Lovie and out the door, leaving her mouth gaping wordlessly.

"I cannot stand that woman," Harper said once we were a safe distance down the sidewalk.

"She didn't know any better." Not everyone knew my history with Lily, and I found it necessary to remind myself of that. To them, she was just a famous designer, up on a pedestal.

"Still, she's always butting into everyone's business. It doesn't creep you out that she's basically spying on your house at all hours?"

"Everyone was at the house this morning. Why not her?"

"You're bummed about the estate, huh?"

"Ugh." I threw my hands up and flopped on the sidewalk bench near where we stood. "What am I'm going to do? I left everything to come here. This is all I have now."

We sat in silence for a moment until I felt the courage to continue. "Before I came here, I went through a pretty tough year. My mom died, my marriage failed, and I retreated inward, basically severing ties with my entire social circle. When Arthur left me this house, the timing couldn't have been more perfect. I needed a place to live. It might seem callous to say, but his death was a windfall for me. I'd inherited some money from my mom already, and nothing was keeping me in that city anymore. This was supposed to be a new beginning. I must have been crazy thinking I could just pick up and move to a new place and everything would be fine. Bad luck seems to follow me around."

"Just because your sister thinks she's God's gift, doesn't mean bad luck follows you around."

"You don't understand. Losing my mom was bad enough, but my marriage broke up because my husband had an affair—with *Lily*. My husband and I had built a life. We ran a hotel business together—small, but successful—and she ruined it. She took everything from me—my relationship, my career. I didn't think she could sink any lower or try any harder to make me miserable, but she did. Even if this comes to nothing, she's once again inserted herself into my attempt at happiness for the sole purpose of bringing me low. It's unbearable." I felt my eyes welling, and by sheer will I held back the tears, determined not to give Lily the satisfaction of making me cry again.

"Well, your sister made a big mistake, because she's underestimated you." Harper gave me a massive hug, squeezing me tight until I laughed. "And your new friends."

A loud crash brought our attention across the road to the hardware store. Cars lined the street, obscuring most of the view, but we could still see a scuffle through the front windows. We rushed over and through the doors to find old Walter laying on the floor with a large man looming over him. A merchandise display board lay on its side and small tools and boxes of nails lay strewn across the floor.

"If you say one more word, Walter, so help me, I will finish you," the man spat. "I want it back by tomorrow. Or else."

"Walter, what's going on?" Harper leaned down to help him up.

"What are you doing?" I demanded to the other man.

"None of your business," he shot back, then turned and stomped out of the store, leaving me, Harper, and a very shaken Walter behind.

"Are you all right?"

"I may look like a frail bit of skin and bones, but I'm made of tougher stuff."

"What was that all about?" asked Harper.

"Kenny's just riled up about some business."

Harper scoffed. "Some business? That seemed pretty serious, Walter. Do you want me to call Vernon?"

"No," he snapped. Harper looked shocked, but he

quickly continued much more calmly, "Don't call Vernon. He'd only fuss. I'm okay, just help me up."

Walter took a moment to get to his feet. Even with our help he toddled a moment before regaining a steady footing.

"Are you sure you don't want me to call Vernon?"

"I'm sure. You've done enough and I'm just fine. I'm going to stop by Shelby's for a bite and then head home."

We watched as he hobbled out of the hardware store and turned, not toward Shelby's Diner, but in the opposite direction.

"Maybe he's dropping off the bag at his car," I wondered aloud.

Harper's eyes narrowed. "Walter doesn't have a car."

"The *car salesman* doesn't have a car?" I asked, incredulous.

"Yeah." She shook her head. "He rides a bike everywhere. He's definitely up to something."

Six

THE COOL BREEZE brushed my face as I sat on the front porch stairs the next morning. Mayor Dewey perched casually on the wooden railing a few feet away, staring at me with those vibrant yellow eyes. Blink, blink. I blinked back. He blinked again. "Are you trying to tell me something, Dewey?" One more blink and he was off, fleeing into the bushes behind the house.

I cupped my mug of coffee close to my chest as I watched the sun rise over the trees to the east. It was a small comfort. The previous night I'd slept in the living room on my inflatable mattress and now felt a bit worse for wear after two days of unpacking.

Today would be worse, at least mentally, since I'd have to call my lawyer and I also needed to find time to drive to Vista, a larger town up the highway where I could pick up the blueprints I'd ordered of the house. The other letter I'd received was from the County Recorder's Office informing me that they were ready. I knew from my experience in the hotel business that understanding what I had to work with before knocking down walls was important, so I needed a starting point before rushing into renovations.

My legs and back ached, and sitting in the steps wasn't helping. I need to stretch my legs out, which would give me an opportunity to get to know the property. I took the steps from the porch gingerly and hobbled my way around to the back of the property. Ocean waves crashed far below the cliff, but I couldn't see around the overgrown bushes near the southwest corner of the house. A small opening between bushes afforded me a magnificent view of clear blue ocean, but it was a tiny vantage point—I'd have to remember to clear out the shrubbery and set up a sunset viewing spot for future guests.

While surveying the spot more closely, I spied something shiny on the ground peeking out of the bushes. It appeared to be a fairly new hammer, since there were few dents or scuffs around the head. By the weight of it I could tell it was well made, the tool of a professional, not one of those flimsy things you buy at the box store. Nick must have dropped it while working on the nearby electrical panel yesterday. This might give me the perfect excuse to see him again. Just for fun.

A bit later I arrived at Shelby's Diner to pick up breakfast. Even with my electricity finally on, I still hadn't found time to drive up to Vista to the big grocery store to stock up, so I'd been surviving on cinnamon rolls from Angie's bakery and meals from Shelby's Diner since I arrived. Despite being a weekday, the diner bustled with locals and there was a buzz in the air from the moment I walked in.

Lovie and Shelby stood across the counter from one

another, so I headed their way to put in my order.

"Blunt force trauma," came a whisper as I came upon them. The whispering stopped, and the two straightened when they noticed me standing nearby. Both turned hon-eyed eyes my way.

"What can I get you, dearie?"

"I'll have the French toast and a large coffee."

"Are you going to eat here or takeaway?"

"Takeaway. I'm looking for Nick Christos, the handyman. Any idea where I could find him?"

My request resulted in two sets of sharply raised eye-brows, and I quickly realized I probably should have been more discreet with Lovie listening in.

"He left something at the house and I wanted to re-turn it."

The eyebrows rose higher.

I sighed. "He left his hammer when he turned on my gas and electricity yesterday."

Lovie and Shelby shared a knowing look. "Watch out for that one, dearie."

"Thanks, but I've already been warned."

"Are you sure you want takeaway?" Shelby asked. "Because he's sitting alone in the booth at the back right now." All three of us turned to the back booth, and Nick met our stares before hastily looking down at his food. "My guess is he wouldn't mind the company."

"Great. I guess I'll eat here then."

I headed to the back of the diner and stood by Nick's booth. "Mind if I join you?"

"Of course not." He gestured to the seat across from him.

"Thanks." I placed my backpack on the seat and sat

down on the cushy bench. "I thought I'd have to search high and low for you. I have your hammer. You left it at the house yesterday."

"My hammer?"

"Yeah," I replied, digging in my backpack. "I found it on the ground behind the house."

Nick took one quick look at the hammer. "That's not mine." His eyes darted to the other tables nearby where a fair number of people were enjoying their meals.

"Really? Are you sure?"

"Yeah. Definitely sure."

"That's odd. It didn't look like it had been there very long, so I just assumed it was yours."

"Look, I gotta go," he said hastily. "I forgot I have to be somewhere." He gathered his keys and phone off the table. Before I could respond, he added, "Sorry to rush off, really. Maybe another time?"

"Sure," was all I could squeak out before he dashed away. I sat there silently and watched him leave, confused by his sudden departure.

"I dunno what you said to scare him off," Shelby said, sidling up to the booth. "But he left his food behind. Such a waste." She tsked and gathered up his plate.

"I'm not sure either," I replied softly.

"Is that the hammer?"

"Yeah."

"Why didn't Nick take it?"

"He said it wasn't his."

"Let me take a look." She set the plate back down and took up the hammer. "You know, I think this might be one of Bobby's hammers. I called him over a few weeks ago to fix some loose boards, bless his soul." She put a hand to her heart. "Look, here," she said, lifting her spectacles and squinting to get a closer look. She pointed to the end of the handle. "There's a little 'T' carved into it, just there. Teach."

"Why would Bobby Teach's hammer be at the house?"

"Well now, I don't know, dearie, but anything of Bobby's could be considered evidence." Her eyes widened and she exclaimed in a hushed tone, "This could be the murder weapon." Shelby quickly handed the hammer back to me as though it were poison. Nearby faces turned our way. "You better call Deputy Todd right now." With that, she wiped her hands on her apron before gathering Nick's plate and disappeared through the swivel doors into the kitchen.

Seven

DURING THE ENTIRE drive to Vista, I replayed my recent call with my lawyer in my head. Yes, he received the picture of the letter I sent. Yes, Lily may have a case, if slim. Yes, he would look into it. The very last thing I needed was more legal fees on top of renovation costs, and despite my optimism upon arrival at Starry Cove, I was now questioning if I should give up on the whole harebrained idea and just walk away. Just let her have it. I shook myself out of it and clinched my hands on the steering wheel. Lily always won, but not this time—I wouldn't let her.

I arrived at the County Recorder's Office in Vista around midday, renewed in my conviction to see this project through. Many of Starry Cove's residents worked in this larger town, which sat more inland and to the north roughly ten miles—just far enough for folks to consider it separate. Despite the name, Vista offered little vista of its own, just a larger blip on the map along the highway with a bank and a grocery store and the other necessities that I couldn't find readily in Starry Cove.

As I entered the building that housed the county offices, I spotted Deputy Todd down the left hallway speaking to a man I didn't recognize, also in uniform. The deputy caught my eye and hurried over before I could look away and escape down a side hall or into a waiting room.

"Miss Lewis," he said, tipping his hat.

"Hello, Deputy. I didn't expect to see you here."

He gave an indiscernible grunt and cuffed his thumbs into his belt loops, leaning back slightly to add height to his short frame. "I work here. Now, I am aware that you may have a weapon in your possession. Is that correct?"

Of course he already knows, I thought. "I have a hammer in my backpack, if that's what you mean?"

"That'll be it. Please hand it over."

I rustled in my bag before pulling it out and handing it to Deputy Todd, who produced a tissue from his pocket and took the hammer cautiously by the handle.

"I found it behind the house this morning. It was in some bushes."

"Interesting…" Deputy Todd trailed off, looking closely at the hammer. "Bushes, eh?"

"Yes, the ones near the electrical box behind the house. It was lying on the ground, sort of peeking out. The shiny metal caught my eye."

Another grunt.

"I thought it might be Nick's since he was working back there yesterday, but he said it wasn't his."

"Did you notice anything else?"

"Hard to say, really. Everything is new to me at the house. I don't think I could say if something was out of place or not."

"Uh-huh," he mumbled, nodding his head and that

ridiculous hat. "I'm going to take this," he held up the hammer, dangling it by his fingertips, "and I'll probably want to come back out to the house and have you show me exactly where you found it."

"I have a few stops to make here in Vista, but I should be back at the house later this afternoon."

"That'll do, Miss Lewis." He tipped his hat before walking back down the hall.

After a long wait in the Recorder's Office with no one in sight, a young man appeared from the back and stopped short when he spotted me leaning up against the counter.

"I'm sorry to keep you waiting. We don't get many folks in here."

"That's okay, but might I recommend a bell? I'm here to pick up some blueprints I ordered a few weeks ago. I received a notice that they were ready."

"Name?"

"Poppy Lewis."

He rustled through a stand of cardboard tubes along the back wall and eventually drew out one of the larger cylinders. "Is this for Main Street, Starry Cove?"

"That's it."

"Popular location."

"Popular?"

"We don't get a lot of business in here overall, but this plan's been requested, oh, maybe three times in the past month."

"*Three* times?" I asked, incredulous.

"Including yours."

"I'm not sure who would want the plans to this house. Is that even legal?"

"Oh sure. They're public records."

"Can you tell me who requested them?"

"Unfortunately, that is *not* public record." He tapped a few keys on his computer before adding, "That'll be fifty dollars."

I paid the fee and gathered the long tube, wondering who on earth would have interest in blueprints to an old house—musty and dusty and wearing down.

The Recorder's Office had set aside a stark side room for public use and, being that it was relatively quiet in the office that day, I found it to be a suitable spot to review the plans without interruption.

I popped open the tube and unfurled the pages, spreading them out on the sole table within the room. I'd hoped to gain an understating of the house and its structure, but as I flipped through, I knew I'd have to get a contractor squared away quickly. Electrical, plumbing, roof lines—it was a different language. Although I'd worked on renovations in the past and retained a rudimentary knowledge of reading plans, I had to admit that it was an indecipherable jumble of words and numbers.

As I rolled up the pages to place back in the tube, I spotted a page that showed something surprising—a revised print filed on the house more recently. I flipped back a few sheets to confirm this was separate from the kitchen renovations a few decades prior. The print showed a room addition to the basement's original footprint. I hadn't even been down to the basement yet, but this indicated there should be a small room on the east side which, if my mind could place it, meant it was underneath the living room. A quick glance at the other plans confirmed this.

Piled full of more of that fancy furniture, I hoped. Or it could be a nice wine cellar for the bed-and-breakfast. I filed that little nugget in the back of my mind and decided to check it out once I returned to the house. For now, I needed groceries. I stuffed the blueprints back into their cylindrical case and left the county offices behind me.

**

On my way back to Starry Cove, I took the scenic drive along the Coastal Road, which Angie said skirted the cliffs and offered breathtaking views of the waves and craggy rocks that spanned this stretch of coastline. According to Angie, eventually it would bring me back into town after it transitioned into Second Street.

With the windows rolled down, I let the salty wind blow through my loose hair. My fingers floated on the air outside the driver's window as I meandered along, following the road's sinuous curves. While driving through a particularly beautiful section of redwoods, I spotted a sign poking out from the thickness of trees ahead. "Treasures of the Coast" it read. This was Vernon Dogger's shop, I recalled, so I angled the car to a stop in the empty dirt turnout out front used as a makeshift parking area clear of the road traffic, although there seemed none today.

Trinkets and driftwood and shells made into the shape of turtles and sharks loaded the front porch of the rickety wooden building. There were sets of wind-worn decorative corbels set haphazardly against the side of the porch. Fifty dollars for each set, the tag read. Salvaged from a large old house like Arthur's, I assumed. Next to that sat an enormous piece of wood carved into the shape of crashing waves. Smaller wave carvings lay at its base along with a bundle of ceramic carved garden stakes. An orchestra of wind chimes filled the air with their pleasant tones with each breeze that passed through the forest. The eclectic offerings were enough to distract me for days, and I hadn't even made it inside yet.

Through the front door of the shop, I was met with stacks and displays of more eye-catching merchandise. Each piece was unique or made with slight differences, or even damage, that gave them the distinct feeling of being handmade. I could easily spend a fortune here if I didn't pace myself.

Way in the back, hidden behind stands of maps and ceramic pots, there was a small door leading to a separate room and since I didn't see Vernon in the main store area, thought he might be there. I popped my head around the corner and saw that it was just a small office, but it too was stuffed with trinkets and pictures and various other bits and bobs. My eyes darted everywhere, taking it all in. The drawers of a filing cabinet near the door lay open. Papers were half pulled and falling out and I realized I stood on loose pages scattered across the floor. My eyes continued, settling on the desk against the far wall. Vernon sat in a small chair with his head on the desk. As I stepped forward, I saw to my horror a large pool of blood soaked the surface and now dripped down the front edge and legs of the desk. A wound marked red Vernon's salt and pepper hair and his limbs hung limp, unmoving.

My breath caught. I staggered out of the back room and through the store before darting out the front door. I leaned against the car, heaving air as though underwater, unable to fill my lungs enough before another desperate gasp overtook me. A minute passed, maybe a few, before I gathered myself enough to dig my phone out of my backpack and dial 9-1-1.

"9-1-1, what is your emergency?"

I supported myself on the car, red faced with tears in my eyes. I felt the adrenaline easing from my system and my hands shook, like coming down from a bad high.

"There's a man, Vernon," I sobbed into the phone. "He's been shot—I think he's been murdered."

Eight

I SLUMPED ON one of the decorative concrete benches that bordered the turnout parking lot for Treasures of the Coast. Deputy Todd had already interviewed me by the time the crime scene crew arrived. Despite the time that had elapsed, I still trembled and found it difficult to breathe.

A car pulled up and screeched to a halt on the side of the road. Angie and Harper burst out of the doors and quickly made their way to my side. Their wide eyes scanned around the scene as the crews in their special gear entered and exited the store, bringing out boxes and bags and other evidence. I stared at the ground, avoiding the eyes of others.

"Are you all right," asked Angie, her voice quavering. "I can't believe this could happen. Not in our little town. Oh, poor Vernon."

"Poppy, we should take you home. Let's get you out of here." Harper wrapped her arm around me and urged me off the bench.

"Oy, you there." Deputy Todd was heading our way. "You can't be here."

"We're here to help Poppy. And don't worry because we're leaving."

"Miss Lewis," he directed to me, "as a reminder, you need to remain in town while the investigation runs its course. I may have further questions."

"I understand." My voice was frail and shaken. The deputy had no reason to worry—I had nowhere to go anyway.

"Can't you see she's traumatized, *Deputy*?" Harper spat. Deputy Todd flinched and Harper added, "Angie, you take your car back and we'll meet at Poppy's house. I'll drive Poppy back in her car."

"Right, I'll see you both there in a few minutes. You hold on, Poppy. It'll be all right."

***

The sun set as we three reunited at the big house. Mayor Dewey perched on the rail next to the steps as we approached, and Harper and I gave him a quick pet as she helped me inside and sat me down on Arthur's old furniture in the living room. He followed us in and took up a spot on the arm of the couch. I suspected he'd been a regular visitor to this house his entire life, coming and going as he pleased.

Angie arrived with three coffees in a carrier, and I couldn't have been more relieved at that first glorious sip, like a warm blanket enveloping me in its embrace.

"I see Mayor Dewey is here. Right on the mark, as usual," said Angie, giving him a soft scratch behind the ears. "He always knows when someone needs comforting."

Harper had shushed me each time I tried to talk, sparing me the act of rehashing events on the drive. But now that we were at the house together and safe, it all spilled out. "It was awful, just awful," I said. "He was just sitting there with his head down, like he was taking a nap or something." I shook my head, disbelieving, trying to purge the memory from my brain. "Everything was so… messy."

Angie shook her head, dejected. "I can't believe what is going on around here. This is a quiet town. Nothing like this has ever happened that I can remember."

"It's creeping me out," said Harper, arms folded. "You know what we need? A distraction. Angie, have you seen what Arthur's been hiding in this house?"

That roused me from my dark thoughts. "Oh, it's wonderful. You've got to see it."

"Okay, you have my attention. What is it?"

"We can't tell you. You have to *see* it to understand." Harper grabbed Angie's hand and led her upstairs to the side bedroom.

I trailed behind, still shaky on my legs. When I reached the top of the landing, I heard Angie exclaim, "Holy smokes!" and a smile spread across my face, remembering my own similar reaction and that of Harper.

"Poppy, did you have any idea this was here?" Angie asked as I entered the room.

"Nope. It was a total surprise. The rest of the house is just normal old furniture."

"Can I sit on it?" Angie asked with pleading eyes.

"Of course. I'm not sure how rickety everything is, so just be careful."

"I will." Angie ran her hand along the top edge of the sitting chair before gently placing her bum on the cushion, her feet barely brushing the floor. She settled in, listening for any creaks or cracks. "These must be the real thing."

Harper splayed herself across the duvet and the wood frame groaned. "I don't know how he squirreled all this stuff up here. It must have been in the dead of night or else Lovie would have seen it and told the whole town."

"There's always been a rumor that he had something hidden away, but I just chalked it up to being a grand old house. Harper's right about Lovie, though. Arthur must have taken precautions to keep this from everyone. I suppose he didn't talk a lot about his life or share much. But why hide *this*? Everything is so beautiful. I'd want everyone to see it."

"I don't know. I've only been here a few days so I'm still learning things about the house." I paused. "And about Arthur. Did you know there was a buildout of the basement about forty years ago? I looked at the blueprints today—that's why I was in Vista—and saw a small room was added."

"In the basement? That's odd," said Angie, perking up in the chair.

Harper sat up straight. "Maybe it's a wine cellar full of bottles as old as this furniture. Have you been down there yet?"

"No, I've barely had a chance to explore the main house, let alone the basement or the storage shed by the driveway. I'm sure it will take me years to find every nook and cranny in this place."

"Does that mean you're going to stay here in Starry

Cove?" Angie's face was hopeful.

"Not if Lily has her way."

"Why is she doing this? I can't imagine anyone being so cruel."

"She's always been cruel," I said and relayed to Angie our history.

"Oh," Angie said in a hushed tone. "That's pretty bad. I'm sorry, Poppy."

"Forget Lily. That harpy can try but you've got a solid hold on this house. What did your lawyer say?"

"He said she may have a slim case, but he'd have to look into it. I'll probably hear back in a few days. I'm reluctant to spend money on the house if there's even a remote chance that I'll lose it."

"So, what will you do in the meantime?" Angie asked.

"I can still get things through the planning stages—interview contractors, that sort of thing."

"*In the meantime*, let's go explore the basement," said Harper, jumping up excitedly and heading for the door. "What if Arthur hid more great stuff down there? Don't you two want to find out?"

At the main floor, Harper and Angie looked my way, unsure of where the basement access was located.

"I think it's through a door in the kitchen. I saw it the other day when I was unpacking. It might be locked, so I'll have to find the key." I led them down the stairs and into the kitchen, motioning to the corner as I riffled through the drawers.

"Looks like we don't need a key," Harper said. "It's already open."

"What?" The door stood open a few inches. "That

door was closed when I checked it last."

"Maybe it was a draft," said Angie.

"Maybe…" I was doubtful. "Some of the doors seem to open by themselves, draft or no."

Harper backed away from the door. "Wait, is your house haunted? Because I don't do haunted houses."

Angie tsked. "Don't be silly. It's not haunted. It's just *old*. When you get old, your body will do unexpected things too."

I stepped up to the darkened doorway. A set of wooden steps led down at a steep angle. Cobwebs and dust coated everything within the small cone of light trickling into the stairwell from the kitchen.

"Is this a light?" Harper flipped a switch near the doorway. A light flickered on, illuminating the basement in a dim glow. "Better than nothing, I guess."

The steps looked shaky, so I tested the first with just my toe for stability before adding more weight. Seemed okay. I took another step down and stopped. On the next step below, I noticed an impression in the dust. A large tread mark cut through the grime. Then another on the next step. And another. Based on the direction of the tread, some led down the stairs and some, I noted, led up.

"Someone has been down here," I said. "Recently."

"Recently? How recent?" Harper's voice cracked. "Could they still be down there? Because I *definitely* don't do haunted houses with killers in the basement."

"I don't think so. There are treads going down and back up. Looks like a man's boot."

Angie looked at me in confusion. "But you said the house has been all locked up."

"Hello?" I called into the basement. No response

followed. "I'm going down. The light is enough to see. Just be careful on these first steps—they're a little shaky."

I took each step slowly, gingerly setting my feet one after another until I reached the bottom of the stairs. The floor was concrete and slightly rough, but the ceilings were tall and I could stand upright with ease. Everything lay under a thin layer of dust, so it was easy to follow the man's footsteps.

I didn't see any other prints leading off the first set, so it appeared whoever left these headed directly to a point at the back wall of the basement. Someone had disturbed an area of dust in that one spot, as though they'd spent a great deal of time there. But as I looked around, there was nothing there, just a smooth wall. I oriented myself to the floors up above. If I was standing in this corner against this wall, I should be directly below the living room, which meant…

"This wall shouldn't be here," I said. "This is where the plans led. This should be a door to another room, but it's just a wall."

"What are you talking about?" Harper asked as she and Angie finished descending the stairs.

"The blueprints. The room addition I was telling you about. It should be *right here*." I pointed to the wall.

Angie looked around. "Maybe they never built it."

"The footprints led directly here, like they were looking for something."

"But found a wall instead."

Harper ran her hands over the rough texture. "It's hard to tell, but this may have been covered over." She knocked on the concrete. "Hollow," she said, followed by a sharp intake of breath. "Something's behind here."

"I don't like this." Angie was already eyeing the steps back upstairs.

"Why would Arthur build and then wall up a room in his basement?"

"I can think of a few reasons, and none of them good." Harper stepped away from the wall as we all stared. "And someone else was probably wondering the same thing. Even these footprints look confused."

I crossed my arms. "This doesn't make sense. Whoever was down here knew what they were looking for. The footprints lead straight to this wall and then back up the stairs. Clearly they didn't find what they were expecting." After a moment of silence, it hit me. "Of course, that's it."

"What?" Harper asked.

I turned to both of them. "When I was in Vista today to get the blueprints, the clerk told me that *two* other people recently ordered plans of this house, too. Whoever they were must also know this room exists. Or existed."

"But who were they?"

"The clerk wouldn't tell me. Either way, I don't like people coming into Arthur's house uninvited."

"*Your* house," said Harper firmly.

"Have you noticed any break-ins?"

"Other than the one we're experiencing right now?" Harper asked sarcastically.

"Maybe that's what the hammer was about."

"What hammer?"

"I found a hammer out back under the bushes this morning, but I handed it over to Deputy Todd. He seemed to think it might be important about Bobby Teach."

"Bobby Teach…" Angie wrung her hands. "I don't

like this."

"There is some weird stuff going on in this big house and I don't like it either," said Harper.

"What are you going to do, Poppy?" Angie huddled close by, eyes scanning the basement, as though a monster may jump from the corner at any moment.

"I'm not sure, but let's head upstairs. This place is freaking me out."

"Agreed," said Harper.

Nine

HARPER STAYED WITH me that night since events in the basement had left me too shaken to be alone, and I think Harper needed a friend as well. Angie stayed until late that night but returned home to Roy so they could open the bakery early the next morning. Her hours meant she was usually up at four o'clock to get the bread rising and she said Roy wouldn't be as understanding if she left him to open the bakery by himself again. I can't blame her. Or him.

No surprise that I was the first to wake the next morning and, with the fog already burning off the coast, set about making enough coffee for us both. I'd packed two mugs for my initial stay—one was never enough—so I pulled them both down and filled my favorite, the over-sized blue mug with a hummingbird-shaped handle. I rested the other next to the pot of steaming brew on the counter before easing into the chair at the small breakfast table to enjoy the first sip.

Harper plodded in, rubbing the sleep from her eyes.

She'd slept on Arthur's old sofa in the living room to stay near where I set up camp with my inflatable mattress. My own furniture wasn't due to arrive until the weekend, and I hadn't yet figured out all the room arrangements. There was also Arthur's furniture to deal with, but that would have to wait for another day.

"How'd you sleep?"

"I don't know how Angie does it. I am stone dead in the mornings."

"I'm sure she's not feeling too great this morning either."

"I could certainly go for a cinnamon roll before work. Want to head down to the bakery after we finish up here?"

"Sure, I could do for a quick walk too."

We polished off the last of our coffee and stepped out onto the porch and down the walkway into the fresh light of morning. Mayor Dewey must have stayed close the previous night since he meandered out of the bushes nearby and onto the porch, laying belly up in a patch of morning sunlight that peeked through the railing. In the distance, we spotted Deputy Todd making his way in our direction.

"Great," said Harper, eyes rolling.

"I guess I'll have to skip that cinnamon roll."

"Want me to stay for this?" Harper shot a thumb in Deputy Todd's direction.

"I'll be okay, thanks."

"There's a town meeting tonight. We have one every month. It's basically the highlight of everyone's social calendar, but I'm sure this one will be particularly interesting. Want me to swing by beforehand?"

"I doubt I'll be up for getting cross-examined by the

town."

"Angie and I won't let that happen. I'll come by later, okay?" Harper stepped up and gave me one of her signature bear hugs. "Take care and call if you need anything."

"Thanks. I appreciate all you've done. Both of you."

Harper sauntered down the walkway onto the main stretch of road and beamed an enormous plastic smile at Deputy Todd, waving vigorously. "Good morning, *Deputy*," she shouted across the roundabout. He tipped his hat—bulky monstrosity that it was—in her direction and continued onward toward me. I remained under the trellis until he arrived.

"Good morning, Deputy."

"Likewise, Miss Lewis. I hope you're doing better after yesterday's events."

"I'm doing okay, thanks. Are you here to look around or do you have more questions for me?"

"Both, actually."

"Then before you start, I want to tell you I think someone has been inside the house."

"What makes you think that?"

"There are footprints in the basement."

"Well now, that's not strange, is it?"

"They were made recently."

"Recently? Are you a footprint expert, Miss Lewis?"

"Well, no, but I—"

"I thought not. Now, why don't you show me where you found that hammer? That's what *I'm* interested in, so we'll start there."

The blazing light of this small man's ego made me clench my jaw. But I thought better of responding with the words that came to mind. He clearly thought he knew best, and I was more than willing to let him flounder along. "Fine, this way."

We rounded the house and I pointed to the ground near the tall bushes. "I found the hammer there, sticking out from that bush."

Deputy Todd bent down and rustled in the bushes near where I'd pointed. He knocked a few of the longer branches out of the way to get a better look and one slipped, smacking him in the face, leaving a long red mark across his check. "Dammit," he grumbled.

Oh, sweet karma, I thought.

He stooped down, face inches from the ground. "Did you notice any prints when you found the hammer?"

"Gosh, I'm not sure," I said, tapping my chin. "But I'm no expert."

He shot me a disapproving look and I composed myself. "Sorry… Nothing seemed suspicious at the time, so I didn't look too closely."

"All right," he said, straightening up. "I'm not seeing anything distinctive either. This grass is too thick to hold any prints. I do have a few more questions regarding Mr. Dogger, if you are feeling up for it?"

"I'm fine."

"Mm-hmm." A note pad and pen appeared in his hand, and I noticed many more of the pages appeared used since I'd first spotted it. Deputy Todd must have been busy. "Now, you've already told me you arrived at Mr. Dogger's shop at approximately two o'clock in the afternoon and found Mr. Dogger's body in the office at the back. Is that correct?"

"Yes."

"And you've already stated that upon finding Mr.

Dogger's body, you retreated outside and called authorities. Is that correct?"

"Yes."

"And you stated that Mr. Dogger's body lay slumped on the desk and blood was dripping down the desk legs. Is that correct?"

How could he say it so casually? I relived the discovery of Vernon's body in my mind, the small room splashed with blood sliding down the walls like rain on a windowpane. "Yes," I replied after a moment. "That's what I saw."

"And you stated—"

"I don't mean to sound rude," I interrupted, my patience waning, "but do you have any *new* questions for me?"

His steady gaze met mine. Without breaking eye contact he scribbled something in his notepad then asked, "Was there any indication that there was someone else in the shop when you arrived?"

"I didn't see anyone else and there were no other cars there."

"That is very interesting, isn't it?"

"What's interesting?" I asked.

"That not even Vernon's car was parked at the shop."

"I guess not, although I have no idea what Vernon's car looks like. There were definitely no other cars there— at least not parked on the turnout."

"Trust me, you'd know if Vernon's car was there— it's unmistakable. Were there any other cars on the road that you saw?"

I thought for a moment. The Coastal Road ran from Vista to Starry Cove and I was on the strip the whole drive. "I may have passed a few cars on the road." There had been a few, hadn't there? I struggled to recall, but I had probably paid more attention to the captivating ocean view than the passing cars on the other side. "It's hard to remember."

"Hmm. All right. How about any pedestrians?"

"Like, hikers?"

"Anyone on foot."

"None that I recall. Although, honestly, I may have passed them without noticing."

"Right," he drawled. "Now, Miss Lewis, do you own a firearm?"

"A *what*?" I reeled at this unexpected segue.

"A gun, Miss Lewis."

"No, absolutely not."

"Did your uncle, Arthur Lewis, own a firearm?"

I answered immediately and said, "No, I…" but I trailed off. "I'm not sure, actually. Am I a suspect here, Deputy?"

"There are no official suspects yet, Miss Lewis. This is a general line of questioning for investigations of this nature. The fact remains that you were alone when you discovered Mr. Dogger's body."

His words flowed out like a well-rehearsed speech, which meant he'd either had to say it a bunch of times recently or he expected I'd flinch at the insinuation. "I didn't shoot Vernon. I barely knew him," I said through clenched teeth.

He nodded. "No doubt, Miss Lewis. No doubt." That ridiculous hat flopped to-and-fro. Now I wanted to snatch it off his tiny head and cast it over the cliff into the ocean, but I took a deep breath and gave myself a moment to calm down. It would do no good to lose my temper in front of a deputy asking me questions about a recent murder, especially since I discovered the body, and we both knew I had no alibi.

"I have nothing to hide," I said coolly. "Take a look at whatever you'd like." I swept my arm toward the house, clearing the path for him to the steps.

"That won't be necessary at this time."

I crossed my arms, trying to keep myself composed but truthfully, I wanted to shake like a leaf—not out of guilt or fear, but out of incredulity. It was absurd that anyone could think I'd kill that nice old man. But then again, who here really knew me? Who really knew anyone? Regardless, I didn't do it and I had nothing to hide, so the deputy could spend his sweet time investigating dead ends all he wanted. It wouldn't solve the crime any faster.

"That'll be it for questions for now. Thank you for your assistance, Miss Lewis." Deputy Todd turned to go before stopping and adding, "Hope to see you at the meeting tonight. It would be good for you to make an appearance. You know, acquaint yourself with everyone in town."

"Right. I'll do that."

Ten

I MET HARPER and Angie under the trellis at dusk and shared the details of my interrogation.

"There's a murderer on the loose and he's going around harassing Poppy." Angie took a quick sip from her coffee as we walked along the sidewalk toward the community center. "Unbelievable."

I slammed my empty cup into the trash bin as we passed. "I know I'm new to town, but I don't think I come across as a crazed killer."

"If anyone in town is a crazed killer, it's him." Harper's steps were heavy on the sidewalk, as though marching to war. "Wouldn't surprise me if he did something crazy to boost his *law enforcement* profile, if you know what I mean."

We came upon the building tucked into the strip at the end of Main Street between two shops just before the meeting was set to begin. People milled about outside, making hushed conversation. Light streamed out from the double doors, exposing a room filled with chairs made into perfect rows, some seats full and others empty, waiting to be filled. It appeared from the crowd that it would be standing room only tonight.

"I had no idea there were this many people in Starry Cove."

"There aren't," said Angie. "Some are just here for the spectacle, unfortunately."

All eyes turned our way as we stepped into the room. I shrank a little inside but felt strength with my two friends supporting me on either side.

"Let's get this over with."

"We should grab seats before it's too late. I've been on my feet all day at the bakery. Roy's somewhere inside, but he's a big boy and he'll be fine on his own."

"I want to stop at the snack table. Usually Shelby's brought some little pies or something."

"Do you like Shelby's pies more than mine?" Angie asked, wounded.

"I absolutely love your pies, my dearest baking beauty. But you don't bring them to the town meeting and let me eat as many as I want." Harper shot her a smile.

"Bah. Come on, Poppy. Don't mind the stares." Angie's voice rose and she looked around conspicuously. "Apparently, they've got nothing better to do."

We found three seats on the edge of one row near the back. Angie sat to the right of me, and an empty seat remained on the left for Harper on the aisle. Soon enough, she scurried up with an armful of pies and cakes wrapped in loose napkins. A cookie hung from her lips.

"Want some?" she mumbled.

We both shook our heads and Harper shrugged. I scanned the room and spotted Nick seated a few rows ahead. A commotion rose behind us and Nick's head swiveled around. I tried to catch his eye, but his focus seemed to be on the hubbub beyond. I turned to see as well. Standing in the doorway, as though framed in a painting, stood Lily, commanding attention in a red jumpsuit. She wore her ebony hair in a severe bun perched under a black feathered fedora, with her eyes concealed behind dark sunglasses. Only Lily would wear sunglasses in the evening.

Harper rolled her eyes.

"Is that her?" asked Angie. "You two sure look alike."

My eyes narrowed. "We're nothing alike."

"Of course, sorry. You know what I meant."

"Sorry, Angie. I didn't mean to snap. She's here to dig under my skin and I shouldn't let her get to me."

"That's right," said Harper. "She's wasting her time if she thinks she's going to get your house."

"I hope so."

"Shh, it's starting."

Mayor Jim stepped up to the podium and tapped the microphone. A blast of feedback filled the room and everyone winced.

"Good evening. Thank you for coming. We've had some items added to the agenda for tonight, so I'm going to request that we keep the questions to a minimum."

The crowd grumbled. Apparently, they had arrived with many questions.

"I want to start by saying that we, as a community, mourn the loss of two of our members—Bobby Teach and Vernon Dogger—and we will take a moment to remember them in silence."

The masses hushed and bent their heads to chest. Some clasped hands and others shed tears. Sobs sprinkled throughout the large room and a wailing from the corner cut the air like a rusty knife. Lovie, head buried in her hands, shuddered through her tears. Shelby, who stood next to her, patted her on the shoulder and proffered a tissue to staunch the theatrics. Thankfully, moments of silence last only a moment. I'm not sure the crowd could take another second of Lovie's wailing.

Mayor Jim cleared his throat and continued, "I'm sure you're all eager to hear what is being done, so I'll turn the floor over to Deputy Todd, who's leading the investigations."

Deputy Todd sauntered to the podium as Mayor Jim stepped aside. "Ahem," he began. "On or about two o'clock yesterday afternoon, a citizen of Starry Cove discovered the body of Mr. Vernon Dogger at his place of business. This is being investigated as a homicide. We do not believe robbery was the motivation, although it is still under investigation. Anyone who may have information about the occurrences on or about two o'clock yesterday afternoon—"

"Excuse me, Deputy?" A shrill voice rang through the air. All eyes turned her way. A slim woman with short bobbed blonde hair and red-rimmed glasses stood near the back with a voice recorder in hand.

Deputy Todd glanced at the woman once and continued, "—should contact the Sheriff's Office immediately."

"Deputy, if I may…" she started again.

"No, Miss Valentine," he spat. "You may not. Questions will be addressed at the end."

Miss Valentine, as Deputy Todd identified her,

smiled sweetly and whispered something into her recorder.

"As I was saying," he continued. "Anyone with information should contact authorities immediately. I also recommended citizens refrain from solitary activities and that doors remain locked whether or not you are at home.

"Now, regarding Mr. Bobby Teach, the investigation is currently underway into the circumstances of his death. No details will be shared at this time due to the nature of the investigation." He stepped back from the podium as Mayor Jim took the lead.

"Are there any questions—"

"Mayor!" Miss Valentine shot her hand in the air. "Veronica Valentine, reporting for the *Vista View*." Her voice pierced through the murmuring crowd. "There have been reports that Bobby Teach's manner of death was the result of, and I quote 'blunt force trauma.' Can you speak to these reports?" She thrust the voice recorder toward the front of the room to capture his response. Mayor Jim looked nervously toward the deputy as though caught in headlights, begging him to take over.

Deputy Todd glared at Veronica, then his eyes darted toward Lovie who quickly shrunk into the crowd in the back corner. No surprise where that information leaked out. He stepped to the microphone.

"I have no comment on those *supposed reports*. Mr. Teach's body was found on the rocks below the bluff and, as you can imagine, it was in rough shape. His car was found nearby, which has been towed as evidence."

She continued, "And can you verify that a Poppy Lewis was the individual who *discovered* Vernon Dogger's body at the Treasures of the Coast shop on the

Coastal Road?" Veronica's voice languished on the word. It sounded deceptive when she said it, as though another more sinister would be more fitting in its place.

I sat upright, alert. I hadn't expected to be called out by name, by a reporter no less, and in front of the entire town. I mean, I was sure they probably knew I discovered the body. Lovie was, after all, Deputy Todd's wife. But this woman was questioning my involvement in public, and insinuating that the facts weren't really the facts, and that raised my hackles.

"Now just a minute, lady," Harper began. "Poppy Lewis is a victim here. She's completely traumatized, as are we all after losing Bobby and Vernon."

Veronica considered her, then turned the recorder their way. "Strange though, how her arrival coincided almost precisely with these two unprecedented events. Or so I am told."

Angie puffed up like a bulldog. "Nonsense," she said, her face red.

The room buzzed with excitement. People in the front stood up to get a better look at the confrontation. Lily, I noticed, stood like a marble statue, arms crossed, face unreadable. Ugh, of course she would hear all of this. I slid low in my chair, trying to shrink away.

"Order. Order." Mayor Jim pounded his fist on the podium. "Would everyone please be quiet? This line of questioning is over." He waited for the crowd to settle and retake their seats.

"The next item on the agenda—" Before he finished, a hand rose from dead center in the front row. Unmissable.

"Yes, Doctor?"

The man stood up and turned to face the larger group. He seemed to me to be about average height, with brown mousy hair, glasses, and wore a neat periwinkle V-neck sweater. Very proper. Lines barely creased his face, and I figured he couldn't be over forty.

The man ran his hands down his sweater, straightening invisible wrinkles, then cleared his throat.

"Thank you, Mr. Mayor," he said in a thick Scottish accent. My jaw gaped open. That was about the last thing I expected to hear from this unassuming man's mouth. "Bobby Teach's death may have been a tragic accident, but our friend Vernon didn't shoot himself. Now, I—and I'm sure everyone else—would like some assurances that the people of Starry Cove are safe."

I leaned closer to Angie. "Who is that?"

"That's Dr. MacKenzie. He's the new pharmacist now that Arthur's gone. He's only been here about two months or so. Nice guy, though, from what I can tell."

Harper crowded in. "Pretty cool accent, eh?"

Deputy Todd took the podium microphone again. "I can say that we recommend all citizens refrain from activities that may pose a danger."

"Aye. I understand that you want us to be careful and use common sense, but what are *you* doing to ensure the safety of this community?"

Deputy Todd stiffened. The doctor clearly struck a nerve.

"I am serving this community as I always have, though you may not be aware since you're new in town. I am using professional investigative techniques, of which I have been properly trained in my capacity as a law enforcement officer. However, the person, or persons, responsible for the death of Vernon Dogger are not currently in custody. Yet. If that's what you're getting at, Dr. MacKenzie. Now," he said, turning to the crowd at large. "Are there any other questions?"

"One more—"

"Not you, Miss Valentine," he snapped.

The air was still as Mayor Jim hustled to the podium. "Thank you, Deputy. The next item on our agenda is Starry Cove's very own Pie Parade, which I'm sure you've all been looking forward to…"

His words faded as I stared off, lost in thought. *Person or persons responsible*, he'd said. They're still out there. With the suspicious break-in at the house, I wondered if I was truly safe. And does the town think I'm a murderer now? I glanced around at their faces, but none seemed to be looking my way too intently, their interest captured by the next topic. I scanned to Lily again, whose eyes met mine like daggers until I broke my gaze. I imagined the gears working in Lily's head, plotting her next move, planning how to leverage this to her own advantage.

Tapping on my shoulder brought my attention back to my friends. "What?"

"I said," repeated Angie, "do you think it's too basic if I did an apple pie for the parade?"

"What parade?"

"The Pie Parade. Does it seem selfish to think of the parade with all this murder business going on?"

"Angie," Harper said, butting in. "You could bake a turnip pie with dog food crust and you'd still win first prize."

Angie blushed. "Thanks. I think."

"This meeting's over. I'm going to hit the snack table one more time." Harper jumped up from her chair and was off.

Indeed, the meeting had adjourned, and people shuffled from their seats to the exit doors.

"I need to talk to Roy really quick, but I'll be right back." Angie scurried off toward her husband, who was also scavenging at the snack table. I watched as she smacked a cookie from his hand.

"Miss Lewis," came a perky voice from behind, "may I ask you a few questions?" I spun around to find a recorder thrust a few inches from my face.

"Uh, no comment." I eyed the device in front of me. My face got hot and my cheeks turned red.

"I haven't even asked my questions."

"No comment," I repeated, turning and rushing toward the snack table to seek safe harbor with Harper or Angie. Harper spotted me first.

"What's going on? Is that lady bothering you?"

"She wants to ask me questions."

"Oh yeah?" Harper's eyes narrowed and a grin spread across her face. "I'll give her some answers."

Veronica had followed me along my path, intent on getting her story, but Harper stepped between us, grabbed Veronica's hand and shook it vigorously. "Hi, I'm Harper Tillman. T-I-L-L-M-A-N. Big fan, really big fan. I'm sure you've got tons of questions…" Harper wrapped her lanky arm around Veronica and led her off to the other side of the room.

I silently thanked Harper for being such a wonderfully annoying person when she wanted to be. Sighing in relief, I once again found myself alone in the sea of people. Angie was still at the snack table. Beside her, Nick leaned casually against the wall. His hair was messy, like the first time I'd seen him at the house. Hands in his pockets, he stared at something across the room, unfazed by the crowd of people noisily herding past him to the door. Maybe we could pick up where we'd left off at the diner, but before I took a step in his direction, he shot off through an emptied row of seats to the far side of the room. My eyes followed as he strolled up to Lily and introduced himself. Lily, always obliging to attractive men, greeted him with a smile. My heart sank. *Typical*, I thought.

"Miss Lewis?" came a distinctive voice beside me.

"Dr. MacKenzie. Hello," I said half-heartedly.

"Call me Ryan, please. I wanted to say hello since I heard you're new in town, like me. I promise it gets better." He shared a wink.

"You seem to have ruffled the deputy's feathers a bit."

"Oh, he's all bluster and froth." Ryan glanced the deputy's way and pushed his glasses up at the nose. "There's not much to be said of the law around here, so I wanted to be sure he's doing something proactive."

"I've had my own encounters with our deputy."

"Right. Nasty business yesterday. I'm sure it couldn't have been pleasant."

"No," I replied before changing course. "I hear you've taken on the pharmacy in town. My uncle, Arthur Lewis, was the previous pharmacist before he passed away."

"Aye. Sorry to hear about your uncle. I thought a quiet town would be just what I needed. Guess I was

73

wrong about that, eh?"

I smiled at this—similar thoughts crossed my mind recently. Here was a man faced with the same new town and new people and he seemed to have made it work, or at least he was faking it pretty well.

"Well, I've got to run," he said. "It was very nice meeting you, Miss Lewis, even under the current circumstances. Hopefully I'll see you again soon." His blue eyes twinkled behind his glasses, and I noticed his smile was crooked just to the left side, genuine and unassuming.

"You too. And call me Poppy."

"Goodbye then, Poppy."

I watched him wander away and disappear into the crowd before turning back to the snack table ready to search for Harper and Angie, but they stood only a few feet behind me, staring at me like a teenager caught after curfew.

"What?" I asked, blushing.

Eleven

THE NEXT MORNING Harper and I joined Angie at the bakery intending to start our day the right way—with coffee and cinnamon rolls. This was becoming a routine. As we chimed through the door, we found Angie bent double, fidgeting with the display of scones and cookies in the case, which had shifted in the bustle of the early morning rush. Angie's eyes popped over the top at our entrance.

"Oh good. Glad you're both here. Tell me if this line of scones is straight."

Harper held up an arm in line with the scones and squinted. "Straight as an arrow."

"Excellent." Angie slapped her hands on her apron, releasing a puff of flour. "What brings you two in here bright and early? Shouldn't you still be asleep, Harper?"

"I *am* still asleep, can't you tell? I'm sleepwalking and the only cure is coffee and a cinnamon roll." Harper splayed herself dramatically over the front of the case and pretended to snore.

"Same for me, Angie."

"You both seem in good spirits. I assume you haven't read the *Vista View* yet this morning?"

"Ugh, don't tell me that horrible reporter lady with a stick up her you-know-what is spreading rumors about our town?"

"Why do you think she was at the meeting last night? We've had one—maybe two—murders in town in the last few days. That makes for headline news around here." Her eyes darted my way. "And she mentioned Poppy." Angie grabbed the newspaper from the back counter and handed it to me.

There, front and center, bold font and dripping with drama, read the title: "Killer in the Cove: Can the Community Survive Another Murder?" I scanned for my name, which appeared three quarters through the article on the front page.

> Poppy Lewis, who discovered the body of Vernon Dogger at his trinket shop on the Coastal Road, had only recently moved to Starry Cove. According to reports, Poppy Lewis was alone at the time of the discovery and there are no other witnesses to corroborate her story. The County Sheriff's Office is investigating the death as a homicide and, although authorities identified only one person in the vicinity of the body, they report there are no suspects at this time.
>
> In addition, the discovery of the body of Bobby Teach occurred on the exact day Poppy Lewis arrived to take on the grand

Victorian mansion left to her in the will of her late uncle, Arthur Lewis. Poppy Lewis's sister and famed women's hat designer, Lillian Lewis, is contesting the will. According to Lillian Lewis, Poppy Lewis may have obtained the mansion through means that could only be described as deceptive or fraudulent. Poppy Lewis declined to comment on this story.

I slapped the paper down onto the table. "She makes me out like a conniving murderer."

"Let me see that." Harper, seated across the small table from me, snatched the article and read it for herself. "This isn't journalism. What a load of rubbish."

Angie's cheery voice broke in as she proffered two plates from behind the counter. "Sorry to ruin your morning. How about some pie instead of cinnamon rolls? Another coffee too?"

"Just what I came for," said Harper. "Thanks, Angie. I'm sure you'll bring home the prize this year. It looks delicious."

"Presentation is only part of the competition. There's still the aroma, taste, composition, and crowd's choice categories, all of which I have to nail if I want to win the trophy."

I took the plate and waved it under my nose. "Aroma is spot on. Beautiful lattice, flaky crust. I've never seen a piece of pie that looked more perfect."

"Do you smell the toasted nutmeg? It has to be noticeable."

Harper frowned. "I don't even know what nutmeg

smells like. You can't expect us laypeople to know all your fancy herbs and spices. This smells like apple pie, that's all I can tell."

"Can you at least tell me if it tastes like apple pie?"

"Gladly." Harper heaved a spoonful into her mouth.

"What did you do last year for the competition?" I asked, taking my first bite. It was amazing.

"Last year I made a blackberry honey lattice pie à la mode with homemade vanilla ice cream."

"That sounds spectacular."

"Thanks, but I didn't win. I think the ice cream was a miscalculation. Shelby won. I like her as a person but she's basically my archnemesis in the Pie Parade, so don't share any details with her. This is all super top secret. There's another fellow over in Vista who brings his A-game each year, too. It's been down to the three of us to take home the prize for the past five years."

"Last year, Angie's entry came in second to Shelby's double layer chocolate banana cream pie with torched marshmallow whipped topping and toasted coconut sprinkles."

"Sounds like this thing is really competitive."

"You have no idea," said Angie. "It stresses me out preparing for it each year. Roy has to deal with my hemming and hawing over recipes. Last year I berated him so badly when he couldn't tell me if the whole blackberries in the filling were too big or too small that he ran out of the house and didn't come back all night. That may have been the last straw—he told me to have you two be the testers this year."

"No complaints here." Harper smacked her lips. "You got anything else for us to try? This one is a seven out of ten for me. I think you can do better."

"A seven?" Angie shook her head. "I *knew* apple pie was too basic for this year."

"You need to do something dynamic. Unexpected."

"Yeah," I said. "It's the best apple pie I've ever had, but at the end of the day, it is just apple pie."

"Back to the drawing board, I guess."

"Chin up, Angie. I heard from Shelby that Lovie was planning on entering this year. Anything you make will shine like a heavenly beacon next to whatever garbage-infused monstrosity she bakes up."

"Lovie? Why on earth would she enter a baking contest? Forgive me," Angie said, holding up her hands, "but even the baked goods she buys at the grocery store always seem to be stale."

"I've never heard you sound so ruthless," said Harper, grinning. "At least it's someone you can easily beat."

"But I doubt even the distraction of a pie competition will take Lovie's mind off spreading the gossip in this article. What am I going to do? The entire town will think I'm a murderer and a house thief."

"What you are going to do," Harper mumbled, mouth full of pie and brandishing her fork, "is fight Lily in court. Or on the battlefield with weapons of your choosing, whichever you'd like. Either way, you're going to win, and you're going to renovate that great big house and open your beautiful bed-and-breakfast and shut everyone up."

"I need to call my lawyer again."

"And find out who broke into your house," added Angie. "Maybe it was Lily trying to get a peek at what she was fighting for."

"That's just it, though. When I think about it, nothing was broken into at all. The house was locked up tight, all the windows and the front and back doors."

"But what about those creepy footprints in your basement?"

"Maybe I was wrong about how old they were."

Harper crossed her arms. "That doesn't change the fact that they bee-lined to the walled-up doorway and then skedaddled without looking at anything else. We should break down that wall and see what Arthur was hiding."

"What if it's something awful?" asked Angie. "I couldn't bear it."

"Harper's right. We should find out what's behind the wall."

"But how does that help to clear your name?"

"Maybe it doesn't, Angie. But I'm sick of all these lingering questions and at least this could give us some answers."

"Ok, we're agreed. More pie?" Harper asked, holding up her plate.

"Sorry, but I don't serve seven-out-of-ten pie in this fine establishment. How about a perfect-ten cookie instead?"

***

Later that morning I searched the property for anything that might be useful in breaking the basement wall. If Arthur built it, then maybe he owned tools to tear it down. But I found that the basement itself was mostly empty, just the usual used paint cans and obsolete electronics and gadgets. I'd even sifted through the moldy shed that sat at the end of the driveway, but only found an old lamp with

a frayed cord and crumpled shade, a collection of din-
nerware (mostly broken), and crumbling books and papers crammed into the remaining space. The only exciting
find was a classic Vespa scooter tucked in the back, which
I thought was pretty cool but needed a ton of work in a
skill that I did not possess. Ultimately, nothing in the shed
seemed useful.

Which is why I found myself at the hardware store,
which sat next to the general store, which sat next to the
bookstore. Everything in a neat row, everyone watching
everyone else's every move. I'd just mosey in and explain
that I needed a sledgehammer for some renovation work.
This would be my first renovation project, after all.

"Hello there, Miss Lewis," came a man's voice behind the counter as I walked in. He was a tall, older gentleman, slightly balding, his skin darkened by years of
gritty work, no doubt. He wore overalls, although his
were much grimier and distressed than mine, probably
also due to years of hard work, which I could not claim.

"Hello. I'm not sure we've met."

"No, I guess we haven't. I'm Trevor French."

"Nice to meet you, Trevor. Is this your store? I was
in here a few days ago but must have missed you. Mr.
Dogger—Walter—fell and I came over to help."

"Ahh yes. I spend a lot of time in the back room and
must have missed the whole commotion. Came back out
front and the store was quite a mess."

"Sorry about that."

"Oh, no harm. Poor Walter, though. Can't imagine
what he's going through right now, losing his brother and
all. They were real close, those two."

"Did you know Vernon well?"

"Sure did. He was in and out of here all the time. The three of us went to school together, back in the Dark Ages. Did some business together, this and that." He shook his head. "Now, who knows."

"Were you doing any business together at the time of his death?"

"We had a project planned for next month. Something about selling craft cheeses to tourists, but that probably won't go anywhere now. Vernon and Walter were always coming up with these wild money-making schemes. Always trying to get folks to buy in to their ideas. Some worked, most didn't. I'm willing to invest if the time is right and the project is sound, mind you, but there were plenty of deals I'm glad I wasn't a part of." Trevor shook his head again. "Those two sure were something together. It'll be strange without Vernon around."

"I'm sorry you lost such a good friend, and I'm sure he'll be sorely missed. Bobby too."

"Now, Bobby I didn't know so well, which is odd considering I run a hardware store and he was a handyman always working on projects around town—he even fixed up my bicycle, once. Bit of a rough side to that one, always scrounging for work, never really settling on anything. I remember he bought a real nice set of tools from me a few weeks ago, including some fancy pieces I ordered special. Paid cash. I recall he shared a place with Nick Christos. I think they worked together since I've seen them come in together quite a bit. Or did, but they were always quiet and weren't much for talkin'."

"So, Nick and Bobby at least must have known each other pretty well."

"I'd say so." Trevor's voice lowered to a whisper

even though we were alone. "There were rumors around town, on account of them living together, but I didn't pay those no mind. Nick's well known to like the ladies. He always seems to be with some new young thing every week. Tourists driving through our little town looking for some weekend fun, that sort of thing."

"I've met Nick. I can see why the ladies would like him."

Trevor chuckled. "No doubt. But listen to me blather on like an old fossil. What can I help you with today?"

"I need something big that can break concrete."

"Doing a bit of demolition on the house?"

"Er, renovations. I'm thinking of pulling up a small patio in the back." It wasn't technically a lie since I did plan to tear up one of those patios eventually. I just wasn't sure who in town I could trust, so I figured it was better to hold back where I could. Trevor seemed nice enough, but I wasn't willing to chance it.

"I have a selection of tools along the back wall that'll do the trick. Let me know if you have any questions."

I waded through the aisles to the back and perused the heavy weaponry when after a minute or two I heard the shop door open.

"Hello there, Doctor. What can I do for you?" I ducked my head slightly, trying to hide among the rows. I didn't necessarily want to hide from anyone, but I also didn't want to have to explain myself to anyone either. Like any not-at-all-suspicious person, I just wanted to grab my sledgehammer and go on my merry way.

"Good morning, Trevor. Nice to see you again. Just need to pick up a few things to finish that gazebo I've been working on."

"Not done with that thing yet?" Trevor chuckled.

"Sadly not. I may have bit off more than I can chew on that project. Should have started with something a wee bit smaller, like a nice, easy spice rack."

"You just holler if you want any help. I know a few folks who'd be happy to lend a hand."

"Thanks, but I think I've finally got the hang of it."

His footsteps approached along the aisle, and I braced for impact.

"Ah, Poppy. What a pleasant surprise. What brings you here?"

"Just here for some tools. For the house. For the out-side of the house. Er, for a patio." I stumbled, my tongue tying itself in knots. "How is your gazebo?"

"Heard that then?"

Whoops, I thought, scrunching my face in embarrass-ment. "I wasn't trying to overhear."

He leaned in close and whispered, "To be honest, it's a mess. Don't tell Trevor though—I'd never hear the end of it."

"Your secret is safe with me," I whispered back.

"You should come by and see it. Once I've finished, of course. On the other hand, that may be never. I may end up setting the whole thing on fire and be done with it."

"Why don't you take Trevor up on his offer then?"

"I'm too chicken to let on that I'm a failure. Months later and I'm still struggling with first impressions and fitting in. Actually, since you're in the same boat as me and you're already privy to my carpentry secret, would you like to grab dinner with me sometime? You know, the two new folks comparing notes."

It took a moment for the question to register. I'd spent the past decade in married obscurity, so I was a little out of practice, but I think the doctor was asking me on a date.

"Like, a date?"

I must have looked puzzled because Ryan quickly responded, "Well, maybe just a friendly dinner shared by two people who have something in common?"

I quickly corrected myself. "Sorry, yes. Dinner sounds great. Where?"

"Not scared of Shelby's, are you? Best food in the county, or so we've been told."

Despite my desire to say yes, I was reluctant to accept such a conspicuous location for our not-date. He looked so pleased with himself though, as though he'd faced a great trial and come out the victor.

"Shelby's would be perfect."

"Fantastic. Tomorrow at seven then?"

"Sure. Seven o'clock."

"Well, I've got to grab these screws before I head back next door. I might grab a flame-thrower for that gazebo too. See you then, Poppy."

"Ryan," I said, stopping him. "Did you happen to work with Bobby Teach or Nick Christos on your gazebo?"

"No, neither. I've been trying to do it all myself. That's why it's turned out so badly."

"Oh, right. Did you know Bobby at all?"

"I don't know anyone here well outside of my professional capacity. Is there something about Bobby you want to know?"

"No, I was just curious about him."

"Okay, see you then." He walked back down the aisle toward Trevor, who waited for him at the checkout, leaving me to wonder just who Bobby Teach was to the people in town. Did anyone really know him?

Twelve

"So, when is this glamorous date at Shelby's Diner?" Harper asked, seated at the single table inside the bakery.

"Tell us again how he asked you," said Angie, batting her eyelashes. "Do the voice."

I laughed at Angie's insistence. He did have an exotic and sexy accent, and all the more intriguing coming from such an unassuming man. "It's not a date, and I'm not going to do the voice again, okay? He was very nice, and dinner is tomorrow. Which means," my voice grew serious, "we're breaking the basement wall tonight."

"Right." Harper clapped her hands together. "I'm ready."

"How late are we going to be? I hate to leave Roy to open the bakery alone again."

"That depends on what we find, right Poppy?"

"I suppose so. Don't worry, Angie. I'll make a big pot of coffee."

Angie looked toward the door that led to the kitchen. The sound of Roy struggling with a tray cart drifted into the front of the bakery. "Okay. I'll let Roy know I'm leaving. But next time we decide to explore a scary basement, let's do it in the early afternoon or on my day off."

We left the bakery and walked down to the house as the sun set beyond the horizon. As promised, I brewed a fresh pot of coffee and set out some snacks. Before coming to Starry Cove, I couldn't say I had many friends—any good friends at least—who weren't also friends with my ex-husband. And I left all of that behind. Now, I thanked my stars for Harper and Angie and the immediate and natural friendship we'd formed. It certainly wasn't something I'd expected, but I was thankful nonetheless. With the unexpected events over the past few days, I couldn't imagine facing this new town without the two of them at my side.

"Look," Harper said, holding out her thin trembling hands. "I'm already shaking, I'm so excited to see what we're going to find."

"Let's get to it. I bought some flashlights along with the sledgehammer so we'll be able to see properly." I handed one to each of them as we stood staring at the door to the basement. It loomed in the corner, daring us to enter and take our chances below.

I led our intrepid team down the stairs, flashlight in one hand, sledgehammer hung in the other, and soon we found ourselves back in front of the bare basement wall. I had handed Harper the blueprints and now examined them again to ensure we were in the correct location.

"I can knock on the wall again and make sure we're in the clear."

"Okay, knock and I'll give it a go." I handed my flashlight to Angie, who pointed them both at the wall, the light they cast quavering slightly along with her hands.

Harper knocked once chest high at the center of the wall. "Yep, still hollow. Hit it right here."

I stepped up to the wall and swung the sledgehammer to the side behind me before bringing it swiftly around like a home run hitter to crash squarely on the wall. We peered forward in the dark. A tiny crumble of concrete dribbled to the floor.

"This might be a long night," said Angie.

"Let me try." Harper stepped up to the plate. She took the hammer and gave it a mighty swing, grunting as the weighted head hit the wall, buckling a large portion.

"Nice job," said Angie. "Hit it again and I think we might be able to peek inside."

"Wait, do you both think this wall is secure? Is the house going to come down on us?"

"No way. Arthur added this afterward, and it's a doorway anyway. We're just making it a doorway again." Harper slammed the hammer around once more and the concrete tumbled away to reveal a dark hole. No light came from within, and the air was cold and dusty with concrete particles.

I stepped forward with a flashlight and shone it inside while also trying to peek through the small opening.

At first, I thought it was empty. The room certainly wasn't full of more Victorian furniture or ancient wine, much to my disappointment. "I can't really see anything."

"Let me open it up further." Harper smashed the hammer a few more times until she created a hole large enough for us to fit through.

One by one we crawled through the opening and into

the hidden room. It was dark, the only illumination came from our three flashlights. But even those were enough to show us the room was small, perhaps only ten feet by ten feet square. The ceiling height was even with the rest of the basement area, and I was sure now that this was directly under the living room.

"There's something in the far corner here," said Angie. Her flashlight lit on a rectangular metal box lying on the floor, fixed with tarnished hinges and what appeared to be a substantial lock.

"Yes," Harper squealed. "It's a treasure chest."

Angie sighed. "It's just a box, Harper. It could be full of rusty nails for all we know. Or something sinister. What if Arthur wasn't a nice old man after all? What if he stored mementos of his past illicit deeds in this very box, never meant for anyone's eyes ever again and we're about to find out all about—"

"Angie," I scolded. "Focus. I don't see anything else. This chest must be all that was walled-up in here." I leaned down to get a closer look. The box was a bit larger than a shoebox, except the metal was scored and beaten, definitely old. Dust lay in a thick layer upon the top and nestled in the crevasses of the hinges and locking mechanism.

"Let's get this out of here so we can see what we're dealing with. The kitchen would be best."

"Can you lift it?" asked Harper.

"I think so," I said, hoisting it off the floor. "Something's definitely inside. It's got a little weight to it, that's for sure."

"Maybe it's gold doubloons."

"Not likely, Harper."

"Well, it's not a Victorian armoire."

"I didn't see a key. Did either of you?" I asked.

Angie swung her flashlight around, focusing on the floor and the dark corners. "I don't see a key."

"Then let's get out of here and up to the kitchen. I want to get this opened if we can."

We made our way back through the broken doorway and up the stairs into the kitchen, where I set the box in the center of the table and lifted the lock. Rusty and dusty, but secure.

"I don't suppose Arthur left you any old-timey looking keys, did he?" Harper asked.

"There was a keychain with all the house keys on it, but those are all accounted for and none would fit this lock."

"Of course not," said Angie. "Why would he put this lock on the box and wall it up in a secret room in the basement just to leave the key to it on a ring that anyone could get to?"

"I suppose we could break it open. Shame, though." I looked over the lock mechanism and wondered what the best way would be to break it open without damaging the contents. "If we try to smash it open, we could break whatever's inside." I tapped the box with a finger. "I think this might be steel."

Harper handled the lock in her long fingers. "Well, we're not opening this with our bare hands. Do you have bolt cutters? Those should work."

"I rummaged in the shed earlier and Arthur didn't have any tools. I don't think he was very D-I-Y."

"No, I wouldn't say he was either," said Angie. "He was such a quiet man. Which makes this all so strange.

The basement, this box, that furniture upstairs. Really strange."

"I can get bolt cutters tomorrow at the hardware store," I said. "It's closed now."

"If we're cutting this lock off tomorrow, then we're doing it before five o'clock. You promised."

"That shouldn't be a problem. Maybe earlier if you're both free."

"I will make myself free," Harper said. "I'm dying to see what's inside. I'm not sure I can wait until tomorrow—I might gnaw this lock off with my teeth."

"I probably won't be able to sleep tonight now anyway, thanks to this mystery," said Angie. "Let's get it done as soon as possible. My nerves can't take much more."

***

That night I lay awake on the inflatable mattress in the living room. I set up my small pile of belongings in one corner of the room, like an island in a sea of Arthur's old life. His chairs, his sofa, his bookcase with his books and memories. *What were you up to, Arthur?*

My head rested on the pillow and as I drifted to sleep, I imagined making this house into a charming bed-and-breakfast retreat. Arthur's old room could be the honeymoon suite, the Victorian room needed nothing more—I would advertise it as an authentic Victorian escape. The other two could be classic, but still retain the homey feeling one expects from a bed-and-breakfast. Images filled my mind, colors, the ocean, and the sea breeze…

A crash startled me awake. Had it come from the kitchen? I sat up slowly to avoid making noise, the air mattress giving way easily to my movements. I sat for a moment, listening. Nothing. It might be silent now, but I was sure I'd heard a noise in the kitchen.

I raised myself off the mattress. A faint squeak escaped as it shifted on the floor. I waited another moment then inched into the foyer. From there, I peeked into the kitchen. No lights were on, but my eyes had grown accustomed to the dark. I made out the edge of the counter and the small table against the wall. Movement caught my eye as something jumped off the counter and scampered past me into another room. Just Mayor Dewey.

Stepping forward lightly into the kitchen doorway, I felt along the wall until I found the switch and turned on the light. The sudden brightness made me squint, but I saw something on the floor. It was one of my ceramic birds, shattered to pieces across the linoleum. I rushed over to gather the fragments and felt a gust of cold sea air hit my face. The window was open. Not just open, it splayed wide and the other birds lay scattered and disturbed upon the sill.

I sucked in a breath. I was sure this window was closed last night. *Did someone come in through here?* I thought. That would explain the cat, but he couldn't have opened it. Another gust blew through the room and a faint squeal of hinges made me turn to the basement door. It was ajar. *Were they still here?*

With everything going on in this town in the past few days, and the history of this house, I wasn't taking any chances. I grabbed a knife from the block on the counter and readied myself for the worst. Although the door was just a few feet away, each step toward it felt like an eternity. Light peeked into the stairwell from the overhead kitchen fixture, but I couldn't make out anything distinct. I reached for the doorknob, knife at the ready in my other hand. Just as I placed my fingers on the knob, the door crashed open in a blur. The knife flew from my hand, skittering to the other side of the room as I was knocked back onto the floor. A darkened figure leaped over me toward the open window, but I grabbed the person's pant leg and held on tight, all sense of reason and self-preservation gone.

"Who are you?" I demanded.

A dark gloved hand came down heavily on my arms. I heard heavy grunts as the shadow struck me repeatedly until I gave way and its leg came free.

I winced in pain. In the chaos I tried desperately to make out a face, but the figure scurried over the sill and into the night, leaving me prostrate and panting alone on the kitchen floor.

Thirteen

ANGIE HELD THE ice pack against my head while Deputy Todd continued his questioning.

"And then you said this figure jumped through the open window?"

"Yes."

"Do you remember if the window was locked before you went to bed?"

"I can't say I checked. There are a lot of windows in this house." I glanced at Harper and Angie. I'd called them both after phoning the authorities and they arrived swiftly after that. "But I was a bit distracted so I may have forgotten."

"Do you have any idea who this individual was?"

"All I heard were grunts, but they were low and gruff. The figure was also taller and bulkier than the average woman, so I'd say it was most likely a man."

"That could be anyone, though," said Harper.

"Do you have any idea why this individual wanted to break into your home?"

Harper and Angie shot me a quick look.

"No," I said. "And *nothing* is missing that I can tell." I tried to stress the words, hoping Harper and Angie understood that the box was still safe and undisturbed.

Deputy Todd grunted and scribbled in his notebook. "I'll log this report and check for any footprints outside, but the weather's been pretty dry, so I don't have much hope. And I'll remind you that you should lock your doors and windows at all times."

"Thank you, Deputy." I did my best to feign a yawn. "I'm so grateful for your assistance. Right now, I'm just a little shaken and probably need to get some rest."

"Of course. Call me if you think of anything else. Lots of strange things going on lately. Could all be tied together."

"I will be sure to let you know." I showed the deputy out and hurried back to the living room.

"The box is safe, right?" Harper asked.

I nodded. "Yeah. I stowed it away last night."

"Things are getting serious, Poppy. You could have been hurt. Really hurt."

"Angie, if he wanted to hurt me he would have. But he just darted out. He was after the box, I know it. He must have snuck in through the unlocked window, gone down to the basement and discovered the broken wall and empty room. The wind or Mayor Dewey must have knocked over one of my birds—that's the only thing that woke me up."

"So, he could think that nothing was ever in the room."

Angie added, "Or he could know that you have whatever was in there."

96

"Either way, this couldn't have been the person who was in the house before, otherwise why come back?"

"Maybe he was going to open the wall, like we did," said Angie.

"But there're no tools or anything left behind. I mustered enough courage to look before the deputy got here."

"Where is the box now?" Harper asked.

"It's on the other side of my mattress, under that little table." I motioned to a small side table sitting beside my air mattress. I realized now how pathetic this all looked. That I needed to set up a permanent space for myself. This temporary setup could not continue for much longer.

Harper leaned down and hefted the box into her arms, inspecting the lock. "I don't see how we could break this lock without more substantial tools, otherwise I'd say let's break this sucker open and get it over with."

"We already decided that we'll open it at a reasonable time and use bolt cutters." Angie checked her watch.

"Sorry about all this you guys. I didn't mean to drag you over here in the middle of the night."

"You didn't drag us anywhere. Someone attacked you, remember? Do you want to stay with us tonight? Roy won't mind."

"No, I'll be okay. I just need to check every lock in this house again."

"I'll stay," said Harper. "It'll be another girls' sleepover."

"Okay, but let's not tell scary stories. I've experienced enough excitement for one night."

***

The remainder of the night was uneventful, and I went

back to sleep easily knowing Harper was nearby. Perhaps the perpetrator thought better of trying again after I fought back, or maybe he knew that whatever was behind that wall was now gone. Either way, I woke to a foggy coastal morning, perfect for enjoying the first cup of coffee of the day. I halted a moment as I entered the kitchen, remembering the events of the previous night, and mourned my lost bird.

Harper popped into the kitchen to share a quick greeting before darting out the door, running down the steps, already late for her route. I didn't mind that she left so suddenly—I had plans for today, too. Big plans. Plans to get to the bottom of whatever was going on and whoever was responsible. Last night gave me vision and clarity. My safety was on the line and that meant I needed to act.

I locked the house up tight—I checked twice—and headed to Shelby's Diner, where I hoped to find the place full of patrons enjoying a hearty breakfast. Sure enough, the place was packed. The first person I spotted was Walter, who sat alone nearby at the counter staring at his food. He must be going through a rough time, losing his brother and all, so I eased into the seat next to him gently.

"Hello, Walter. How are you doing today?" I asked in a soft voice.

"What…" Walter seemed to emerge from a daze. "Oh, Poppy. Hello there."

"Do you mind if I join you?"

"No, no I don't mind. Vernon used to sit there. You just startled me a bit."

"You must miss him terribly."

"I do." Walter hung his head a bit lower.

"Do you have any idea who may have wanted to hurt Vernon?"

Walter took a moment to respond. He stared through the food on his plate, lost in thought. "There ain't nobody I can think of who'd want to hurt my brother. Well, almost no one. We had business partners who probably wished we'd suffer something pretty terrible, or so they've threatened. But that doesn't make you someone's enemy, does it?" His voice trailed off as Shelby arrived at the counter to take my order.

"French toast, please. And a large coffee."

"More coffee for you, Walter?" Shelby asked gently.

He nodded and she filled his mug and left to put in my order.

"Walter, did Vernon have business partners who'd threatened him recently?"

"They all do, but it's just hot air. Or so I thought. Trevor's always harping on us; and I think Nick and him were working on a deal together, but I didn't hear that anything went south."

"Any idea what kind of deal they were working on?"

"Something about tourists. Some scheme to get tourists to spend money, probably at Vernon's shop."

"And you don't think they had a falling out?"

"If you're suggesting Nick did something to my brother, then no, I don't think he'd touch him. I didn't think anyone in this town would, but here we are." Walter slammed a hand down on the counter.

"I'm sorry, Walter. I've upset you." My words had gone too far. Walter was still struggling to cope with Vernon's death, and I'd steamrolled in with all sorts of questions. What an insensitive dolt.

"You're all right," he said. "I'm just… Well, I don't know what I am right now."

Shelby swung by with the carafe ready to fill any mugs that had an inch to spare and saw Walter struggling. "Walter, why don't I bring you out a big slice of my apple pie?"

Walter nodded slowly. "That'd be real nice, Shelby. On the house, right?"

"Sure thing. Whatever you need, Walter."

"Could I get it to go?" he asked. "I think I'll just head home."

"Sure, Walter. How about you, Poppy?"

"A slice of your pie sounds just wonderful. Thank you."

As Shelby headed to the back to prepare the pies, I wondered why Nick's name kept coming up in conversation. As far as I knew, he was a just handyman who was also pretty handy with the ladies, and he certainly didn't come across as a shrewd businessman, let alone a cold-blooded killer. This was the first time I heard that Nick had any connection with anyone other than for his handyman services. And according to Trevor, most of the work, handyman or side venture, went Bobby's way. I had to admit, Nick definitely had something to gain by getting Bobby out of the way. But Vernon?

Two clamshells appeared before us and Walter thanked Shelby for her hospitality. He gathered his coat before I gambled one last request. "Walter, if there's anything I can do, please let me know. And if you think of anything more about Vernon, would you let me know that as well?"

"Sure thing, Poppy. But I doubt I have much more to

share. We'll have to see what Deputy Todd finds out."

"Right, Deputy Todd. I'm sure he's working diligently." I handed Walter his pie and watched as he shuffled out the door. The chime seemed too cheery for the
mood of the day and Walter's face mirrored that mood as
I watched him pedal away down the street.

I spent the rest of my breakfast in thought about what
Walter said, and what Trevor had said. What everyone
said. Maybe Vernon's murder was one of those fly-by-
night thrill killings that probably only happen in places
other than Starry Cove. I sighed, still lost. So many questions and so few answers.

As if prompted by my downcast mood, Lovie rung
through the diner door's bell and sidled up to me at the
counter. "Good morning, Poppy, *so* glad to see you're doing well after last night."

"What happened last night?" Shelby asked, having
come by as soon as Lovie walked in.

"Our poor Poppy was accosted in that big house last
night. Absolutely awful to think of you, weak and fright-
ened, attacked by an unknown intruder." Lovie's curls
bounced with each jarring exclamation.

"That's not really an accurate—"

"And Todd, er, the deputy, ripped from our bed in the
middle of the night, sped to the crime scene to investigate."

It was easier to sit back and sip my coffee, letting
Lovie spill it all out than it was to correct her. Shelby bent
over, elbows on the counter and head in her hands, drink-
ing it in, clearly enraptured by the story. "Poppy, I had no
idea. And here I was yammering on about pie."

"It's okay, Shelby. It wasn't quite as dramatic as

Lovie makes it out to be. The person just ran off, anyway."

"But he was in your house. And with everything going on around town, weren't you a little scared?"

Truthfully, I was a lot scared, but I wasn't weak and frail the way Lovie described me. I was strong and fully intended to find the culprit. "I was scared, Shelby. But I acted to protect myself, which we should all keep in mind right about now."

"That's God's truth, there."

"I hope you're both taking precautions to stay safe," I said. "Vernon's death was shocking. It's hard to imagine anyone in a quaint town like this capable of that type of violence, but you never know."

Shelby nodded. "Oh sure, dearie. Everyone knows everyone around here. And while we aren't all the best of friends, it's hard to think of these folks shooting anyone, let alone a neighbor."

"Shelby's right. I don't think anyone in this town is capable of murder, except maybe Kenny."

"Oh, right. Kenny." Shelby nodded knowingly.

"What about Kenny?" I sat up a little straighter, my interest piqued. Finally. I knew the diner would pay off eventually, and I'd be sure to get something good out of the town gossips.

"Kenny's a bit, how do you say it? Volatile."

"He's got a temper, dearie."

"Yep." Lovie leaned into the counter closer to me and Shelby. "And I heard he had some harsh words for Walter the other day."

I remained silent. I didn't want to share what Harper and I witnessed at the hardware store, so I kept it to myself.

"And," Lovie continued, "I saw his car drive past here headed to the bluff the night Bobby died—or was murdered. That small road. You know Shelby, the one just past the fish stand before you get to the beach? I remember I turned to Walter beside me and said, 'Look, there goes Kenny, probably angry and drunk and headed in the wrong direction.'"

"Oh yeah. Tiny road, barely even a path. One car at a time, that sort of thing."

I nodded along with their words, letting it all sink in. "What do you think it means? Do you think Bobby's death wasn't an accident after all?"

"Well," Lovie said, smirking and looking around to check if anyone might overhear, "I don't know about you two, but I'd take a closer look at Kenny and what he's been up to."

"And what about you, Lovie?" I asked. "What were you doing when Bobby died and Vernon was murdered?"

"Me?" Lovie exclaimed, eyes bulging. "Why, I was with my husband all night when Bobby died. And I was probably here with Shelby the other day. You were here that morning too."

Shelby nodded vigorously. "Yes. I was here all day, working."

"Right, I don't mean to suggest that you had anything to do with Vernon's murder. It's just that, well, were you here for that long, Lovie? I mean, I was gone for hours between breakfast here at the diner and when I found Vernon."

"I will have you know I volunteer most afternoons at the church." Lovie leaned back and folded her arms. "The mayor was there too. He can vouch for me."

"Sorry," I said, having riled her up too much. "I didn't mean to come across that way. We're all in this together, right? To find out what happened to our friends?"

"Er, yes. I understand, I guess."

"Me too," said Shelby. "Vernon was a good friend and a valuable customer."

"Good. I hope you'll both tell me if you find out anything new. Anything at all."

"Absolutely," Lovie said. "I'm entirely devoted to finding out who could have done this to our poor Vernon. And Bobby, of course."

This new information gave me at least a few more leads to follow up on. As I was packing my things to leave the diner, my phone rang. It was my lawyer.

"Hello?" I answered, exiting through the diner door.

"Ms. Lewis, glad I caught you."

"Do you have an update on the estate?"

"I do, and I think you'll be happy to hear what I have to share." I could definitely use some good news. I waited for him to continue. "It appears your sister, Lillian, failed to establish protocols when she went overseas."

"What does that mean?"

"It means, I think we can show she had an obligation to manage her incoming mail while in Europe. After all, what if she received another legal document such as a summons or a subpoena? I don't think our case is any different."

"That's great news. What do we do now?"

"With your permission, I'm going to contact her attorneys and request they drop the case."

"And if they don't agree?"

"Then we go court and ask the judge to do the same."

"All right, keep me posted on what her lawyers say. I'm not holding my breath though. I'm sure her intent is to cause me as much grief as possible, not to actually walk away with the house in her name."

"I will certainly keep you apprised. Talk to you soon."

I hung up the phone, a little relieved, but not totally in the clear. I knew Lily didn't care whether she won or lost this case, only that she could dig her claws further into my new life. The woman had no shame. Vile, monstrous, hateful woman. But I intended to win this time.

Fourteen

THE HARDWARE STORE opened at ten o'clock, and I waited by the door until Trevor arrived with a smile to unlock it.

"Good to see you again bright and early, Poppy."

"Thanks, Trevor. Do you have bolt cutters? There's a lock at the house I need to remove, but I can't find a key." Technically true. I hated telling more lies, so I chose my words carefully.

"Oh sure, I've got those. Just over here." He showed me to the selection hanging on the display and I grabbed a set of cutters that looked brawny enough to snap the lock on the secret box.

A colorful flyer hung next to the checkout advertising the Pie Parade. "What's this about anyway?"

"You're in for a treat. The Pie Parade is a baking competition, and this town has a lot of bakers, not just Shelby and Angie. They let outsiders enter their pies too. It's real competitive—a point of pride for the winner and the town. And most of the well-known bakers keep their entries a secret until the day of the parade."

"Is it an actual parade?"

"Yep. Huge event, you'll see. All the town—and lots from other towns—come down to line the street for the parade. Each contestant walks their pie down Main Street, sweeping it under the noses of the spectators. Then, a panel of judges decides who the winner is."

"Who are the judges?"

"It's a secret. They always keep it a secret so the contestants can't try any funny business, if you know what I mean."

I nodded. "Sounds like fun."

"Oh, it is. The *Vista View* comes down and does a story on it every year, too. Big picture on the front page of the winner with their pie. They take those pictures at the starting line, since at the end of the parade the pies get eaten."

"I'm sure Angie will win. She's the best baker in town."

"She sure is one of the best, but like I said, it's real competitive. Now, can I help you with anything else?"

"This'll do it. Thanks, Trevor." I swung out the door and onto the sidewalk. I wanted to go straight to the house and break the lock. Curiosity gnawed at me, but I'd promised Harper and Angie that we'd do it together this afternoon. It was hard, but I held back and instead walked up the sidewalk until I arrived at the church which, according to the sign, was the non-denominational Fellowship of Faith, a mossy stone building straight out of the Middle Ages, except a digital marquee ran out front and it had contemporary essentials like running water and an indoor toilet.

Lucinda Harrison

The church was quiet at this time midmorning on a weekday. Most folks made their sole weekly visit on Sunday. Except for the sound of the trees waving in the sea breeze high above, there was no other sound as I approached. The fog had worn off and the sun shone brightly above me, giving the well-tended flowerbeds along the walkway some much-needed light.

The doors stood open during the daytime hours, desperately urging passersby to step inside and connect with their faith. I wandered into the entryway but saw no one inside. "Hello?" I called out. A moment later a balding head poked out of a door at the back of the nave.

"Hello. I'm Basil Meyers. I'm the pastor here." He wore what was left of his stringy gray hair in a low ponytail, delicate rimless glasses perched on his nose. A tie-dyed shirt peeked out from underneath his shabby cardigan, which draped loosely on his thin shoulders, wrinkled and moth-eaten. I noticed the cardigan hung slightly askew, buttoned off by one buttonhole. Knobby knees poked out from his shorts and on his feet were simple flip flops.

"Just who I was looking for. I'm Poppy Lewis. I just moved to town. I took over the purple Victorian that used to belong to Arthur Lewis."

"Yeah, yeah sure. I know who you are. Welcome to our little slice of heaven, Poppy." He extended his arms out to the expanse of the church. "Groovy name you've got, Poppy. Were your parents part of the movement?"

"The movement?"

"The enlightenment movement. Poppies are a gateway to a deep and meaningful level of enlightenment for those seeking its embrace."

"Uh, I think my parents just liked flowers. My sister's name is Lillian, or Lily, as we call her."

"Far out. Flowers are God's embellishments on Earth," he said, bobbing his head up and down in a slow rhythm. "What can I do for you? You said you were looking for me."

"I was hoping you could help me with some questions I have. See, I'm new here, and I'm eager to get involved. I heard there are volunteer opportunities here at the church, particularly during the afternoon hours."

"Yeah, sure. We have regular volunteer hours. Mostly packaging non-perishables for distribution to the food pantry in Vista or preparing handouts for Sunday services."

"Do you have many volunteers?"

"They come and go, but some are fairly regular, bless them."

"I thought I saw Mayor Jim in here the other day, and Lovie Newman. Do they volunteer here often?"

He thought a moment. "They do come in a lot, but I can't really remember them volunteering in the past few days. I've been expecting more people to come in seeking the comforts of the church, with everything going on, you understand, but it's been pretty quiet around here. I would remember if they'd come in, so you must've seen someone else."

My internal eyebrows rose at this revelation. Why would Lovie lie about where she was during the murder? What was she trying to do anyway, saying she was at the church with the mayor volunteering?

I took the pastor's hand and shook it quickly. "Thank you, Pastor. I'll swing by whenever I have time to volunteer."

"I hope to see you on Sundays, too," he winked. "All flowers need the light of God to flourish." And with that he shuffled back to his office.

The pastor had been surprisingly helpful, but my back hurt from last night's scuffle so I sat at a nearby pew for a moment, just to give myself a rest. Soon after, I heard two people entering through the open doors behind me.

"I'd never have said that to Kenny. He'd have blown his lid." The voice belonged to a woman, but whispers inside a nearly empty church had the odd effect of amplifying that which you wanted to keep quiet.

"I know, but you should have—" The voice of the other woman cut out as they greeted Pastor Basil at his office.

"Ahh, Georgia, Beatrice, groovy," he said, his voice mellow. "So nice to see you on this beautiful sunny day. What a glorious gift from God."

"Yes, isn't it? We came by to talk about Saturday's bell choir practice…" The sound of voices disappeared as he shut the door behind them.

I wasn't sure which woman was which, but it seemed to me just more evidence that Kenny was violent. First Walter, then both Shelby and Lovie mentioned it, now this. My sole interaction with him when he assaulted Walter was all I needed in order to know Kenny was a dangerous person. If I were to ask him questions, I wanted to be sure someone was with me, or at least that I was in a public place, although that hadn't helped Walter very much.

I clutched my bag and headed to the back of the

church toward the exit to the street. As I approached the doors, I heard a set of heels clacking on the walkway. Unsure of who I would encounter, I quickly hid myself behind the door just as a figure cast a shadow onto the church floor from outside. A slim and severe silhouette topped with a wide-brimmed hat, tilted slightly to the side. I recognized it immediately.

Lily entered the church and slowly made her way down the pews, choosing one near the front. I stayed hidden. The last thing I wanted was a confrontation with my sister right now, in a church no less. But what was Lily doing in a church? As far as I knew, she had never been much for religion or faith. Probably trying to weasel her way into Pastor Basil's good graces. *Good luck, Lily*, I thought as I slipped out the door and into the open air. *God will see past your flower's deceptive beauty.*

Fifteen

I HADN'T WALKED far before I spotted Mayor Jim schmoozing with a couple on the sidewalk. Since this could be a fruitful chance encounter, I loitered some distance off, pretending to be interested in the flowers growing in the decorative planters that ran alongside Main Street. The mayor finally finished his chat and headed my way, striding confidently, self-assured smirk on his face.

"Hello, Mayor Jim." I feigned surprise as I flagged him down.

"Miss Lewis, so nice to see you out and about."

"I'm glad I ran into you. I had a question about the Fellowship of Faith church, and I was hoping you'd be able to help me."

"Well, sure thing. I'll answer what I can."

"Thanks," I gushed. "I ran into Lovie Newman earlier today and she mentioned you two often volunteer there."

Mayor Jim cleared his throat. "That's right. We were volunteering there just the other day. Preparing fliers, if I remember correctly."

"I was thinking of taking some time to volunteer my-self. Do you find it to be worthwhile? How much of your time does it take each day?"

"I'm not there each day, but I do go by often, usually for at least an hour or two. I'm sure Pastor Basil would appreciate any amount of assistance from his flock."

"Of course. I don't have any special skills to offer, but I can probably work on fliers, too."

"As a new member, that'd be a great way to support the town."

"I'm certainly trying," I cooed. "That reporter woman—What was her name?"

"Veronica Valentine."

"That's the one. That woman made me sound like a criminal at the meeting the other night, and I think it may have turned the town against me."

"Rumors can be nasty things," he said, shaking his head.

"I don't suppose there's been any progress on that murder case. It would be great if that could get cleared up so I can try to fix my image around town, being new and all."

"Well now, I can't say as I should share details with civilians."

"Oh, gosh, I'm not asking for details. I was just won-dering if there'd been any progress."

"Deputy Todd said that he'd found some helpful clues. I'm sure he's working diligently on cracking the case."

"I'm sure. Well, thanks anyway. I should be going. I've got to get started calling contractors for the house."

Mayor Jim's head perked up. "The house, yes. Any progress on that front?"

The mayor's sudden interest wasn't lost on me, so I tested the waters. "First, I need to get plans drawn up. I've got an idea to gut the basement and put in a wine bar down there. For the future guests, of course."

"Oh? Sounds like a big job. You should make sure you have the right folks on hand. May I suggest someone? Very well respected and knows his stuff."

"Sure, what's the name?"

"Brock Small. He's a contractor up in Vista. Did some work for me before."

"Thanks, I'll look him up."

"I'll catch you later, Miss Lewis. I'm off to an important meeting just now."

"Sure, no problem. See you around." I waved as the mayor strode off. I certainly had no intention of calling Brock Small, whoever he might be. Any interest in the basement raised my hackles, but it could still simply be curiosity. But, more importantly, I'd confirmed another suspicion—Mayor Jim was also lying about volunteering at the church with Lovie. Why would they both lie about being at the church unless they had something to hide? The time of a violent murder isn't exactly the time you want to muddle your alibi.

I mulled it over as I headed to the bakery. It was about noon and I was craving some coffee. And maybe one of Angie's cinnamon rolls.

"Got the you-know-what?" Angie whispered as I stepped in. She glanced to a customer perusing cakes along the back wall, indicating I should keep my voice down as well.

"Yep." I held up the plastic bag, the bolt cutters stretching the plastic into an unnatural shape.

"Great, I'll see you at your house when we close up at two o'clock."

"There's something else I want to tell you," I started, but quickly stopped as the customer drew nearer.

"Anything else for you, Mrs. Perez?" Angie asked as the woman approached the checkout.

"Just the cookies, thank you, Angie," she said, digging in her purse. "I always like to stop in and grab one of your treats when I come into town. Tell me, are you doing something special for the Pie Parade this year?"

"I sure am. I've got something really spectacular up my sleeve, but it's a secret."

"I just can't wait, it's so exciting. See you there."

Angie watched, expressionless, as the woman left the bakery then turned to me. "Ugh. What am I going to do? The Pie Parade is in just a few days and I *still* don't have a clue what I'm going to make."

"You'll think of something, I'm sure."

"I'll have to. Anyway, you said there was something else you wanted to tell me?"

"I guess I should tell Harper as well, so I'll save the details until later, but I've been snooping around this morning and I've found out some very interesting information."

"About what?"

"I'm not sure if any of it matters yet. I'll tell you both when you come over. Can I get some coffee and a cinnamon roll?"

"Yeah, sure. Hey, if you buy everything we can close up early." Angie grinned and batted her eyelashes.

"Alas, one sweet treat will have to do for now."

***

One more stop remained that day before Angie, Harper and I would settle down and hopefully solve the mystery of Arthur's secret box. Nick Christos and Bobby Teach were roommates, and I had a few lingering questions for Nick. Problem was, I didn't have an excuse to casually drop by his place. Instead, I headed back to the shed behind the house and dug out that musty lamp Arthur had stashed away. Broken switch, frayed cord, and the shade had long since deteriorated. It was perfect.

Since Bobby was dead, that left Nick as the only handyman in town. I got the address from Harper—friends in high places and all—and that's how I found myself in front of a rundown home away from the hub of town, farther down the same street that boasted Angie's delightful green cottage. Such a difference a little love and care could make. The yard was unkempt and browning, and dark paint peeled from the side of the house like shedding skin. A few shutters dangled off their hinges, giving the property a general sense of abandonment. I wondered how successful a handyman could be when his house looked like such a ruin.

I strode up three little steps to the porch, lamp in hand, and knocked lightly on the door. After a moment, the door opened and Nick appeared, shirtless. I'm not one for speechlessness, but this was twice he'd left me with no words. I looked away—at the lamp, at anything—before I could talk. "Hi, uh, Nick, I was hoping you could take a look at this for me. I found it in Arthur's shed and thought you might be able to get it working again. I hope

I'm not disturbing you."

"No, no, you're not disturbing me." Nick stepped out onto the porch and quickly closed the front door behind him before I could get much of a glance inside. He took up the lamp and turned it around in his hands. "I can probably fix this pretty quickly. I can bring it by your house once it's done, if that works?"

"Yeah, sure. I appreciate it." Nick started to go back indoors, so I added, "I heard you and Bobby lived here together. Roommates, right?"

He stopped. "That's right. We worked here together too."

"Worked here?"

"That's right. Our workshop is out back. Bobby did most of his tinkering back there."

"What happened to all his stuff—his tools—now that he's gone?"

"Uh, I'm not sure. He didn't have family that I knew about, so I guess they stay here."

"Did you know Vernon at all? Seems like he was pretty popular around town. You know, a real character."

"Yeah, he was one of the nice old guys, always hanging at the diner and talking about the good ol' days or whatever crazy plan he was up to that day."

"Someone mentioned to me all the odd businesses Vernon and Walter used to run."

He scoffed. "If you could even call them that. Those two were always scheming on one thing or another. Tried to pull Bobby into a few of them, too."

"And did he?" I leaned in closer, finally getting somewhere. "Get pulled in, I mean."

"Oh yeah, a few times. I think they had something

brewing recently, but he rarely shared details."

"And did you ever work on any of these *schemes*?"

Nick clammed up quickly at my question and diverted his eyes from mine. "Maybe once or twice," he said. "But they were always on the up-and-up, so don't worry about that."

"Oh, I'm not worried," I said, keeping my voice light and cheery. "Everyone's got to make a living, right?"

"Right."

"Such a shame, though, what happened to Vernon. Seems completely random, don't you think?"

"Maybe. I'm sure Deputy Todd will figure it out. He already asked me if I knew who'd want to kill him."

"And do you?"

"Well, no, but I told him I thought some people were kind of suspicious. Like Kenny Trotter. I saw him and Vernon together a lot up until his murder."

"Does that seem odd to you?"

"Very odd. Vernon and Kenny didn't much like each other ever since Kenny lost a bunch of money when their plan to sell those talking fish to tourists didn't pan out. I guess they got over it, though. Like I said, they were always up to that kind of thing. Just seemed odd that it was Kenny and Vernon only. Usually, Vernon and Walter were always around together. Anyway, Vernon and Kenny would talk on the street corner away from others. Kenny never went to the diner or anywhere much. Not the nicest guy."

"So I've heard. I'm sure Deputy Todd already wondered, but what were you doing when Vernon was murdered? I mean, could you have seen someone suspicious that day?"

"I had a job at the church that day. Pastor Basil asked me to finish up a job Bobby had started to tighten up the bolts on the pews. I saw you at the diner before that, re-member?"

"Yes, I remember. Did you see anyone else at the church?"

Nick furrowed his brow. "Bea Trotter came in. I re-member because she sat on a pew I hadn't fixed yet and I asked her to move. Other than that, I don't think I saw anyone except Pastor Basil. I guess some folks could've been really quiet, but I was working inside the church the whole time and would have seen them, I think."

"Bea Trotter. That's Kenny's wife, right?"

"Yeah, nice lady. She's always at the church. They're an odd couple, her and Kenny."

"Love is blind, I guess."

"I guess."

"And you were at the church all afternoon?"

"At least until three. I worked kind of slow, but it was something I'd never done before."

"Sure, sure, that makes sense. Look, Nick, I've got to be off, but thanks again for working on the lamp. Bring it by the house whenever you're done, and we'll work out the fee."

"Will do. See you later, Poppy." He waited until I'd left the porch before opening the front door and disap-pearing inside.

***

I arrived back at the house, a beautiful gleaming purple behemoth in the bright sunlight, and parked the car on the gravel driveway. I immediately spotted a bob of bright blonde—or gray, I still wasn't sure—curls waiting under the trellis. Lovie scurried up to me as I got out of the car.

"Poppy, glad I caught you."

"Hi Lovie, what's up?"

"Remember how you said we were all in it together to discover what happened to Vernon? And Bobby, of course."

"Yeah. Did you find something out?"

"Well, I remembered that last night Todd—I mean the deputy—was reporting into the main office and he mentioned that Vernon was found slumped over a blueprint of *your house.*"

My heart skipped. It was Vernon all along. But why? What if he was scheming with someone to get to whatever Arthur sealed away in the basement? I was sure Vernon intended to take whatever was there. Was that why he was killed? Was that why I'm still being targeted? So many questions swirled in my head. Thankfully, Harper and Angie would be here soon, and we'd at least find out what the fuss was all about. And hopefully get some answers.

"Poppy? Are you all right?"

"Thanks, Lovie," I said, keeping my composure. "That's an odd thing for Vernon to have."

"It sure is. Todd—I mean the deputy—also said they still haven't found Vernon's car. If that means anything to you."

"That certainly is a missing piece of the puzzle." My voice was calm but I groaned inside. I'd completely for-gotten about the missing car, and now it was going to gnaw at me. "Let me know if you hear anything else, Lovie. Anything at all."

Lovie took her leave as Angie arrived about half a

second after the bakery closed. She brought the remaining bakery items that didn't sell, and I wondered how long I could sustain eating nothing but enriched dough for every meal. Perhaps it was time to put my culinary skills to the test, but tonight we had a bigger priority than dinner.

Harper arrived not long after Angie and the three of us gathered around the box, which we'd placed on the kitchen table under good lighting.

"I've been waiting all day for this," said Harper.

"Me too," said Angie, her eyes shining brightly.

I brandished the bolt cutters steady in my hand. "Here goes nothing."

Angie clung to Harper in anticipation while Harper stood ready with her teddy bear camera.

I strained, squeezing with both hands before I heard a snap and the lock popped off. The rusty hinges and locking tongue were still intact, so I gently lifted the tab away from the tongue and slowly raised the metal lid.

Sixteen

"HUH, THAT'S INTERESTING," I said, unimpressed.

"I was expecting something... I dunno, more exciting," said Harper, lowering her camera. I too was disappointed, but I scolded myself for getting my hopes up that it would be something that offered immediate gratification and value.

Angie heaved a sigh of relief. "I'm so thankful it isn't a severed hand or dead animal or some other gruesome thing."

We stared down at the object that had given us so much grief. Within the box lay a tattered tome no larger than a simple notebook, bound in discolored linen. No title graced the front, and bits of scrap paper peeked out from the edges, as though the binding was giving way.

"What do you think it is?" asked Angie.

"Other than a book?"

Angie leveled an exhausted look at Harper. "Yes, other than that."

"I'd say it's very old."

Harper frowned. "So much for my doubloons."

I wondered why Arthur would go through so much trouble to lock away a simple book. "He could have stored this in a cabinet or something, safely stowed away out of harm's way. Why the box? Why the secret basement room? There's got to be more to it than this."

"And no doubt the people who broke in knew something about this, or at least thought it was worth something," said Harper. "Otherwise, why bother for this shabby thing?"

I gently picked up the book—it could fall apart at any second—and opened it to a random page.

"It's just symbols. Maybe it's a sketchbook."

"Awfully old and sealed away for a sketchbook, don't you think?" Angie asked.

Symbols, sketched images, and notes covered each page, none making any sense at all to us.

"Wait," Harper said. "Go back to that last page."

I flipped back to a page that showed an oblong shape with dashed lines and scribbles in the margins.

"That's a treasure map. Look, there's an 'X' marking the spot."

Angie didn't seem convinced. "And if you turn it upside down it looks like a bunny eating a carrot. So what?"

"It could be a map to anything," I said. "Or not a map at all. This part here says, 'Head to P byway the line' then it gets too hard to read."

"How disappointing," Angie said, wilting into a chair by the table. "I don't see how this helps us find out what happened to Bobby and Vernon."

"It just might, though. I forgot to tell you both what Lovie told me this afternoon. She said that Vernon was found hunched over a blueprint of *this house*."

"One of the rogue blueprints," cried Harper.

"Exactly. I must not have seen it when I was there because his body was blocking it, and I didn't stick around very long."

"Of course you didn't." Angie laid a hand on my arm. "That must have been awful."

"Okay, but why would Vernon, or anyone really, want this?" Harper held up the grubby notebook, baffled.

"It could be worth a lot more," Angie said. "Maybe it's some famous artist's sketchbook."

"Then why not put it in a safe deposit box or something?" Harper shrugged. "Isn't that what old people do with their valuables?"

"There's more I need to tell you," I said. "I saw Lovie earlier at the diner and she told me she was at the church volunteering during the time Vernon was murdered. She said Mayor Jim could confirm it."

"She does volunteer there a lot," said Angie, nodding.

"Except that when I went to the church and asked Pastor Basil, he said Lovie and Mayor Jim were definitely *not* volunteering at the church that day."

"Pastor Basil? He's a bit of a hippy-dippy if you know what I mean." Harper bobbed her head side-to-side and stuck out her tongue. "Are you sure he had the right day?"

"He was positive. Plus, Nick confirmed the same for me later."

"Why would Lovie lie about volunteering?" Angie asked.

"What's even more suspicious is that when I asked

Mayor Jim, he also said that they were volunteering that day. So, either Pastor Basil and Nick are lying, or Lovie and the mayor are lying."

"I know who I'd put my money on," said Harper. "And, by the way, I'm cringing inside wondering why Lovie and Jim might be lying. But how does this help us?"

"It might not," I admitted. "But it tells us that there were people who have no alibi during the time of the murder and are willing to lie about it."

"Did you find out anything else? I hate that I'm stuck at the bakery all day. I feel like I'm no help at all."

"Your beautiful face is all we need, Angie. Plus, how are we supposed to stay energized without sugar and carbs to keep us fueled?"

"Don't be silly," Angie admonished, trying to hide her smile.

"Okay." Harper rubbed her hands together. "So, what's next?"

"I went to see Nick, like I said. The place was a mess, not what I was expecting from two handymen, but I guess par for the course for a couple of bachelors. Anyway, I wouldn't say Nick was dodging my questions, but he wasn't exactly forthcoming either. He confirmed some of what I've heard elsewhere—about Bobby and about Kenny. Apparently, the guys in town—Vernon, Walter, Bobby, and Kenny—were always trying to pull off random money-making ventures. Nick said he saw Vernon a lot with Kenny recently. And Harper, remember what we saw in the hardware store? Walter and Kenny. I never knew Bobby, so I can't say if anything was going on there."

"Yeah, now that you mention it, they were always working on something together. Bobby, too. And, I've never seen inside that house either. And I deliver mail there, like, every day."

"What if one project they were working on was acquiring the notebook?"

"You think they were trying to get to this?" Harper looked at the notebook, doubtful. "On purpose?"

"It's just an idea."

"So, you think the blueprint guys are them? Why not four blueprints then? Why only two?"

"That's a good question, and I don't have an answer yet, but I know what I'm doing next."

"What's that?" asked Angie.

"I'm going to Vista tomorrow to put this into a safe deposit box."

"Shouldn't you do it today? Are you going to risk another attack tonight?"

"If they're going to attack, then they'll do it whether or not the thing is here. But maybe you're right—at least it won't be here for them to take if they do come snooping around. Can I get to the bank in Vista before it closes?"

Angie checked her watch. "If you leave soon. I can go with you."

"I've still got to finish my rounds at some point," said Harper. "But you two go ahead. We'll catch up after."

After Harper pulled away in her mail truck, Angie and I piled into my Prius with the book gently cradled in her arms. We'd grabbed some bubble wrap left over from the meager boxes I brought with me to town and wrapped it securely in a cloud of bubbles. If we got to Vista in time, I could open a safe deposit box and leave it under the lock and key of the bank—much more secure than the stately old mansion with its drafty doors and secret visitors.

"Let's take the Coastal Road. Traffic might hold us up if we take the highway."

"Sounds good." I eased out of the driveway and followed Second Street, the only other road in Starry Cove, which eventually turned into the Coastal Road meandering through the redwoods and ferns, just wide enough for one car each way.

"Do people live out here or is this all just forest?"

"Sure, people live out here. We'll pass some mailboxes and driveways every once in a while. Mostly folks who make it into town only a few times a week. They stay at home the rest of the time. Not really hermits, just those who find it inconvenient to drive into town."

"That must be why the town meeting was so full. I guess everyone can't live on the two or three streets that make up the town proper."

"Right. See, up here is the Trotter place. It's locked at the road since Kenny doesn't like visitors. Only lets a few people in and then only if he has a really good reason." Angie pointed as I slowed the car and stopped where a metal pipe gate met the road. A long dirt driveway led onto the property, and I could just make out a building through the trees and brush. A large "No Trespassing" sign hung prominently on the gate.

"Hang on," said Angie. "Can you see that?"

"See what?"

"There, to the left behind that redwood to the side of the house. There's something orange peeking out from under that big tarp."

"Okay," I said, curiously. I saw the orange spot she

was pointing at but wasn't sure why it mattered.

"That's Vernon's car. I'm sure of it. The color is distinct. He drove it forever and Walter used to give him so much grief for not buying a new car from him, but Vernon just wanted to drive his old orange car. I guess if there's nothing wrong with the car and the gas mileage is okay, then there's no reason to consider a new car. I mean, taxes are higher, the car payments alone—"

"Angie," I cut her off, "why would Vernon's car be in Kenny's yard? Deputy Todd mentioned that it was odd that the car wasn't found at the shop on the day of his murder."

"Well, Kenny's a mechanic."

"He is?"

"Yeah. There are cars all over his lot. Look." I scanned through the dense trees. Sure enough, snippets of cars and trucks peppered the property. I couldn't see much through the dense foliage, but I saw enough to realize Kenny's place was nothing more than an old car lot.

"We can't stay here. Kenny might see us. And we've got to get to Vista before the bank closes anyway."

I knew Angie was right, but I wanted to find out why Vernon's vehicle was in Kenny's car cemetery. And I wanted a word with Kenny—I just needed to find a way to do it safely.

Vista proved to be a quick stop with no surprises at the bank. Angie had to hold my hand as we drove by Vernon's shop along the Coastal Road, but I made it through. A few signatures later and I had my very own safe deposit box, with a special item stored securely inside. I had half a mind to post signs around the outside of the house that read, "Don't bother. It's no longer here," but thought better of it. Besides, I still needed to get back to Starry Cove for my date-but-not-a-date with Ryan. Admittedly, it was hard to concentrate on dinner when I'd discovered so much today. All I wanted to do was ask more questions and get more answers.

Back at the house, shirts flew from a box and onto the sofa as I rummaged through the scant clothing I had. My full wardrobe was probably being loaded onto the moving truck now somewhere far, far away.

"I don't think so," said Harper as I held up a wrinkled jade blouse. She had rejoined us after her rounds and now sat in judgment over my wardrobe.

"This is the best I have. The others are worse, trust me. I didn't expect to need to gussy myself up at any point. All I brought were coveralls, jeans, and T-shirts."

Angie put her hands on her hips. "Here's what we're going to do. I'll get the kettle on—you have one of those at least, I've seen it—and we'll make our own steamer and get those wrinkles right out."

"Actually, can we do that to a T-shirt? I might as well just put forward the worst I have to offer. That way, if it doesn't scare him away, I'll know he's not a complete jerk."

"Ryan MacKenzie is not a jerk," said Angie. "He's nice, you said so yourself."

"Yeah, but you can never really tell. I thought my ex-husband was nice once too."

"Never mind that. I'll get the kettle started."

"This one," said Harper, holding up an ugly stained shirt with a faded nineties album cover on the front. "If he doesn't run away screaming, then you'll know he's a veritable angel."

"Oh, shut up," I laughed, snatching the shirt from Harper's hands.

Harper continued to dig and finally pulled out an entirely inoffensive black shirt with no logos, no hideous album covers, no holes, and only a few wrinkles.

"Perfect. Add some jeans and I'm set—that's proper attire for Shelby's diner, right?"

Harper plopped down on the sofa as I searched more boxes for a pair of pants. "So, did you find anything else other than Vernon's car?"

"No. And I don't see a way to ask Kenny any questions without coming on too strong."

"He doesn't come to town much, that's for sure."

"And he doesn't like visitors," added Angie, who returned from the kitchen with a whistling kettle. She motioned to the coat rack that sat in the corner. "Hand your clothes up here, and I'll steam them."

I draped the shirt on the sole hanger I'd found in one closet, and Angie got to work. We sat in silence watching the wrinkles fade before Harper suddenly shot up like a rocket, her face barely holding back her delight.

"Ladies, ladies," she said, waving her hands. "May I present to you the only institution allowed on Mr. Kenneth Trotter's property that he won't chase away with a shotgun—the United States Postal Service." Harper bowed with a dramatic flourish.

"Of course," Angie exclaimed.

"There's only one minor problem. The Trotter's don't get any mail," Harper said. "Like, ever. Well, sometimes Bea Trotter gets one of her Christian newsletters, but I deliver mail there once in a blue moon. Once in a purple moon with frosting. It could be forever before I'm able to legitimately go on the property and get a close look at the cars."

"Oh." Angie's face fell.

I tapped a finger to my chin. "But couldn't *we* send him mail? A letter or a package or something."

"That's a great idea, Poppy. We could mail it tomorrow and Harper would have it to process within a day or two, right?"

"That sounds about right. It's got to be a package, though, otherwise I'd just leave regular mail in the mailbox by the road."

"Then let's get to work. We need to script this perfectly so he doesn't catch on. Not to mention I have to be at the diner in thirty minutes."

Seventeen

I ARRIVED AT the diner a little later than planned and spied Ryan at a booth against the wall. He buried his head in a book, brown hair unremarkable, glasses teetering on his nose. He wore a pale V-neck sweater, similar to what he wore when I first met him at the town meeting. A thoroughly ordinary and unassuming guy, accent aside. *Totally safe*, I thought.

His eyes looked up when the door chime clanged as I entered the diner. Our eyes quickly met, and he raised a hand to gesture me over to the table.

"Glad you made it. I hope you don't mind I already ordered a drink. You look lovely by the way."

An angel, I thought, scooting into the booth. "No of course I don't mind."

"How has your day been?"

"Um," I paused, replaying the events of my whirlwind day in my head. "Uneventful. I took a stroll around town and did some planning for the house. How about you?"

"Oh, boring pharmacy business."

"Sounds exciting to someone who knows next to nothing about pharmacy business."

Shelby arrived at the table and gave me a sly grin. "Can I get you a drink, dearie?"

"Can I have a coffee?"

"Sure, it's never too late for coffee at Shelby's. Coming right up."

"So, tell me about the house. What plans have you made?"

"Oh I, uh, decided I'll need to set up a space for myself once the moving truck arrives, hopefully tomorrow." I could hardly believe those words. Had it only been a week since I drove up to the house for the first time?

"You don't have your own room?"

"Well, no. Arthur left his furniture and everything to me in the will, so I have a house full of his things and none really of my own. I don't even have much coming in the truck, but at least it's mine and it's familiar."

"It must be hard to live in what feels like someone else's house."

"Yeah, it's like an extended stay at a relative's without them being around. I'm not sure if I should use this or that or if it's okay for me to touch anything. It still seems surreal that he left everything to me. I barely knew him, but he also didn't have a lot of family."

"Maybe he saw something special in you and wanted you to have what meant the most to him."

I'd never really thought about it that way. Arthur's house was spectacular, and there was no doubt that it was well kept. He must have really loved it, and felt I was the right person to have it. A tear threatened to well in my eye, but I tried to wipe it away casually so Ryan wouldn't see. "That's a nice thing to say to someone you've only just met."

"Sometimes, you don't need to know much about someone to know they are a good person. Arthur and I might be similar in that way."

"Thank you. I hope to do him proud by giving the house new life. I expect I'll add another room to the ground floor that will eventually turn into the living space for me until I can find an on-site manager. The guests will stay upstairs in the four large rooms—one of which will be a honeymoon suite, and one I have special plans for."

His eyebrow went up at this. "Special plans?"

"Well, there's something special about that room that Arthur left, and I want to honor that for him."

"Interesting. I've been hearing a lot about Arthur, being that I replaced him at the pharmacy, and he sounded like a well-respected man. Universally liked, it seems."

"I get that impression as well. I just wish the sentiment carried over to me. I'm not sure if you caught the article that reporter from Vista wrote, but it didn't paint me in a very good light." I looked down at the table, slightly ashamed to admit the article had gotten to me.

"I saw the article, but I don't pay those much mind, especially those that serve no purpose but to rile up the masses. I like to think others are above that too. Just remember, you can't please them all."

"I know you're right, but it's still hard to be new and suddenly get cast as a villain."

"It seems you have friends, though, right? The baker and the postie."

"Postie?"

He rolled his eyes and shook his head a little. "Sorry. Sometimes I slip back to Scotland for a moment. I meant the woman who delivers mail."

"Harper, yeah. And Angie. They've been great friends and have helped me acclimate to the new town. I guess I do have things to be thankful for after all. You have an excellent bedside manner, Doctor—you've turned my mood around completely."

"No problem," he said, beaming. "I'm still new here too, as you know, and I have yet to acquire two best friends, so you're ahead of the curve."

"Have you made *any* friends here?"

"Acquaintances, sure. But I'm not really a man's man. I think the sweater turns them off."

I laughed. "I think it distinguishes you."

"Thank you." He smiled, and I couldn't help but blush in response.

Shelby broke the moment as she plodded up to the table with coffee, the squeak of her shoes like rubber on rubber. "All right you two, what'll it be?"

"Oh, I forgot to look," I said. "You go first."

"It will come as no surprise, but I'll have the burger and chips. My favorite."

"*Fries*, Doctor," she corrected.

"Whatever you say, Shelby," he said, sharing a grin.

"And I'll have… the same."

"These'll be up shortly." Shelby snatched the menus out of our hands and squeaked away into the kitchen.

"It's fun to give her a hard time with the fries," he said. "I think she likes it though."

"I wonder if Shelby has a little crush on you."

"Not likely, although I would be honored. I believe

she has a beau hiding somewhere already. Truth is, I love the food here, so it's hard not to show it. I love food in general, though you probably can't tell by looking at me, all skin and bones. American food is great, but I'd give anything to have takeout from a decent Thai or Italian restaurant these days." He sniffed the air as though the hot food was in front of him already, all spices and thick sauces.

This man was speaking my language. When I first separated from my ex-husband, I ordered takeout every night. I went through every restaurant in the city, every ethnic cuisine. "That sounds great. I like to dabble a bit cooking various cuisines. I should use you as a test subject."

"I'm all yours," he replied. "I'll try anything."

"I'll remember that, I promise. But tell me more about where you came from. How did you get from Scotland to here?"

"I went the long way, let's say. My wife—"

I about spit out my coffee. "Your wife?"

"I guess I should have mentioned that I'm widowed. My wife passed away a few years ago."

"Oh, I'm sorry."

"My son and I finally moved here to be closer to his grandparents, who live in Vista. I was lucky enough to find a job here. Sorry, that's rude. I didn't mean to say Arthur's death was lucky."

"Don't worry about it. I understand."

"Well then, that's my story. I found the job here and it's been going well."

"How old is your son?"

"He's twelve—just old enough to get into real

trouble."

"I'm sure he'll be fine. How much trouble could there be in this small town?"

"Where I'm from, when there's nothing to do, the kids make trouble. But his grades are good, especially considering he changed schools during the winter break, so I'm thankful he hasn't rebelled yet. Do you have any children?"

"No," I said slowly. "My ex-husband and I didn't have any children. We were pretty focused on our business. I guess it never came up."

"What business was that?"

"We ran a few small hotels, nothing big. That's why I'm hoping I can bring the house back to life. I know a thing or two about running a hotel, I figured it would translate to a bed-and-breakfast."

He nodded. "Sounds reasonable."

"I managed through a renovation before at one of our sites, so I have a good idea of what to expect. I imagine I can find the skilled labor in Vista and have the place up and running in time for autumn, before the weather gets bad."

"There's plenty of people who love the coast year-round. I'm sure you'll have a lot of interest. You mentioned an on-site manager. Are you not planning on staying on yourself?"

"I haven't decided yet. I'm in a bit of limbo right now. I know I'll be here for a while to complete the house. After that, who knows? I have to admit I hadn't planned on staying permanently. Now, I've made some friends, and the house is growing on me." I sighed. "But the town also thinks I'm a crazed murderer, which might be a problem."

He scoffed. "The town doesn't think that. A small-town newspaper needed to sell some copies, that's all."

"I hope so."

Shelby arrived at the table with our food. "Here you go, two orders of burgers and *fries*."

"Chip fries, excellent. Thank you, Shelby."

Shelby sighed and gave Ryan a beleaguered look, but sauntered back to the kitchen with a grin on her face, nonetheless.

He chuckled and shook his head. "Never gets old."

Eighteen

EARLY THE NEXT morning I arrived at the bakery carrying a cardboard box under one arm.

"Tell me everything," Angie demanded. "And say it in his voice."

"Good morning to you, too, Angie. And I'm not going to do the voice."

Angie wiped her hands on her apron and a puff of flour escaped into the surrounding air. "I can withhold cinnamon rolls."

"You wouldn't."

"I would, but I'm *choosing* not to. You still have to tell me how the date went."

"Yeah, I know. Let's wait for Harper. She should be here soon, but I *will* tell you that Ryan is just as nice as you suspected."

"I told you. Not all men are scum."

Harper swung through the door, massive sunglasses shading her face. "Egad, it's early. Everything is so bright. Shouldn't there be actual fog on this foggy coast?"

"Good morning, sunshine," said Angie. "How about some coffee?"

"Yes, sweet nectar o' the morn', give to me your essence." Harper flopped down on the café chair beside me and Angie came around with two coffees. We each took a sip and sighed deeply.

"Okay, spill it," Harper said, flicking down her sunglasses to stare at me. "I want all the gory details."

"There are no gory details. We ate dinner and talked about life. You know, the things you do on not-date-dates."

"My dates are a lot different than yours."

"Did he pay? Did you have dessert?" asked Angie.

"Yes, he paid and yes, we shared dessert."

"That makes it a date-date. Are you going out again?"

"We didn't talk about a next date. I suppose I'll see him around town. I just met him, after all. And I'm coming off a divorce, so I'm not looking for anything serious. You guys know that."

"You're right, Poppy. Sorry to push it."

Harper waved us off. "Well, I'm not sorry. What you need is a distraction."

"I think the house and one—possibly two—murders is distraction enough. I brought the package, by the way." I held up the box.

"What's in it?" asked Angie.

"I grabbed a random book from Arthur's shelves."

"Knowing Arthur, the book is probably worth thousands of dollars," said Harper.

"It's not. It's a newer copy of Treasure Island. No marks or anything on the inside, so it could come from

140

anyone."

"Kenny's going to be so confused," said Angie. "Books are probably foreign to him. But I guess that's not the point. We want to get onto the property without getting shot, right?"

"Right. And Harper's our ticket in. Is this box big enough?"

"Yeah. So, you'll mail this today and I'll deliver it when it comes through the mail service, probably tomorrow or the next day. I'll call you both when it's ready."

"I'm going to mail it from Vista with no return address."

"Perfect."

"I've also got the truck arriving today—they called earlier   so I'm finally going to have my own stuff."

"That's good news," said Angie.

"Yeah. One bedroom upstairs is entirely empty, so I'll set up there. I don't have much stuff, so it won't be a problem. I downsized when I moved into a studio apartment after the divorce. We sold off most of our joint property. I feel like I'm starting from scratch."

Angie patted my arm. "New beginnings can be a good thing too, remember that."

"You two have been great. Ryan mentioned it last night. He said I was lucky to have two friends so soon after moving to a new town, and he's right."

"You mean you were lucky enough to stumble upon the only two normal people in this town."

"Two very normal people who break into secret basement rooms and concoct elaborate plans to spy on their neighbor's property. Did I get that right?"

"Exactly," Harper replied from behind her shades,

sipping casually from her coffee. "That's normal for around here."

***

Vista was uneventful. I took the highway, not because it was faster but because I did not want to drive past Vernon's shop again. The memory ran through my head and shaking it was difficult, so I didn't need any more triggers. Thankfully, I mailed the small package—no return address, no fuss—and made it back before the moving truck was due at the house. There was even time to tidy up before the movers arrived at ten o'clock sharp.

"Nice color," one of them said as they began unloading. I ignored the sarcasm dripping from his voice and guided them upstairs to the empty bedroom and had them place everything against the walls. I would need time and space to set up my bed, which I'd broken down for the move. The small table I used for meals remained downstairs, placed next to Arthur's table in the kitchen. Thankfully, there was enough space for everything. The house was, after all, enormous and could fit the entire contents of my personal belongings ten times over, but I didn't feel comfortable integrating my things into the wider house. Not yet. I'd get rid of the tattered furniture eventually, but I wanted to keep some of Arthur's charm for the bed-and-breakfast. His taste was so eclectic—on one hand he owned an entire collection of Victorian bedroom furniture, on the other he used a sunken tweed sofa long past its prime.

I stood by the window, fluffing out the dusty drapes, hoping the motes that sunk like lead to the floor would instead dissipate and disappear completely. It felt to me like everything needed a deep cleaning. Perhaps, I thought, I should just flood the basement and throw in a few gallons of detergent and all the furniture and fabric and hope for the best, but I knew it would come down to bare-knuckle hard work. The road ahead seemed so long.

I could see the roundabout from the window, with the flagpole at its center, flag whipping wildly in the breeze. A large-brimmed hat cast a shadow on the ground beneath the wavering flag. Deputy Todd was making his rounds.

I did not want to run into him today. Besides, Lovie would share any new details that came into play in the investigation. I didn't need the deputy, and his ego probably wouldn't allow him to see me as anything other than a bumbling idiot. I waited until he finally left the area before I went downstairs and outside.

Shelby greeted me as I came through the door at the diner. "Hi there, dearie. Here for some lunch?"

"Yeah, or maybe an early dinner." I bought enough groceries in Vista to cook for myself but hadn't been able to get my feet wet in Arthur's kitchen. Plus, the attack there still left me a little shaken, and I wanted to avoid the space as much as possible, at least for a little while.

"Is Lovie here?"

"No, dearie. She was in here earlier but said she and the mayor were going to volunteer today and she'd be gone for a while."

"Is that so?"

"Yep. So, what'll you have?"

"Coffee, burger. In that order."

"Gotcha," she said, giving me a wink. "Coming right up."

I left the diner well-fed and intent on finding out what

was really going on with all the benevolent *volunteering* going on around town. I flagged down Pastor Basil who was out front of the church tending the flowers.

"Good afternoon, Pastor."

He looked up from his spot on the ground, where he sat cross-legged on the path, wearing gardening gloves and a tie-dyed apron. "And a groovy afternoon to you, Poppy," he said, standing up. "I've just been tending the *L. Pardalinum*." He pointed to the ground at a patch of green fronds. "They don't bloom until summer, but they've been giving me bad vibes the past few years, so I wanted to show them some extra love and care. I've been meditating beside them daily, hoping it will encourage them to thrive. This flower bed is my favorite spot in the whole church."

"Outside of the church is your favorite place in it?"

"How's that?" he responded, confused.

"Never mind," I said, shaking my head. "I came by to see if Mayor Jim was here by chance."

"Well, I've been by the door all morning talking to the flowers, and no one has gone in that I've seen. I guess my eyes were closed, but I still would have heard—I'm especially attuned to all the senses while zenning out."

As I suspected. Lovie and Jim *were* up to something. Harper might have been right that the most obvious answer is also quite unsavory, but it wasn't a loose end I could let linger. "Thanks, Pastor. I guess I'll have to look elsewhere."

"Be sure to come back before these bloom," he said, motioning to the flowers. "It's a total downer your sister didn't get to see these either. I pointed them out to her the other day when she came by. They're lilies, after all.

Leopard, or Tiger Lilies is the common name. Groovy flowers, just beautiful."

And entirely fitting, I thought. "I'm sure they're lovely when they bloom. Sorry to rush off but I've got to find the mayor."

"See you on Sunday," he said, tapping the side of his nose.

Nineteen

THE MAYOR'S OFFICE was a small room off the interior of the community center where the town meetings were held. Angie pointed it out to me the other night. She called the room the tiniest Town Hall in the state and she wasn't wrong. It was little more than a closet. I approached the closed door directly. Locked. I knocked on the door in two short raps. Faint scuffling and murmurs escaped through the crack under the door. It took a few moments before the mayor's voice replied, "Come in."

I stepped inside and was not at all surprised to see Lovie Newman seated, stubby legs crossed daintily, in one of the two leather chairs facing the mayor's desk. A conspicuous smear of red lipstick encircled her lips and she preened her untidy curls with a shaky hand. "Hello, Poppy. What brings you here?"

"I could ask the same of you."

"According to Shelby, you're both supposed to be volunteering at the church, yet here you are."

They glanced at one another. "Whatever do you

mean, Miss Lewis?" asked the mayor. "Are you feeling all right?"

My eyes fell on his loosened tie and the red stain adorning the collar of his stark white shirt. I sneered. "Don't patronize me, Mayor. One week in this town is enough to know when someone is trying to pull the wool over my eyes."

Lovie licked her lips, eyes darting from Mayor Jim to the door behind me. "What are you two hiding?" I asked.

"You can't tell Todd, please," said Lovie. "He wouldn't understand."

"Out with it."

Mayor Jim inhaled a deep breath and leaned back. "Lovie, you don't have to say anything."

I stared daggers at him and turned to Lovie. "How about I stroll down the street and find your husband, Deputy Todd, and tell him all about the lies you've been telling about volunteering at the church? And now I find you locked in this small room together, blinds drawn, in the middle of the afternoon, all sweaty and disheveled."

"Jim—"

He slapped his hand on the desk. "Lovie, don't you dare say a word. Now, look here, Miss Lewis," he jabbed a finger toward me, "you can't waltz in here and make demands on me. In case you've forgotten, I'm the mayor of this town and I think you'll find that the good deputy would put my word above that of a stranger who's just strolled her way into town."

My jaw clenched with every word. This man thought he could intimidate me, but I held an ace in my pocket. A smile spread across my face, and I leaned in close so he could hear me clearly. "That may be so, but I have the word of the *good pastor*, who can vouch that neither of you have been volunteering during the times you claimed. Something tells me Deputy Todd would be very interested in that."

"Interested in what?" came a drawl from behind me. Deputy Todd stood rigid in the doorway as his hand pushed the door open fully to expose all three of us before him. His eyes moving from Lovie to the mayor and back again. Lovie clutched at her skirt, squirming. "What's going on here, Lovie?" he asked.

"Todd, I—" she started before bursting into tears. "I'm so sorry."

"It's not what you think, Todd. I—" began Mayor Jim.

Deputy Todd cut in. "And what do I think, Jim?" His voice was even and cold. "Miss Lewis, would you excuse us? I believe I have questions for these two."

I dipped out of the office, relieved to be away from the explosion yet to come. Although we were far from friends, I felt more than a modicum of empathy for Deputy Todd. No one should have to go through that. I knew full well the emotions he was about to experience, what would consume him in the coming days. It would start in the pit of his stomach and move outward, like an oil spill, filling his head with memories and then speculations and then mixing the two together so he can't remember what was true and what was not. I wouldn't wish that on my worst enemy. Well, except Lily. I wouldn't mind if she felt that misery for just one despairing moment.

At least I'd found some answers, and I could cross Lovie and Mayor Jim off my list of potential killers on the loose around town since it was now clear they'd been engaging in a clandestine dalliance. The jury was still out on plenty of others, and I planned to continue to dig deeper. Once this was behind me, I could focus on the house, the renovation, and finally move on with starting my new life.

Passing the bookstore along the sidewalk on my way back toward the house, I spotted Kenny getting out of a truck parked on the street. I ducked behind a pillar. I hadn't expected to see him in town. Angie said he rarely drives in. As he opened the shop door, Nick stumbled out, Arthur's lamp firmly grasped in his hands, and Nick quickly bobbed out of Kenny's way before continuing down the sidewalk toward the roundabout.

Once the coast was clear, I slipped by the hardware store and glanced into the truck bed, scanning for anything out of place. There was nothing inside that seemed out of the ordinary, just some basic mechanic tools loose in the bottom of the bed and one of those creeper trays mechanics use to roll themselves under cars. I don't know what I was expecting. A pool of blood? Another dead body? A sign that read "Murderer on Board"? I rolled my eyes at my own foolishness. Of course I wouldn't find anything that conspicuous. Instead, I'd have to wait for the package to make its way into play and see if Harper could discover anything more that Kenny might be hiding.

I scurried along toward the house, knowing that Nick was just a minute or so ahead of me. I didn't want to miss him returning Arthur's lamp, and this could provide a perfect opportunity for more digging.

I turned onto the walk and dipped under the trellis,

overflowing with clematis even at this early time of the season.

Nick spotted me coming up the walk. "Hi, Poppy, I was just dropping off your lamp. Wasn't too hard to fix."

"Great, thanks, Nick," I said, meeting him on the porch by the front door. "Glad it wasn't too big of a job."

"Not at all."

"Let me get this door open." I fumbled to find the right house key, still unfamiliar with the look and feel of the one that matched the front door. I must have turned the knob too quickly, eager to get inside after messing around with the keys, because I heard a snap and the knob loosened in my hand before coming apart completely. *Just great*, I thought.

"Looks like you need a new doorknob."

"Go ahead and set the lamp on the side table there by the door." I left the knob on the table too and grabbed my purse from the kitchen where I'd left it earlier.

"What's the damage?" I asked, opening my wallet.

Nick picked up the broken fixture, peered closely at it, then smiled. "I'd say one old doorknob."

"Very funny." At least I managed a faint grin despite the frustration growing over the old house. "How about for the lamp?"

"Twenty bucks should cover it. And I'll even throw in one doorknob repair for free."

"Thanks," I said and handed him a twenty-dollar bill.

"I'll be right back—I need to grab my tools from down the street."

Nick returned in just a few minutes, toolbox in hand, and got to work on fixing the knob. I stood close by, pretending to straighten up the porch, but in reality I was watching him work out of the corner of my eye.

"Can you hand me the Philips screwdriver?" he asked.

I leaned down to the toolbox, which lay open on the floor of the porch behind me, and searched for the Philips. The tools were heavy, and they matched the pattern of the hammer I'd found behind the house a few days ago. Sure enough, upon closer inspection, I spied a small T carved into the base of the screwdriver. The same T that Shelby pointed out to me as belonging to Bobby Teach. Searching through the other tools, I found a similar mark on each one.

"Did you find it?" he asked, still crouched and inspecting the door mechanism.

"I—" I stuttered, unsure if I should bring up what I'd seen. "I think so." I handed him the screwdriver. He took it up quickly and continued his work. Looking around, I was alone on the porch with him, not a person in sight, not anyone walking along the street within eyesight. No drivers coming in or out of town. No one to witness anything if I confronted Nick about Bobby's tools and things went south. How close was the toolbox? Could I grab a weapon in time?

He jiggled the knob. "That should do it."

"Thanks." I kept my voice calm. I couldn't let this opportunity slip away. If I played my cards right, I could get some solid answers. "Nick," I started cautiously, "when I showed you that hammer the other day you mentioned it wasn't yours. I noticed that these other tools are similar." I hoped my words didn't trigger a reaction and that he'd have some simple excuse for misleading me before.

151

Instead, his jaw clenched and his eyes darted toward the street. Was he looking for witnesses? Was he going to run? He lowered his eyes. "You found me out," he said in a low voice. I steeled myself at his admission, prepared for the worst, but it didn't come. He continued, "I'm so embarrassed. When Bobby died, I took on all the work he'd been doing around town. I hate to admit I wasn't prepared, but I just didn't have the experience, or the tools at least, to do it." He turned away from me.

"Nick, I—"

"No, it's my fault. I took Bobby's tools—I was just borrowing them, though. I really needed them, you understand? I couldn't let Pastor Basil down. I couldn't let everyone know I didn't have the money to get my own, and I needed the work. Bobby always had money coming in somehow, but I didn't. That's why we lived together. He let me stay because he knew I didn't have the money to get my own place. And now I have to pay the rent and everything by myself. I don't know if I can do it without him. I had something going on with Vernon to make some money, but now that opportunity's gone too."

"What was that?"

He shook his head. "I don't want you to think I'm a bad person."

"Please, Nick. Just tell me."

"We were working on a plan to get tourists to the shop—Vernon's shop. I would go to the public beach up the coast and flirt with as many girls as I could, get them buttered up, then suggest they meet me there later on. I wouldn't show up, of course, but they'd be there and any money they spent, Vernon would kick back a little to me. I needed the money, Poppy. I swear it."

As unpalatable as their plan was to me, I knew what it felt like to be poor and on your own. I understood how Nick was struggling. I placed a gentle hand on his muscled shoulder and said softly, "Then you shouldn't be fixing doorknobs for free."

He faced me again and smiled, eyes still downcast. "Thanks, Poppy. And you're right, I've just never had much smarts for business."

"I won't tell anyone about the tools. From the sound of it, you were probably Bobby's closest friend, and I'm sure he'd want you to have them, anyway." I ducked inside to grab another twenty-dollar bill and tucked it in his shirt pocket. "And thank you for the excellent repair work on my door."

As Nick left the house, shiny new toolkit at his side, I received a call—it was my lawyer.

"Yes?" I asked.

"Good afternoon, Ms. Lewis. I have some good news."

"*Good* news?" He must have misspoken. I never get good news when Lily is involved. It always goes her way somehow.

"That's right. I spoke with your sister's attorneys and they've agreed to drop the contestation of the will and estate."

"Really? Did they say why?"

"I like to think it's how I explained to them the utter futility of bringing the case to court. They seemed quite eager to drop it once they discussed it with their client."

"So, Lily's dropping the case? Do I have to do anything more?"

"No, I'll work with them on the paperwork and let

you know when I receive confirmation that they've dropped it. It shouldn't take long. Rest easy and put this behind you. You shouldn't have any more trouble from your sister or anyone else regarding the house or the rest of the estate."

"Thanks. I appreciate your hard work on this. I really thought she'd bleed me dry this time." I ended the call and sat on one of the wooden benches on the front porch, leaning back against the house. A deep breath felt invigorating as sea air filled my lungs. Was it really over? It was hard to accept that she would abandon one of her threats so quickly and with no pushback, so I would just have to wait for the other shoe to drop.

Twenty

ANGIE HAD ASKED Harper and me to stop by the bakery during the afternoon to test out the pie she'd been practicing for the Pie Parade. Twist my arm. Harper was still finishing her rounds, but I headed over for an early sampling. Maybe I was just in a good mood because of the house, or because I now knew Nick didn't have it in him to kill his best friend, but I sauntered along the sidewalk with a smile on my face. I spotted Ryan stepping out of the general store across the street where the pharmacy was located. I stepped off the curb, ready to cross the road to say hello, when I noticed a graceful woman glide out the door Ryan held open. She turned to him and placed a hand on his arm. I stopped dead, one foot in the street. It was Lily. Lily and Ryan. Lily with her claws on Ryan. My Ryan.

The scene unfolded like a bad dream. He returned her gesture, placing his hand on her arm, a tender embrace and a few shared whispers and then she turned to walk away. I quickly retreated and jumped behind a shrub, continuing to watch her slink down the sidewalk toward her roadster parked a few yards further down the street. He watched her go too, his eyes lingered on her frame. I waited until he'd gone back inside and she'd driven off to whatever lair she kept these days before dipping into the safety of Angie's bakery.

"What do you mean you saw Ryan and Lily?" Angie asked after I'd spilled what I'd just seen.

"I mean I saw them. Both of them. Embracing, touching. Things that make me ill."

Angie scoffed. "Oh, I don't know, Poppy. I don't think Ryan would do that."

"I saw it with my own eyes. She probably knew this would hurt more than the house. She knew a direct hit against my new relationship with a man would be the *coup de grâce*. She's evil."

"Who's evil?" Harper asked, stepping into the bakery.

"Lily, apparently."

"Yes, Lily," I spat. "She's now on a mission to steal Ryan from me."

Harper's eyes bulged. "She's what now? How did this happen?"

"I saw them, just now, on the sidewalk."

"Okay... What does that mean?"

"Haven't you two been paying attention? Lily is out to get me. She's out to ruin my life. This is no coincidence, her and Ryan."

"Okay, Poppy. We believe you, just take a minute to calm down." Angie's soothing voice put me at ease only a little. The events of today—the reliving of my own events through those of Deputy Todd—reopened the wound Lily had cut deep within me.

"Yeah, Lily may be out to get you, but Ryan isn't stupid," said Harper. "He's also a nice guy, so have faith that's all it was—him being nice."

It was hard for my mind not to jump to the worst. Maybe Harper and Angie were right and Ryan wouldn't fall for Lily's games. Faith, however, was hard to come by when it came to my sister.

"How about another pie?" Angie interjected. "New recipe I just cooked up—Peaches and Cream Blueberry Sugar Crust Pie."

"Sounds like a mouthful—hand it over." Harper grabbed both plates of pie Angie passed to her over the case.

"What inspired this recipe?"

"After my abysmal seven-out-of-ten apple pie," Angie said, glaring at Harper, "I decided I needed to crank it up a notch."

"It's good, but where did you find peaches and blueberries this time of year?" asked Harper.

"Well, that was a slight problem. It's too early for stone fruit locally, and I couldn't find any distributers to ship any before the parade, so I used frozen." She mumbled these last words, looking away, pretending to clean off her workspace against the wall.

Harper almost choked. "*Frozen* fruit? Frozen fruit will keep you off the podium."

"I know." Angie fussed about, wringing her hands. "But even if I had ordered a week ago, the shipment wouldn't have been here in time."

"I think it's great," I said, licking my fork.

"Thanks, Poppy."

"Poppy, you don't understand," Harper said, turning to me with urgency in her eyes. "Shelby's next door right now whipping up the next greatest thing since coffee, and Angie's using frozen fruit in her pie."

Angie held up her hands in defeat. "Okay, okay. I've got a few other ideas up my sleeve. I just need time to work them out."

Harper shot back, "You don't have time. The parade is in a few days."

"I know. It's just with everything going on I think I've been distracted. And I've been up gallivanting with you two."

"Oh, yeah," said Harper, distracted. "Everything go okay with the package, Poppy?"

"Seamless."

"Great. It will probably be ready by Monday."

"Lovie!" I shouted.

Harper jumped in her chair, long fingers grasping for the fork as it slipped from her hand and clanged on the floor. "What's wrong?"

"I just remembered I forgot to tell you both what happened today." A sudden change in topic to pie and I'd lost my train of thought.

"Was it about pie?" asked Angie.

"No, no. I found out that Mayor Jim and Lovie couldn't be involved in Vernon's murder."

"How do you know that?"

"Because I confronted them today. Lovie lied to Shelby about volunteering again, and I found them both at the mayor's office instead."

Harper's face drained of blood. "It's true, isn't it? They've been…"

"Yes. And worse, Deputy Todd was there to discover it too."

"Oh no," said Angie. "Poor thing."

"Maybe it's for the best," said Harper. "I mean, they clearly aren't happy."

"Well, I thought about keeping it to myself, since it was pretty personal stuff between them, but I thought you should know we can count them off the list of potential murderers."

"Anyone else we can cross off?" asked Angie.

"Yeah, Nick. He wasn't involved either."

"How do you know?"

"Let's just say he was probably the last person who wanted either Bobby or Vernon dead."

"That's good news," said Angie.

"He also fixed a doorknob that came loose at the house."

"I thought you weren't putting any money into the house until you sorted everything out with Lily."

"A doorknob doesn't count," said Angie. "Does it?"

I rolled my eyes. "I can't believe I forgot to tell you about the house, too."

Angie frowned at me. "You seem to be forgetting a lot of things today, Poppy. Are you okay?"

"I'm sorry. I just got so riled up because of Ryan and Lily. I completely lost my train of thought. So much has happened."

"What about the house?" asked Harper, eager to hear my news.

"Right. I heard from my lawyer, and he said Lily's agreed to drop the case."

Angie clapped her floury hands together. "That's

great news."

"Wait, I'm confused. You said she wouldn't drop it. No way, no how."

"I thought so too, but my lawyer confirmed it. We're just waiting for official word from the court."

"This is quite the news day for this small town," said Angie.

Harper held up her empty plate. "Yeah, and I'd say that calls for more pie."

Twenty-one

A KNOCK AT the front door startled me awake. I'd spent the rest of the previous day setting up my bedroom on the second floor. Bed frame assembled, mattress and box spring placed, sheets laid out. I wouldn't say it felt like home, but it was getting closer.

I took the stairs slowly, still groggy from sleep, and a second knock came just as I opened the front door.

Deputy Todd stood rigid in his clean and pressed uniform. He held his hat in his hands, and wisps of his thinning hair blew lightly in the breeze. "Good morning, Miss Lewis. I'd like to have a word."

I wouldn't say his manner was of one who'd just found out his wife was having an affair. On the contrary, he seemed all business. "What can I do for you, Deputy?"

"May I?" he motioned inside the threshold, and I stepped aside to allow him to enter the house. "Ahem," he started. "About yesterday, I'd appreciate if you kept the matter to yourself."

Oops, I thought. "I'll do my best, of course."

"There's another reason I came by. The ballistics came back on the gun used to killed Vernon Dogger. The casings belong to a specific size caliber revolver, and there's only one of those registered to any resident of Starry Cove." Deputy Todd met my eyes. "Arthur Lewis."

"Arthur?" I staggered. "That makes no sense. Arthur was dead before all this happened."

"A-yup."

"But the murderer could have been anyone with that type of gun. It could have been some random crazy person driving through who killed Vernon for the thrill of it. How can you be sure it was Arthur's?"

"Well, first off, the casing found at the scene is pretty old. Almost antique, you could say, so it probably came from an old-fashioned gun, just like the Chief's Special registered to Arthur. Now, you stated before that you didn't know if he owned a firearm. Have you found one in the house?"

"No."

"Okay," he nodded. "So, Arthur had a gun registered to his name of the same age and type that's believed to have been used in the murder. And you can't find it. Now, where does that leave us?"

"Maybe I just haven't found it yet. Or someone may have taken it. I told you before I thought someone was in the house."

"Mind if I look around this time?" He glanced behind me and up the stairwell.

"Not at all."

I follow the deputy as he made his way from room to room checking the usual places people keep their firearms—hall closets, tall cabinets. You can imagine my surprise when, in Arthurs's room, Deputy Todd pulled out a box of bullets from the very back of the bedside table behind a pile of old magazines and crossword puzzles. The box was heavy, almost full, and although it looked fairly new, the date stamp indicated it was from the 1950s. Well-kept, like all of Arthur's things.

"Practically antique," he said. "And if I wagered a guess, these bullets would match the casing found at the murder scene."

I shook my head in disbelief. "I had no idea."

"And there's a spot here for a gun case." He pointed to an empty spot in the nightstand's drawer. "Perfect size."

"I guess it was stolen then. I don't remember him leaving it to anyone specifically in his will, and all the contents of the house transferred to me."

"Miss Lewis, I'm going to ask you one time, and be straight with me. Do you know where this gun is?"

"No, absolutely not," I said. "I've never seen a gun in this house and haven't seen those bullets before either." My shoulders slumped, and I started to sweat a bit, like he'd sat me down under a hot interrogation lamp, guilty as sin. "I know I have no alibi for the murder, but I swear to you, I had nothing to do with Vernon's death."

"I believe you, Miss Lewis. You had no motive and your clothes were too clean, anyway."

"Who *does* have a motive?" I asked. "Who could kill Vernon Dogger in cold blood?"

His eyes looked away from mine, and he steeled his jaw. "Vernon had enemies. Not mafia-level enemies, mind you, but enemies nonetheless. I'm certain that if we find out what happened to this gun, we'll have our murderer."

"I hope so. I can't stand being left in the lurch, with people thinking I've done something horrid and no way to defend myself."

"I understand. I'm going to take these," he held up the box of bullets, "and ask you to contact me if anything else happens—anything suspicious. I'm not so sure that the attack on you the other night didn't have something to do with this mess."

"I will, thanks." I led the deputy to the porch and watched as he disappeared into the fog. The morning air felt chilly on my face, and the town sat silent, like the blanket of mist was weighing it down. Even the coffee I made fresh left me cold and gloomy.

I was still in a glum mood when another knock at the door caused me to jump in my skin. I was about to open it when the visitor rapped again, harsher, and then called out my name.

"Poppy? It's Lily. I'd like a moment to talk."

I crept back from the door without a sound and hid just outside the foyer so she couldn't spot my shape if she peered through the sidelights. She knocked again. I chanced a peek around the corner, watching her distorted shape on the other side of the glass as she waited for my response. Clenching my jaw, I ran the verbal attacks I'd rehearsed through my head—the things I dreamed of saying to her face if given the chance and the courage. My eyes narrowed, but just before I'd built up enough of that courage to open the door and say my thoughts out loud, her shape drifted away and her steps grew softer as she descended the porch stairs and walked away.

***

I waited awhile after Lily's surprise visit before I dared leave the house. I hoped a hearty breakfast would cheer me up, so I grabbed my jacket and walked through the lingering fog to the diner. Shelby's place was packed, a totally different feeling than the loneliness I'd experienced back at the house. Most folks were there in pairs or families filling booths, so I moved toward the single seat at the counter next to Walter—Vernon's old seat.

"Mind if I sit here?" It felt right to ask permission from him, having only been a few days since Vernon sat there last. The loss must still be fresh in his mind.

"Oh, Poppy. Please have a seat. I could use the company this morning. How's the house going?"

"I finally got my own things moved in. Arthur had so much of his own stuff, and he left me practically everything, so I'm still sorting it all out."

"Nice guy, Arthur. Funny that he lived in that big house though, all by himself."

"He seemed to be a big collector. There's some interesting stuff I plan to have out on display once I open the bed-and-breakfast."

"Interesting stuff, huh? Sounds like old Arthur had a bit of a hoarder in him."

"Maybe a little, but he was pretty selective with what he owned. It's all very nice and well-kept."

"Glad you're keeping his legacy going. I think the town could benefit from your bed-and-breakfast, despite what the mayor and the deputy think."

"That's right," said Shelby, bustling up to the counter. "I sure wouldn't say no to more customers." She pulled a mug from under the counter and filled it automatically.

"Thanks, Shelby. I'm pretty excited to finally dip into my inheritance and get the renovations going."

"Don't look now, Poppy, but here comes Ryan. I hope you two had a nice time the other night." She winked as she headed down the counter, filling mugs as she went along.

Oh no, I thought.

"You and the pharmacist, huh?" asked Walter with a grin on his face. "Nice to see two young people having some fun."

"We went on one date, and it wasn't even a date, Walter." I didn't look at the door on purpose. Making eye contact was not in the plan for today.

"Oh, well, you're making lots of friends and that's good. Harper and Angie. Now this fella," said Walter.

"Poppy, hello," said Ryan in his infuriating accent. "Having breakfast too then? Would you like to grab a table together?"

"Hi there, Doctor," said Walter. "You go along, Poppy. I won't mind. I'm leaving soon anyway."

Ugh, I thought. *There goes my only way out.*

"Sure," I said calmly, grabbing my mug. "See you around, Walter."

Of course, to make it more awkward, we took the same booth we'd sat at on our not-date. "How is everything going?" he asked. "I had an enjoyable time the other night. It's so good to talk to someone who understands what it's like to be in a new town, starting a new life."

"Uh huh," I mumbled, staring at my mug.

"And I thought, if you had a nice time too, that you

might want to catch a movie with me in Vista soon. We could grab dinner as well."

"Um," I said, looking away.

"Is everything all right?"

"It's…"

"Poppy?"

"What were you doing with my sister, Lily? Now, you don't know much about me, but you said you were a good judge of character. So, what was that about?"

"Your sister?" he asked, bewildered.

As if he didn't know. "Yeah. Tall, dark hair, talons. Can't miss her."

"I know who you are talking about, but I'm not sure what you want me to say." His voice remained calm and understated.

"I saw you two together and trust me because I know her better than anyone, and I know what she gets up to. Look, Ryan, I'm not interested in competing with my sister for anything anymore."

"Competing? Poppy, I'm not sure what you think is going on, but it's not whatever you're insinuating."

"Then what is it?" I demanded.

"It's—" he started, then shook his head. "It's not what you think it is."

Pressure built up in my ears and behind my eyes. The flood was coming. I knew I was going to blow, so I stood up from the booth. "I think I should go."

Without another word, I left him sitting there, slack-jawed, staring back at me with such a look on his face you'd think I'd just told him the sky was green and the sea was red. I probably could have handled that better. I *know* I could have handled that better, but Lily brings out

167

the worst in me. I steamed my way out the diner's door and to the bakery next door.

"Poppy, great. Try this." Angie shoved a plate of pie into my face as soon as I sat down. "It's wild honey and huckleberry cheese pie. It's made with cream cheese and my own canned huckleberries." Then she saw my face. "What's wrong?"

"I just ran into Ryan at the diner."

"Oh," she breathed. "How'd that go?"

"Catastrophic."

"Oh," she said again, taking the other empty seat at the small table. "Do you want to talk about it?"

"I told him I saw him with Lily, and I knew what was up. He acted surprised, confused even."

"Maybe he was."

"Not likely. There's no way to misconstrue Lily's fawning and his response. I saw it myself."

"Okay, but maybe what you saw wasn't exactly how you saw it. You do get a bit worked up whenever Lily's around, and it's not like they were hiding from people like Lovie and Jim."

"Then what was he hiding? He wouldn't share anything with me."

"Poppy, maybe he couldn't share it with you."

"Or wouldn't." I thrust the first bite of pie in my mouth.

"No, what I mean is, what if he couldn't share it with you because it has to do with his work? You know, as a pharmacist? He can't talk about patients with you."

"Patients? She wasn't picking up allergy pills. She was touching him, playing the sad pouty Lily role she plays so well. I think there were actual tears. And he was giving it back, rubbing her arms and giving her that sad puppy dog face, like he was really feeling sorry—" Then it hit me. Of course he was genuinely feeling it. Ryan was that sincerely nice guy they all warned me about, just doing his job as a doctor to console his patient. Lily as a patient though? That sounded strange.

Angie placed a hand on mine. "See. I'm sure it was something else. I'm not sure what, but it sounds like Ryan was consoling her over something."

"Oh Angie, I think you're right. And I've made a complete buffoon of myself." I smacked my head. I would have hit myself harder if I thought it would slap me back in time so I could change the way it had all played out. "But what was Lily so sad about?"

"I don't know. Everybody goes through life. I know Lily is basically the devil incarnate in your eyes, but I'm sure she has her own troubles. Maybe you should talk to her yourself."

"I'm such a fool." I laid my head down in my arms on the table.

"No, you're not," she said, rubbing my shoulders. "You had a bad day and probably said some things you regret, but Ryan will forgive you once he understands where you're coming from."

I lifted my head, eyes bleary, and stared at her. "I'm a horrible beast who jumps at the throat of the people who've shown me kindness. And you're always so sweet. You really see the good in others."

Angie flashed me a warm smile and squeezed my hand. "And I have pie, too, which makes me extra sweet." She popped up from the chair as I slumped further into mine, defeated. "Now, tell me what you saw at Shelby's.

Were there any pies that weren't for sale? Anything suspicious, like exotic ingredients or special pie tins you noticed in the kitchen?"

"No, I saw nothing of the sort—and I wasn't looking either."

"Bah." She threw her hands up in the air. "This competition will be the death of me. Wild honey huckleberry cheese pie—what was I thinking? Totally basic and boring. It's not even a *pie*—it's just a cheesecake in disguise. I've got to figure this out, Poppy. The parade is tomorrow."

"And I've got to apologize to Ryan. Oh Angie, I can't bear it—I'm so embarrassed, how will I ever talk to him again?"

"You just put one foot in front of the other and go say what needs to be said."

I groaned. "You make it sound so easy."

"And you're making it harder than it needs to be." She slapped her hands on her apron.

"Can I just hide here for the rest of the day?"

"Sure, but you can't mope, and I'll be working on tomorrow's pie since the huckleberry was yet another failure."

"Why don't you just combine them?"

"Combine what?"

"The pies we've tasted. Like a mash-up."

"A mash-up... I couldn't use the frozen fruit. Maybe the apple and huckleberries would work though." She stared off, contemplating the possibilities.

"It sounds good to me."

"Hmm... I have to think more about this combination. I may have an idea to make it stand out."

"Okay, while you work on that there's someone else I need to talk to."

"Who's that?"

"Pastor Basil. I saw Lily at the church the other day—another anomaly. He might know what's going on." I headed for the door. "Thanks for the cheesecake-pie thing. It was delicious."

"Wait," she said. "You always forget to tell me things when you're flustered. Is there anything else you're forgetting?"

I could have slapped myself again. "You're right. Deputy Todd came by the house this morning. He thinks the murder weapon was an old gun that belonged to Arthur. Someone must have stolen it from the house. We also found some bullets in a box left behind."

"Gosh, that's an important discovery."

"Yet we still have no idea who shot Vernon, but once we find that gun, we'll find the killer."

Twenty-two

THE CHURCH STEEPLE appeared as I walked down the sidewalk from the bakery. The fog had burned off and it was proving to be a beautiful day, despite my bleak mood. I just assumed the pastor would be there, but I suppose he has a life too and may not spend all day, every day at the church. More than likely, I'd find him in the garden.

And sure enough, there he was, on his knees with his hands in the dirt, tending to his flowers or whatever Latin name they were called. He looked intense, totally focused, and sweat dripped down his brow from the effort. Mayor Dewey wriggled in the dirt nearby, scratching his back and enjoying the sun and company of the flowers and butterflies.

"Hello, Pastor Basil," I said with a small wave to catch his attention.

"Poppy. Groovy, just groovy. Mayor Dewey and I were giving these flowers some much-needed love."

"I thought I'd stop by and see if you needed any help."

"You could hand me that bag of worm castings. Just there, in the wheelbarrow."

"Worm castings?"

"That's right. Makes great fertilizer. It's just worm poop. Black gold, it's called. In order to give your plants the energy and support they need, you first need to enrich their environment, tend to them with love and care and give them the best that our Lord has to offer—worm poop."

"Interesting." I handed him the bag of soupy black sludge.

"What can I do for you otherwise, Poppy?"

"I was actually hoping you might be able to tell me why my sister was here the other day."

He paused a moment, then stood up and brushed his hands on his apron. "Well, it's not really for me to say. Have you talked to her yourself?"

"No."

"In my experience, that's always the best way to find out about another person—to ask them yourself."

"I can't ask her."

"Why not?"

I looked around. This wasn't the place to spill my heart. "Could we go inside?"

"Of course, let me just ditch these gardening duds." He removed his apron and gloves and set them gently on the wheelbarrow. "My office should do nicely. Dewey, don't dig up the bulbs. They get upset when they're disturbed." Mayor Dewey responded with a gentle mew and continued to lay stretched out, content in the dirt between the flowers.

I hadn't seen Pastor Basil's office before, only

observed him and a few people enter and exit during my previous visit. Now I saw that it was exactly what one would expect a pastor's office *not* to be. Sure, there was a desk and the requisite drawers for filing and seating for members of his congregation. What stood out was the giant tie-dyed peace banner spanning the wall behind his chair and the dream catchers hanging in the window, fluttering slightly in the wind that breezed through. A tiny laptop sat in the middle of the empty desktop. It was an odd mix of hippie and modern-contemporary esthetic.

"We can lounge on the cushions, if you'd prefer," he said, pointing at a stack of vibrant silk-embroidered floor cushions stacked against the wall. "Sometimes they help a person feel grounded, which allows them to better connect with their faith and achieve inner peace."

"The chair is fine, thanks."

"As you wish." He scooted behind his desk and took a seat in his own chair while I chose the nearest to the door. "Now, what did you want to talk about? Something is troubling you."

I took a deep breath and spilled it all out. "I don't know what you and Lily talked about, but she and I aren't the closest of sisters. She's always tried to be better than me, in every way. A year ago, it came to a head—she seduced my husband, just to prove to me she could. It ended my marriage at what was already a tough time. Our mom passed away and Lily, as usual, was too busy to bother with any of the arrangements, so it fell to me. I guess she didn't have time to spare for that, but she found time enough to sleep with my husband. She's an evil person, Pastor. I know that's a bad thing to say about someone in a church, but she is. There's not a redeemable bone in her body."

Pastor Basil leaned back in his chair as he listened. His fingers pitched in front of his face as he was deep in thought. "I see. That's quite a tough burden to bear, and there is little joy in the end of a marriage."

"So, you see, that's why I can't talk to her. She'd lie to me anyway or make up some story. I can't trust anything that woman does or says. She even tried to take Arthur's house from me, if you can believe it."

"Why do you think she does these things?"

"I think she hates me."

"These acts of hers, they may be rooted in hate. Or they could stem from her own self-worth or self-doubt."

"She's a very successful businesswoman. I doubt she needs or wants for anything in this world."

"Does she have friends?"

"Friends?" I'd never thought about it. I couldn't imagine anyone would want to be friends with her, but I suppose it was possible. She had none that I could remember when we were younger, although she was smart and pretty. I also couldn't remember her ever going out to a party or to a friend's house. So what? Maybe she was lonely, but she didn't make it easy. *It's her own fault,* I thought. *She brought it on herself.*

"From that downer look on your face, I'd wager she wasn't Miss Popularity."

"No, but she's not a pleasant person, so that's no surprise. I can't excuse her behavior. I won't."

"Excusing and forgiving are choices we make with guidance from the Lord. Only you know what is possible."

"So, you won't tell me why she was here?"

He adjusted his glasses. "I'm sorry, Poppy, but it's not for me to share. If you can find it in your heart to approach her and discover the answer for yourself, you may find that forgiving isn't so far from your grasp as you might think."

It was beyond my capability to speak to Lily without losing my head. I wanted to wash her out of my life, but this mystery nagged at me. Lily didn't hide from her actions—she was entirely willing to share with me how she seduced my husband, or how she casually dropped by to tell me she was going to fight Arthur's will. With this secreting around—trips to church, to the pharmacist—something else must be going on.

"Thanks, anyway," I said, dejected, and I stood up from my chair. As I swung the office door open, I nearly ran into a woman's small fist.

"Oh, I'm sorry," she squeaked. She must have been reaching to knock as I'd opened the door.

"No, my apologies. I didn't see you there." I let her pass and once again sat at one of the back pews to gather my thoughts. This was a serene place, and it exuded that old charm, like a little English church cobbled together with stones quarried from the area and hand built by sweaty God-fearing villagers.

From the back, I heard the woman say, "I came early to practice the bells, Pastor. Georgia will be here soon, too."

"Groovy, Beatrice. I always love the sound of bells ringing in the bright light of day, like God's sweet kiss."

"Yes, well I was having trouble with my brush damp and practice makes perfect. I'll be in the nave if you need me."

"We'll jam together later once I've finished my sermon."

"Oh, hello again," said the woman as she passed me walking down the aisle.

"Hello, there. I'm Poppy Lewis."

"Bea Trotter."

"Nice to meet you. You play the bells?"

"That's right, I'm here almost every day either practicing or volunteering in other ways. There's always so much to do around this place."

"Kenny Trotter is your husband, right? He's a mechanic, I hear."

At the mentioned of Kenny's name her face went rigid and her voice trembled. "Yes, he's my husband. Why?"

"No reason, I was just putting two and two together. I'm new in town, so I'm not familiar with everyone just yet."

"That's right. You took on Arthur's big purple Victorian."

"He was my uncle."

"Arthur," she said, looking off. "What a nice man. He is truly missed by everyone. Such a beautiful house, too. I'm glad it's staying in the family. I think Lovie mentioned that it was going to be a bed-and-breakfast."

"Yes. I'm planning on renovating, but there's still a lot to do. I've only just moved in."

"I bet. Kenny was always talking about that house. How it was too big and had secrets and might be haunted or something."

"Haunted?"

"Yes, but I don't believe in ghosts. Other than the

Holy Ghost, of course." She dropped her eyes. "I heard
Kenny and Vernon talking about the house a few weeks
ago. They said there was something inside that was important. I can't imagine what they meant. Can you?"

"I'm not sure," I said, trying to keep my face neutral.
"Maybe just superstition. You said you heard Kenny and
Vernon, but were Bobby Teach or Walter Dogger ever
part of these conversations?"

"Not Bobby, bless his heart. And I don't think I saw
either—it was just the one time I heard them talking, anyway. Walter came to our house to borrow Kenny's truck,
but other than that I don't remember seeing either of them
any time recently."

"He borrowed Kenny's truck?"

"That's right. He brought over a rundown orange car
for some repairs a week or two ago and asked to borrow
Kenny's truck for a few days. Kenny made him pay for
the use of it, of course."

"That's interesting."

"Not really. In Kenny's mind, there's a buck to be
made in any situation. I think those guys were all like
that." She shook her head. "Well, I better get some practice in or I'll never improve before tomorrow. Last week
I thought I'd die from embarrassment when I missed the
second cue. And I felt so bad for Pastor Basil—he works
so hard to train our little bell choir."

"It was nice meeting you, Bea."

"You too, Poppy. I hope my bells don't bother you."

"I'm sure they won't."

I watched as this perfectly amiable woman walked
down the aisle and set off toward a set of bells that sat in
a row on a table against the wall behind the pulpit. I

wondered how she survived marriage to someone like Kenny—loud, brash, violent. Her life must be misery behind closed doors. It's no wonder she spends so much time at church. She couldn't have come at a better time, though, otherwise I'd have missed her and the fount of information she had to share. So, Kenny and Vernon were scheming about Arthur's house and it appears they knew that something valuable—or at least interesting—was inside. And I'd bet Arthur's fortune that old orange car was Vernon's, which puzzled me—why would Walter bring Vernon's car to Kenny's house, and why did he need to borrow a truck if he didn't normally drive? At least some things were matching up with the blueprints and the break-ins. And out of Vernon and Kenny, only one of those schemers was still alive.

***

I delayed as long as I could, but dread filled me as I finally left the church. With each step it oozed into my soul, but I knew I needed to smooth things out with Ryan sooner rather than later if I wanted to preserve our friendship. I'd never been any good at apologizing for being an insufferable dolt, and this time would be exceptionally difficult. At this time of day, he'd still be at the pharmacy, being that incredibly nice guy I'd accused him of *not* being, providing medicines for those in need, saving lives and all that was noble and good.

The pharmacy was nothing more than a tiny space located at the back of the general store. I stood at the entrance on the street, leaning against the wall, reliving every moment of my morning's regrettable events. I cringed at each word that had spewed from my mouth, at

Ryan's delicate features crushed by confusion and by the barrier of his convictions.

Twice I walked away out of fear. Twice I came back and leaned against the wall next to the entrance. *Come on, Poppy*, I thought. *You owe it to him.*

"Are you planning on coming inside at some point?" came a Scottish brogue at the door. The shock alone made me jump. "You've been pacing out here for fifteen minutes."

"Have I?" I asked, truly unsure, eying the completely empty street on both sides and in both directions for a plausible reason to loiter—or for an escape route.

"Aye. And I know why you're here, Poppy, but I can't help you. You'll have to talk to your sister yourself."

"Oh," was all I could say. I gathered all my strength. This was it. This was the moment. I just needed to say the words and get them out and a weight would lift off my shoulders like Atlas shrugging off that burdensome Earth once and for all. I took a deep breath and opened my mouth to respond—

"And another thing," he continued. "You made it very clear that your sister hurt you in some way—caused you some sort of deep, visceral pain. But there's something you need to know about me. I come from a place where we hold loyalty and honor dear, where there are still respectable codes of behavior. I am not a person who betrays a trust that I am trying hard to build. Something I am trying to build with you specifically, as a friend."

I lowered my head. I had never been so kindly admonished in my life and never felt so low about my own actions. He was right, totally and completely and utterly correct. Lily had hurt me, and he was that *nice guy* who just wanted to make a friend.

"You're right," I whispered. "About all of it. I came to apologize because I realized how horrible I'd acted earlier."

"Aye. You've got the right of it there."

"And I wanted you to know that I respect that you can't talk about my sister. I should talk to her myself. You're not the only person to tell me that today."

"Good. Now, I hope you've gotten it all out of your system. I can't have you blowing up at me the next time we're out together."

"Next time?"

"Aye. I believe in forgiving and forgetting, but as the old saying goes, 'Fool me once…'"

I nodded, knowing exactly what he meant. I wouldn't have another chance to maintain this budding friendship if I flew off the handle again.

"That offer of dinner and a movie is still on the table, if you're interested. Think about it," he said as he stepped back through the door. "I hope I'll see you at the Pie Parade tomorrow."

But I didn't have to think about it. My entire body tingled, and I think my feet even flittered off the ground for a moment. Apparently, nice guys give second chances, and I wasn't going to blow it this time.

Twenty-three

THE SUNDAY OF the Pie Parade dawned under sunny skies. While still chilly, the late morning felt brisk and bright and I decided it was time for me to cash in my promise to Pastor Basil to finally make it to church. Not being a spiritual person, I was eager to see Angie and Harper to fill them in on the good news about Ryan rather than find a way closer to God. The town elves must have been busy the previous night, as streamers and flags and banners now lined Main Street, awaiting the Pie Parade scheduled for later that day.

"Poppy, over here," came Angie's voice as I approached the church garden. She stood by herself waving a chubby arm in the air to flag me down.

"Hi, Angie. Where's Roy?"

"Oh, Roy," she said, gesturing in the general vicinity behind her. "He's off talking to someone about woodworking or whittling or whiskey or something. Did you get a chance to talk to Ryan?"

"Yes, and thankfully it went pretty well. He said he'd

be at the parade today."

"I'm so glad to hear it," she gushed. "I knew he'd understand."

"How about you? Did you finish your pie for today?"

Angie eyes shifted from side to side then she cupped my arm and led me behind the gladiolas. "Yes, but I can't talk details here. There are ears everywhere. This is church, after all—the chosen hunting ground of gossips and blabbermouths."

"Will Harper be here?"

"No, no." Angie waved dismissively. "Not her thing. But don't worry, I told her to meet us out here after church is over. We can head to the bakery after that so you two can psych me up, get me in the zone."

"Anything you need, Angie. We'll be there for you."

"Thanks. Oh gosh, don't look now but here comes Deputy Todd and Lovie." Angie shifted her eyes toward the street.

We huddled behind the flowers watching as the couple made their way from the sidewalk up the pavers and into the church, arm-in-arm, the deputy staring straight forward and Lovie's eyes glued to the ground the entire way.

"Lovie's usually champing at the bit to jabber with the other ladies."

"Guess the other day took the wind out of her sails," I said. "It's probably less fun to be the one gossiped about, although I can't imagine anyone except us knows unless Lovie spilled the beans herself."

"Not likely if she's kept the affair a secret for this long."

"You're right. So, the penitent wife may truly be

penitent. I hope they can work things out, I really do. It's no fun to experience the end of a marriage."

Angie placed a hand on my arm and gave it a gentle squeeze. "I hear the pastor's gong. Let's go inside."

As church ended, the townsfolk exploded through the doors into the warm sunlight. Pastor Basil's sermon was particularly cheerful, and spirits were high in anticipation of the Pie Parade. Clusters of women encircled Shelby and Angie, chattering about the upcoming parade as I stood a way off along the flower bed, staring at the pastor's carefully tended lilies. They were beautiful, those that were blooming, but a fair number drooped low, shriveled and wilted and in stark contrast against their hardier neighbors. Their color had faded, the vibrant orange turned a dull brown.

"They can still come back to life," said a voice next to me. "God willing."

"Hello, Pastor."

"Penny for your thoughts?"

"I'm thinking about my sister."

"Have you talked to her yet?"

"Not yet," I said. "I don't actually have a way to contact her—I just sort of have to run into her, I guess."

He nodded. "I see. Would it be helpful if she came to you?"

"Yes, but I—"

"Hello, Poppy," came a voice behind us.

It was her—it was Lily's voice. I spun around to see her standing just a few feet away on the cobbled path. She wore a beautiful day dress in lavender and a wide-brimmed hat, elaborate and luxurious, perched securely on her head. A wave of long black hair cascaded dramatically over one shoulder.

"Lily." It was all I could say. I hadn't prepared a greeting or a speech or a line of questioning. I turned to Pastor Basil for help, but he'd already floated away.

"I'm dropping the inquiry into the house."

"Yes, I know," I replied. "Although I'm not sure why."

"Because I'm tired."

"Oh? Tired? That's rich."

"Poppy, there are things going on in my life—"

"Wait... Your life? This isn't your life." I gestured to the surrounding town. "This is *my* life." I couldn't stop myself. I wasn't ready for this. "You have invaded my new life—a new life I had to start because of *you*."

"I know, but if you'll just listen—"

"No, you don't get any more of my time. I'm done. I have no idea why I'm even talking to you." I threw my hands up and walked away. Angie was somewhere in the crowd, and I needed to get to her fast before I blew up.

"Wait, Poppy," Lily's voice called softly behind me. "You should know that I'm dying."

Twenty-four

IT WAS LIKE hitting a wall of bricks. I stopped dead in my tracks. I didn't turn to Lily, I simply stood there motionless as her words sunk in. *Dying*. Had my heart stopped? The air was thick with the muffled sounds of the church-goers a few yards away. I tried to pinpoint what I was feeling right then. Did I even care? When I realized I'd stopped breathing, I let out a strangled gasp and I knew— Yes, I cared.

"Dying," I responded, still not facing her.

"Yes, that's why I'm here. For treatment. There's a specialist in Vista who's trialing a new type of therapy treatment."

"Dying?" I repeated, finally turning back to face her.

"Are you glad?" She steeled herself for my answer.

I couldn't respond right away. Part of me wanted to shout Yes! And to tell her how thrilled I was that she'd finally be out of my life. But the core of me had no will to shout or to scream or to cry. The news was numbing. "No," was all I said.

"I don't want to fight anymore, Poppy. I know I've been wretched to you and I don't deserve your sympathy. If I've learned anything from the past few months, it's that life is short and I need to atone to those I've wronged, including you. Especially you. If it means anything, I'm sorry, so truly sorry."

I stared at her for a moment before Angie appeared at my side, out of breath. "Poppy, I was talking to the ladies and I didn't see you here." Her eyes flickered to Lily. "I came as soon as I saw."

"It's okay, Angie," I said emotionless. "Lily was just sharing some news with me."

"Oh, okay," Angie said, confused. "Do you want me to go away?"

"No. Actually, I'm ready to go if you are?"

"Sure." Angie cradled my arm and led me away.

"Poppy?" Lily called from behind and I turned back to her. "Can you forgive me? You're all I have left."

I stood dumbfounded, confused. It was too much to process. I said nothing and let Angie steer me in the direction down the path.

We left Lily behind next to her namesake flowers, some wilting, some flourishing. Pastor Basil had returned and took up her hand in his, and as Angie and I walked away, I watched them locked together in prayer.

"Come on," Angie said. "I'm not sure what that was all about, but I'll take you to the bakery and we can make some coffee and you can have a cinnamon roll. That'll help." She led me in silence to the bakery and sat me down at the little table inside.

She handed me a cup of freshly brewed coffee. "I'm sorry I wasn't there for you. What happened?"

"She's dying."

"She's dying?" Angie repeated, shaking her head. "What does that mean?"

"I have no idea. I didn't get details. She said something about treatment and Vista, but I was only half listening at that point."

"Oh, Poppy. I'm so sorry. Are you okay?"

"I don't know. I feel sort of numb right now."

A knocking came from the storefront and we looked to see Harper, face and hands squished up against the window peering in. Angie hustled over and turned the key in the lock to open the door.

"Roy said you two went this way. What's going on? I thought we were going to meet outside the church?"

"There's something going on with Lily," Angie said softly.

"Lily? What now? I hope she hasn't gone and screwed things up again."

"No, not exactly. She told me she's dying."

"Dying?"

I nodded. "I guess it could be true. That must be why she's been in the area—to see a specialist in Vista for treatment. She must have been getting medicine from Ryan. And she must have been meeting with Pastor Basil to…"

"To seek comfort," said Angie.

"Jesus," Harper said, exhaling.

Angie nodded. "Yes, Jesus too."

"I'm sorry, Angie," I said, shaking my head. "This is your day and I've made it all about me and Lily."

"Don't be ridiculous. This is heavy news to take so suddenly. But," she said, her voice cheering up, "if you two will sit there, I'll show you what I have in store for today's parade."

"Yes, please. Something to take my mind off this."

Angie bustled behind the counter and opened a door in the underside of the pastry case, hidden from view. A second later she reappeared carrying an enormous pie. Her eyes twinkled as she placed it on the table between me and Harper.

Tiny purple flowers dotted the top layer of crust, which sparkled from the generous grains of sugar coating the surface. She'd strategically cut holes out of the top crust to reveal the colorful fruit filling inside and a glorious sweet aroma wafted up and into our noses.

"It's an apple huckleberry sugar pie with an edible flower butter crust."

"It's beautiful."

"It's a winner," said Harper, drooling.

"It's something I couldn't have done without the both of you."

"Can we eat it?" asked Harper, reaching in to touch the delicate flowers embedded I the crust.

Angie's slapped her hand away. "Of course not, this is for the parade. You can eat it afterward or I can make another. This is going to bring home the trophy this year. I can feel it."

**

As the afternoon closed in and the time of the parade approached, Roy arrived at the bakery to signal it was time to get going. Angie closed up and we headed to the starting line, which was a covered booth with sawhorses set up to create starting blocks on the road outside the church.

The sidewalks had filled considerably and as Angie walked by, covertly carrying her pie, an occasional cheer erupted as she passed. Each time her smile widened until I thought it might take over her face completely. She could hardly contain her excitement and pride over this year's pie as her feet skipped across the ground. I couldn't blame her—the pie was beautiful and smelled great. Definitely a winner.

"I've got to head into the registration booth to sign in my pie and get a number bib."

Harper nodded. "Poppy and I will find a spot in the crowd and catch up with you later, once you've hoisted the trophy."

"Thanks, you two—I really mean it," said Angie and she turned away under the fold of the tent cover.

Harper grabbed my hand and led me off into the crowd, which mostly congregated around the starting line, but there were chairs and blankets lined up all along Main Street to the opposite side near the roundabout where the finish line was located.

"Are we going to the finish line?"

"No, it's better to walk along with the competitors until they reach the end. I just wanted to get clear of this first big crowd. Looks like there're a lot of entries this year."

"How can you tell?"

"Over there, by the start line. All the people with bibs are entrants. There're only a few real competitors—Angie, Shelby, that guy from Vista whose name I can never remember. Maybe some others. But that's about it, the others are just here for fun."

We stopped at a distance and I looked back toward

the start line. Shelby stood to the side with her entourage from the diner, her pie carefully covered to keep its secrets. A large shape covered by a tarp sat off to the side of Shelby's group. It piqued my interest, but Harper was already moving down the street and I wanted to keep up.

"Look," Harper said. "There's Mayor Dewey."

"Where?"

She pointed across the street where a small opening in the crowd revealed the side of a storefront, an old bike leaned up against a mailbox. Mayor Dewey sat perfectly on the bike's seat staring at us indifferently, his plump ginger outline stood out against the starkness of the black mailbox behind him.

"He's creeping on me again," Harper said, waving her spindly fingers in his direction. "I see you seeing me, Mayor Dewey."

"Does he just wander around?"

"Of course. The mayor's got to know what's going on in his town, right?"

"How does he eat? Does he catch mice or something?"

"Nah. The fish stand has him covered. He eats like a spoiled prince. Hey, there's a spot we can push in. C'mon, it's about to start."

From the edge of the road we could see the competitors in a row at the starting line. Angie was in the middle, number nine according to her bib. Her head leaned out, looking nervously to the end of the row where, to our great surprise, was Shelby, not standing, but seated on a wheeled contraption decorated in the shape of a giant pie.

"What the heck is that?" asked Harper.

"It looks like one of those motorized grocery carts."

"Shelby's gone full on this year. She's made an actual float for the parade—can you believe it?"

"Does that count?"

"I guess you can do anything. I don't think you get extra points, just extra favor from the crowd for being a massive showoff. Probably trying to make up for her inferior pie."

"There's Lovie, too," I said. She stood on the opposite end, grim-faced, wearing her Sunday best but also in tennis shoes. Blonde-gray curls blew into her face with each wind gust and strands of hair stuck to her red lipstick.

"I wouldn't want to be one of the judges today," said Harper.

"Who are the judges today? Trevor said they were a secret."

"Here comes Mayor Jim to announce it now."

Mayor Jim stepped up to a podium and microphone set off to the side from the starting line. His voice boomed from the speakers set along the sidewalk.

"It's my pleasure to welcome you all to Starry Cove's annual Pie Parade. Please be respectful of our competitors and allow others a chance to come to the front to see the pies up close. This year we have over twenty entries, all of which look amazing, and I'm sure our judges will have a heck of a time deciding the winner. Let's give our competitors a round of applause."

The crowd clapped on cue and the competitors cautiously held up their pies and beamed back, nodding in thanks.

"And I'm sure you're wondering just who those judges are this year. Well, I'm happy to announce that one of your judges will be none other than yours truly. That's right, ladies and gentlemen, I'll be judging this year's competition with the other member of the panel—Starry Cove's own deputy sheriff, Todd Newman. Let's give him a round of applause."

Mayor Jim nodded to Deputy Todd, who stood stone-faced next to the podium. A smattering of half-hearted claps broke out from the crowd. Lovie didn't move an inch, she just stared forward toward the finish line as though wishing the whole ordeal were already over.

"Oh, this should be good. I'm sure those two get along just peachy now," said Harper. "No wonder Lovie entered. She probably found out from each of them that they were on the panel and thought she'd be a shoo-in to win. Joke's on her, I guess."

The soft clapping subsided, and the mayor continued, "Ladies and gentlemen, please be sure to enter your vote in the crowd's choice category at the booth set up next to the judges' tent. Don't forget, your vote could decide our winner. And with that, let's start the parade." Upon his last word the starting ribbon fell to the ground, and the competitors made their way to the sides of the street to display their pies to the masses.

"So, do we just look at them?"

"Yeah, and if you're close enough you can smell too. We'll put our entries in for Angie later."

A few competitors I didn't recognize walked by and held out their pies for us to view—a pretty lattice-crusted fruit something, a full-top crusted something else with pink goo oozing out the fluting. We were admiring an excellently executed frill crust when a sudden commotion caught our attention nearby. It was hard to tell from our side of the street, but it appeared Shelby's cart had stopped moving in front of the community center. We watched as it jerked mechanically, driving her midway into the street away from the crowd lining the side of the road. She fiddled with the steering column while holding her pie in one hand, all the while shouting to her entourage, who'd remained at the starting line about twenty-five yards away and hadn't yet noticed what was going on.

"I don't think they can hear her," I said.

Shelby's cart jerked again, and one competitor leaped out of her way, juggling their pie before regaining a secure hold.

"Oh no," said Harper. "I think she's out of control."

Sure enough, the cart jerked again, this time in the opposite direction toward the throngs of people lining our side of the street. Shelby's eyes bulged as she clung desperately to her pie, both hands now completely off the controls. A sleek orange figure darted across the road toward the pie float—it was Mayor Dewey—and someone yelled that he was going to get run over. Harper quickly ducked under the tape that held the crowd back in an attempt to either gain control of the scooter or save Mayor Dewey—probably the latter—but the cart swerved again and ran over her foot. Harper yowled and tumbled to the ground as the cat skittered between the legs of the spectators and out of sight.

A trail of Shelby's supporters finally realized what was amiss and now ran her way from their spot at the starting line. Shelby screamed and people scattered as the cart sped up and jumped the curb before ramming into a light pole, narrowly missing many bystanders. Upon impact, the pie slipped from her arms in what seemed like slow motion and crashed face-down on the concrete sidewalk in a splatter of glass, ruby red filling and buttery crumble crust. The carnage was shocking—an absolute massacre.

A collective gasp rose from the crowd and all other competitors who were still behind Shelby stopped in their tracks and watched as the scene unfolded before their eyes. Those in front turned at the sound of the crash to see what the hubbub was about and stared in disbelief.

I ducked under the tape and ran to Harper's side. She nursed her foot, but otherwise seemed okay.

A man from Shelby's team finally reached her side and found her still strapped into the cart, flustered beyond recovery. The pie float keeping her upright, but its mangled body also prevented her from escaping during the crash. Now they struggled to disentangle her from its mangled bulk.

"My pie," she wailed. "It's ruined. Get me out of this thing." She wriggled side to side as the people around her tore the pie float to pieces.

Mayor Jim's voice came over the speaker system, "Everyone, please calm down. It appears contestant number twelve must withdraw from the parade." He eyed the red stain on the concrete before adding, "And from the competition altogether. Please make room so crews can clean up the area. Plenty more pies to see, move along, thank you."

"Guess that's one less thing to worry about," said Harper. "With Shelby out of the way, Angie's definitely got this in the bag."

"I hope Shelby's okay. She was really upset."

"Yeah, I'd be too if I mucked up the competition I'd been working on for a year because of some silly gimmick."

"Here comes Angie." I waved frantically as she approached.

"Hi, guys," she said, passing. "Too bad about Shelby, huh? Looked like she made something with cherries—hard to tell now. It seemed rather basic from what I could tell at the starting line. She must have struggled as much as I did coming up with something unique."

"That's probably why she needed a stunt like that float," said Harper. "You've got this, Angie. Go impress the masses—you've already scored our votes."

As Angie headed up the line, we too moved up the street behind the crowds along the sidewalk to the voting booth at the roundabout. A huge golden trophy sat on full display on a table nearby, gleaming brightly in the sunlight.

"Hello, ladies," said the woman manning the booth.

"Where do we put in our crowd's choice votes?"

"You've found it. Just fill out this slip of paper and drop it into the box here." She motioned to a large cardboard box with a small slit cut into the top to push your vote through.

"At the end of the parade all the votes will be counted and these will be added to their overall scores."

We filled out our vote slips with Angie's name bold and clear and dropped them into the box. The lady at the table stamped our hands to show we'd voted, then we waited at the finish line for Angie to appear.

Other competitors arrived first, their pies still in hand—no more accidents after Shelby's disaster—and they made their way one by one into the judging tent. Soon enough along came Angie beaming and exhibiting her pie steadily in front of her, Roy's head bobbing along behind the line of the crowd on the sidewalk, keeping pace with her as she made her way down the street.

"I made it," she said, reaching us. "I think I won them over. Now it's time for judgment."

Harper gave her a supportive hug. "No worries, Angie. Knock 'em dead."

We set up camp on the steps of the big house in the shade while waiting for the results to come in. Angie remained, along with the other competitors, to present her pie and receive judging. It felt like ages before Mayor Jim and Deputy Todd finally stepped through the tent flaps and took up the microphone set up at the roundabout finish line.

Harper and I jumped up and ran to join the crowd gathering around the judges and the trophy table. All the contestant mingled in a small circle with their support crews, nervously wringing their hands or wiping their brows in anticipation.

"Ahem," the mayor started. "I'd like to start by thanking all the competitors for making this year's Pie Parade something truly special. The deputy and I have reached a decision and, with the crowd's choice votes tallied and combined, we have a clear winner."

Angie bobbed from foot to foot. Harper grabbed my hand and squeezed.

"And the winner of this year's Pie Parade trophy is… Angela Owens for her magnificent apple huckleberry sugar pie."

Harper screamed, "She won!" and jumped up and

down, taking me with her bounding to Angie's side. We enveloped Angie in a blanket of arms and kisses. Tears of joy streamed down Angie's face and I heard Roy shouting her name from somewhere, lost in the crowd.

"Thank you, thank you," Angie gasped, trying to breathe.

"Give the woman some air," said Harper, pushing the others back and finally letting go of her own squeeze.

Angie stepped up to the table and took the trophy from Deputy Todd's hands. She held it up for all to see then hugged it tightly to her chest and waved at the clapping crowd.

"And now," came the mayor's voice, "we invite you all to step into the tent and taste these pies for yourselves. Samples are out for all to enjoy."

A line quickly formed at the entrance to the tent and Angie headed for our small group on the sidelines. Before she could take two steps, Veronica Valentine, the smarmy *Vista View* reporter stepped in front of her with a recorder and a smile.

"Mrs. Owens, first, congratulations on your win. Can you tell me how you're feeling right now? What would you like our readers to know?"

Angie cleared her throat, not used to the spotlight. "They should know—"

"Thank you, Mrs. Owens," Veronica interrupted. "Were you aware that Shelby Shepard was going to be presenting her pie in a parade float? And were you aware that Miss Shepard said you were her stiffest competition, and that she also said your competitive nature really comes out this time of year, almost to a fault? That you're practically a different person."

"That I'm—" Angie began, stiffening.

"Angie has no faults," said Harper, striding up to them. "You must have misheard Shelby."

Veronica adjusted her red-rimmed glasses. "Perhaps. Now, Mrs. Owens, how do you plan to top this next year, knowing that Shelby Shepard will be back in the competition, hungry for blood?"

"Hungry for blood?" Angie wrung her hands.

"No more questions, Miss Valentine." Harper shooed her off and dragged Angie away from the reporter. "So why don't you scurry back under whatever slimy rock you came from."

Once we were at a safe distance, Harper said, "Don't worry about her, Angie. She's just trying to rile you up. And don't you worry about what she said about Shelby, you won this thing fair and square."

"And by a mile."

"I still can't believe it. It's amazing, isn't it? And you know what? I think that even if Shelby hadn't crashed out of the competition, I still would have won."

"No doubt," I said. "So how do you want to celebrate?"

"Definitely not drinks at the diner," said Angie. "Honestly, I'm so beat from today I just want to rest. I'm sure after the initial shock wears off, I'll be dead tired and will fall asleep in my tracks."

"You go rest," I said. "We'll catch up tomorrow and hopefully we'll have a special package delivery and some more news to share."

"Yeah, go on home," said Harper. "You deserve it. Hopefully after a little recon tomorrow I'll be back to report on my findings and we'll find a suitably conspicuous spot in the bakery for that shiny trophy."

Twenty-five

STILL GLOWING IN the wake of Angie's victory, I sipped my coffee idly on the porch the next morning, staring through the fog onto the roundabout. The chain on the flagpole clanged gently against the metal pole in the breeze. The fog lingered, but would surely burn off before long, so I cupped my hummingbird mug firmly and I enjoyed the salty mist while I could.

My morning daydream came to a screeching halt as the figure of Lily came into my sight on the sidewalk. I scrambled up from my chair, but she called out, having spotted me before I could slink inside.

As she came closer, I saw there was no look of disgust on her face, no upturned nose at the smell of clean sea air. Her eyes were downcast, and she slowed her steps as she came up the walkway.

"I'm glad I caught you," she said.

I didn't respond. Words didn't come easy, especially after what happened the day before. To say I had mixed emotions would be a monumental understatement, so instead I remained silent.

"You left yesterday before I finished what I wanted to tell you."

I wrapped both hands around the warm mug, clinging to it for safety, and sat back down on the bench. I sat stiff and upright—my defensive posture. That I remained on the porch, willing to listen to her words was an achievement. I wanted to hear what she had to say, whether it was out of sheer curiosity or something deeper, I wasn't sure. My eyes met hers, signaling her to continue.

"Three months ago, I was diagnosed with a rare form of cancer. It's quite aggressive and there are few effective treatments." Her eyes shifted to the floorboards of the porch. "At least for me, anyway."

My gut reaction for anyone else would've been sympathy, but I was not so easily fooled by my sister's words. "How do I know this isn't just another one of your tricks or schemes? Why should I believe you now? You don't look sick."

Lily nodded, eyes still cast down. "I understand. But it's true." She lifted her hand and stroked the perfect black tresses flowing over her left shoulder, letting her fingers run through the long locks. With one sudden movement, Lily clutched her hair and yanked it off, taking her hat with it. She held the wig limply in her hand. Her head was bald. No, not bald—covered in a gentle layer of wispy fuzz.

I inhaled sharply.

"As you can see, the chemo didn't work. The only thing left for me now are experimental treatments. That's why I've been seeing a specialist in Vista."

A rush of emotions filled me: shock, suspicion,

satisfaction, sadness. I let nothing show on my face and chose my words carefully. "I see."

With the reveal complete, Lily quickly donned the wig and hat again, adjusting it until satisfied. "But now that has run its course as well. You know, when you're sitting in the doctor's office and she tells you there's nothing else she can do, the only thing you want is someone to cling to." A tear sprouted and ran down her cheek. She wiped it away with her hand and looked away from me out onto the lawn. A deep breath followed. "I realized then that I had no one."

A situation of your own making, I thought.

"And I knew it was a situation of my own making."

I shifted on the bench, uncomfortable that Lily seemed to know my thoughts. "You tried to take this house."

"Yes," she said, shaking her head. "I have a tendency to do those things, don't I? The pastor says I'm seeking ways to connect with you."

"Funny way to do it."

She nodded again, head down. "I know. I don't think I know any other way."

My sympathy only ran so deep. "You have everything. You're beautiful, successful, famous even. Why can't you just leave me alone?"

"*I* have everything? No, Poppy, it's *you* who have everything. Friends, a family, support. There are things more valuable than having a recognizable name." She paused and lifted her head to the porch ceiling, eyes closed. Another deep breath. "I was always jealous of you. You were popular. You made friends easily. You care effortlessly."

I wasn't sure I agreed with that last part.

Lily continued, "I know I'm a monster, and that's the worst part. I see myself in the stark light and I hate who I am."

I let the words sink in. "Is that why you dropped the case? You finally realized what a monster you'd been all these years?"

"In short, yes. But more so to try to establish some semblance of a relationship with you."

"Do you expect me to forget everything you've done?"

She shook her head. "No, of course not. I know I've been horrid and you have no reason to forgive me. But I'm here today to apologize and ask for your forgiveness, whether you grant it or not. It's something I have to do."

I dropped my head and stared into my coffee. No one had made a request so weighty of me before and I wasn't sure I'd be able to forgive, as I knew I wouldn't be able to forget. "What will you do now?" I asked her.

"Now? I suppose I pray." She scoffed, clearly bemused at the thought of it. "I've heard of another experimental treatment in Baltimore, so I'll be seeking that out."

"Does that mean you'll be leaving?"

"Yes. You must be glad."

I wanted to be glad. I wanted to finally be able to celebrate this woman extracting herself from my life. But I wasn't. "Glad isn't right," I said. "I'm not sure what is."

"This might be the most we've spoken civilly in the past few years."

"I suppose so."

"You haven't said whether or not you'll forgive me."

"And I won't. Because I don't know."

Lily nodded, understanding. "Then I may not see you again." She rustled in her purse and pulled out a scrap of paper then handed it to me. "My contact information. Personal contact information. Maybe one day you can..." She didn't finish.

"Maybe," I said, taking the paper.

"Goodbye then, Poppy."

"Goodbye, Lily."

She turned and made her way down the porch steps and along the walkway to the street. I watched as she turned onto the sidewalk and behind a building, out of my sight. Would this be the last time I saw her? Did I care? I looked down at the scrap of paper, considering, then tucked it carefully into the pocket of my coat.

* * *

After letting Lily's words sink in, I left the house for the bakery and found Angie humming merrily as she swept around the pastry cases. The gleaming trophy perched majestically on top of the window display case, for all passersby to see.

"I thought you'd at least take a day off after your win yesterday."

"No way. I've got to capitalize on all the publicity. I've already got four restaurants in Vista that want to use me as their bread and pastry supplier."

"Wow, that's great."

"Yeah, but check out the article in the *Vista View*." She handed me a floury copy from across counter.

Starry Cove Pie Parade Thrills... and

Chills

All the star tarts were out in force at the annual Starry Cove Pie Parade this past Sunday afternoon. Every delectable crusted confection under the sun was on display as the competitors made their way along the crowded Main Street from start to finish line.

Local favorite, Shelby Shepard, crashed out early as her unconventional pie float lost control and careened into the crowd early in the procession, tossing her and her double cherry almond crunch-crumble pie, hurtling to the ground, splattering like a can of crimson paint.

With Shepard out of the race, the declared winner, Angela "Angie" Owens, unable to speak at length after winning the illustrious award, had only a few ominous words of warning to share with our readers about her shocking victory:

"They should know… that I'm… hungry for blood."

I slapped the paper down. "That's ridiculous—she's completely twisted your words."

"Keep reading," she urged, so I returned to the article, fuming out both ears.

Shocking words for a town still grappling with two unsolved deaths, at least one ruled a homicide. According to Deputy Sheriff Todd Newman, no suspects have been identified at this time, and no further public comments would be forthcoming from the Sheriff's Office.

"This lady is unbelievable," I said.

"I know, but it doesn't seem to have affected the business, so that's good. But no suspects in Vernon's murder still. It may never be solved."

"We'll see about that. How's Shelby doing?"

"I'm not sure," said Angie. "She didn't come into the diner this morning. We usually arrive about the same time. She may have arrived later. I'd pop over to check, but I don't think I'm someone she wants to see right now."

"Wise. I'll check on her. Maybe one of the staff knows how she's doing."

I jumped next door to the diner and quickly determined that Shelby was not there, nor were the usual welcoming smiles from the diner staff. The atmosphere was decidedly morose.

"Looking for someone, Poppy?" Walter asked from his seat at the counter. Bea hovered nearby.

"Hi, Walter. Hi, Bea," I replied. "Nice to see you both again. I wanted to check if Shelby was okay after yesterday."

"She hasn't been in," said Bea. "I think she—well, they—need time to heal." She gestured to the staff sulking behind the counter. "Service is slow today too. I wanted to grab something before heading to the church, but I'm still waiting."

"I'd be pretty mopey too after what happened."

"It's a real shame," said Walter. "I'm glad for Angie, though. Her pie was incredible."

"Oh no…" I smacked my forehead. "With all the excitement I forgot to try it."

"I'm sure she'll make you another one, you two being such good friends now."

"Actually, I should make her something for once. Repayment for all the pies she's made for me and Harper."

"That sounds like a lovely idea. Oh good, here's my food," Bea said as the server drifted to the register from the back kitchen. "I've got to get going. Kenny dropped me off earlier since he has a job out of town until tomorrow, so I need to walk down to the church by the time Pastor Basil arrives. My bells were so bad yesterday I thought I might shrivel up like a toadstool in front of all those people."

"I thought the bells were lovely yesterday."

"Thanks, but what I really need is a lot of practice and prayer. At least Georgia will be there too. I stay with her in town any time Kenny's away." She gathered her bag of food and headed out the door. "See you both later."

"Bye, Bea. Guess I'll have to catch Shelby another time."

With no Shelby and only a few somber servers plodding around, I popped back to the bakery. Angie held her phone up to an ear and waved at me to come in and sit down. "Okay Harper, sounds good. I'll let Poppy know and we'll see you at the house once you're off work. Bye."

"What'd she say?"

"She has the package and will call us once she's

found anything. How was Shelby?"

"Not there. I ran into Bea Trotter though. She'll be at the church all day then staying with her friend, and Kenny's out of town on a job."

"That's good. One way or another I'll be happy when this is over. These lingering questions are making me ill. I need to be sure no one else is going to jump out of basement doorways or come into my shop and shoot me or Roy."

"Once we find out about that car and anything else hiding on Kenny's property, we can go to Deputy Todd. Without that information he'd just laugh us out of town. This is our best opportunity to find out what happened to Vernon."

"I know." Her arms whisked furiously in an enormous pink mixing bowl. "I need to keep my thoughts on other things."

"Like your big shiny trophy."

That garnered a smile. "Right. Do you think it needs another polish?"

"Couldn't hurt."

"I wish Harper was here, she'd give it a spiffing shine."

"She has a special delivery today, and with Bea and Kenny away, she shouldn't run into any trouble."

Twenty-six

I WAITED THROUGH the afternoon at the house for word from Harper. She said she'd contact Angie and me after she got a good look at the property, so I waited expectantly, practically twiddling my thumbs, for her call. Mayor Dewey joined me inside and immediately set himself up on the worn arm of Arthur's old sofa, almost as though he'd worn it down himself, which I suspected might just be the case. I stroked his fur absentmindedly, wondering what life as Mayor Dewey must be like, when a knock came at the door. It was Angie.

"Phew," she said after I'd let her in. "We've been so busy, I never thought Roy would let us close up today. I've been champing at the bit to get out of there. Have you heard from Harper yet?"

"No, you?"

"Nothing." She dropped her bag on the floor with a thump. "I thought she'd be done by now."

"Me too. Should we call her?"

"I already tried—no answer."

"Maybe her battery is dead."

"Hmm, maybe." Angie looked doubtful.

"I've got a surprise for you while we wait."

"Ooh. What is it?"

"I'm going to make you an early dinner. Come on." I led her into the kitchen. "You've been working hard all day, and you baked all those pies for Harper and me. It's time someone made something for you for a change."

"I never say no to food," Angie said, gleefully. "What are you making?"

"Um, I'm not sure yet. I've got to work it out. I've been trying to learn to cook since I was suddenly single and I promised Ryan I'd make him something eventually, so I guess I'd better start practicing."

"So, I'm not actually the recipient of a thoughtful dinner. I'm a guinea pig."

"That's one way to look at it. How do you feel about Italian food?"

"Love it."

"Great. One Italian-inspired meal coming right up. You and Mayor Dewey get comfortable."

The recipe I tried to follow called for meatballs, but all I had on hand was shrimp, which I thought would be a suitable substitute. Shrimp were fancy after all—they cost a lot in a restaurant, at least. And how hard could it be? They cooked fast, just like pasta. Add a little alfredo sauce and it was well-nigh gourmet.

I presented my dish with a flourish, and set it in front of Angie, who waited eagerly at the kitchen table. But the look on her face when she took that first bite of linguini was a clear sign that something was dreadfully off. Her brow furrowed and I heard crunching as she slowly chewed that first mouthful. She looked up at me once with those sweet, kind eyes of hers then gently spit it out into her napkin.

"What's wrong?" I asked.

"Nothing."

"Something's wrong."

"It's nothing. I'm not very hungry."

"You're a terrible liar. Just tell me."

"Okay," she said, wringing a napkin in her hands. "Don't be mad but, um, did you take the shells off the shrimp?"

Oh no. "I thought they had to stay on. Isn't that what fancy restaurants do?"

"I dunno, Poppy. Maybe not like this." She used her fork to fiddle with the remaining shrimp swimming in noodles and white sauce. "Also, um, did you clean the shrimp?"

"What do you mean?"

"Clean them—like, remove the guts and um, the poop."

"Poop? I didn't even know that was a thing."

"Yeah, it's a thing." She showed me the vein running along the back of a shrimp body she'd just peeled. "I mean, A for effort, but you should probably keep practicing. Maybe Harper can be the next taster. And I wouldn't invite Ryan over just yet."

"Definitely not." What a disaster. I'd nearly poisoned Angie, but at least I learned more about shrimp…

Angie put her fork down. "It's been another hour and we still haven't heard from Harper. It's getting really late, even for her rounds. Maybe you were right about her battery."

"Maybe, but she knows where to find us and it's been plenty of time. Do you think we should go by and make sure everything is okay?"

"Go by Kenny's?"

"Yeah, and her place. Just to make sure," I said.

"What if she comes by here looking for us?"

"We can leave a note on the door."

"What if Kenny's back from his job already?"

"We won't go up to the house. Come on, Angie. Don't be such a scaredy-cat."

A hastily scribbled note taped to the door would have to suffice. If Harper came by, she'd know we stepped out to look for her and she'd wait until we returned.

Angie and I loaded into my Prius and began our search at Harper's apartment, which I'd never been to and had no idea where it was located. Angie showed me and, of course, it was on the same street as her cottage and Nick's rental—essentially the only other street in Starry Cove, which turned into the Coastal Road if you followed it long enough.

Harper's apartment was the back unit of a weathered gray duplex. I parked on the gravel shoulder so I didn't block the road and we walked up to her door together. Angie gave it a gentle knock and we waited. A large rainbow flag served as a window dressing, and I peered in through a gap at the side, but the interior was completely dark, and I couldn't make anything out. We waited for a few moments before knocking again—still nothing.

"Guess she's not here," said Angie.

"What about the mail truck?"

"She doesn't park it here. She parks at the station in Vista and drives her own car. Anyway, I didn't see either in the parking lot when we drove up."

"Let's keep going and check out Kenny's."

The sun hung low on the horizon and it was getting hard to see through the thick brush that ran alongside the roadway. By the time we arrived at Kenny's place, I'd turned on the headlights just to see the road.

"Well, what do you think?" I asked, staring into the dense foliage.

"I can't really see anything. Do you see Kenny's truck?"

"It's hard to tell. I'll tell you what I don't see, though—Harper's mail truck. She must have gone on somewhere else."

"Let's go," said Angie. "I don't want Kenny to come back while we're parked here staring at his house. Maybe we should try her apartment again?"

"Okay." I turned the Prius around and drove back to Harper's apartment. We tried knocking again, even turned the handle to see if it was unlocked, but it wasn't, and no one was answering.

"Maybe her car broke down at the station in Vista," I said.

"I feel like she would have called one of us. Oh, maybe that's why Kenny got called away?"

I shook my head. "I don't think so. Bea mentioned he would be out of town overnight and that was even before Harper called you this morning."

Our brief trip produced no solid answers, just speculation and, ultimately, we still hadn't heard from Harper. I parked the Prius on the gravel driveway, and we started up the path to the house. The note we'd left remained attached to the door and fluttered slightly in the evening breeze, but as we got closer, we could tell the paper had something scratched on it.

Angie hurried up the steps. "It must be a note from Harper."

"Weird. Why not just call?" I snatched the note from the door. We huddled over it in the dark, the faint glow of the foyer light inside gave us just enough illumination to see the scribbled words: "IF YOU WANT YOUR FRIEND BACK COME TO THE TROTTER PROPERTY. BRING NO ONE ELSE. $50,000."

"Oh, my gosh," Angie jumped back, as though the note itself might attack her. "It's a ransom note! We need to contact Deputy Todd."

"But the note says not to bring anyone else. What if this person hurts her?"

"You aren't planning on going yourself, are you? And who has fifty-thousand dollars just lying around, anyway?"

"I do," I mumbled, holding the note limply in my hand.

"You *do*?"

"Yes, from the divorce, from my mom's estate and then from Arthur. It wasn't enough for all the renovations, but it was enough to get started. Along with a small loan that's how I was going to fund the work on the house."

"You can't go there alone, Poppy. If Harper got into trouble you will too. Kenny's no joke—he's got a really short fuse. Besides, you don't have the money with you—it's in a bank or something, right?"

My heart beat out of my chest as my mind raced through options. "Yes, and it's too late to withdraw anything today. Maybe I can go tomorrow—"

"This is serious," she said, shaking my shoulders. "We need to call Deputy Todd or the mayor or someone. It was a harmless adventure before, but Harper could be in real trouble."

I nodded, accepting the truth, knowing Angie was right. We needed more than just our merry band of misfits to save Harper now. "I guess we don't have any more cards to play. And the longer we wait, the more likely Harper could get hurt—if she hasn't been hurt already."

So we took the chance and called Deputy Todd, who rolled up a few minutes later in his truck, blue lights whirling.

"Do you two want to tell me why you've hauled me away from my favorite TV show?"

"Deputy," Angie started, breathless. "Harper's in trouble. There was a basement wall and then Vernon's car and Kenny's place and then shrimp linguini and now there's a note and—"

"Breathe, Mrs. Owens," Deputy Todd interrupted. Angie sagged against me. "Miss Lewis, why don't you tell me what's going on."

"This note was attached to the door," I said, handing him the scrap of paper.

He read it out loud, "Went out looking for you, call if you get this or wait—"

"No, no, that's the part we wrote when we went out looking for Harper. Read the other part—the jagged scribbles. Someone added that part while we were away from the house."

His eyes scanned the rest of the note. "The Trotter property, huh? Who do you think left this note?"

"We think it was Kenny," said Angie, jumping in.

"See, that's what I was trying to say before. Vernon's car is in the yard and Kenny was really mean and Harper was delivering the mail and—"

"Thank you, Mrs. Owens," he said shortly, interrupting her again. "Miss Lewis, would you translate?"

"We spotted what we believe is Vernon's car hidden on Kenny's property, so Harper was going to check it out during her rounds today. Except, she never returned. We checked her apartment but she's nowhere to be found. Then we found this note."

"Hmm," he murmured, turning the note around in his hand. "I'll go check out the Trotter property and let you know if I find anything."

"I'm going with you."

"No, you're not."

"I'm coming too," Angie wailed as she burst into tears.

"And you're definitely not coming," he said. "This is a matter for law enforcement."

"But he'll hurt Harper. The note said not to bring anyone else. I have to go," I said.

He mulled this over for a moment, tapping his boot. "All right, Miss Lewis. We'll go in together, but I take the lead—you're just the bait."

"Oh no, Poppy…" Angie clung to my arm.

Mayor Dewey appeared, climbing on the porch, and curled his body and tail around Angie's leg, purring softly. "He's worried about Harper, too," I said.

"Angie, go home to Roy. I'll be fine. I'll call you when it's over." Or at least I hoped I would call her when it was over. Simply put, I was about to head into a situation I was not prepared for, to face a man who had a history of violence, and with a handler who'd probably never shot a gun in his professional career. Hope was all I had that I would make it out alive.

***

Deputy Todd parked his truck along the road a few yards from the entrance to Kenny's property and eased open his door, the hinges letting out a long high-pitched squeal that pierced the quiet night. He grimaced. I motioned to open the passenger door to get out as well.

"Oh no you don't. You stay right here and let me take care of this," he whispered. "I'll tell you if I need you."

"If he sees you, that'll be it for Harper. It has to be me."

"All right, but we're just going to look for now. No funny business. I want to get a good scope of the property before anyone barges in."

I extracted myself from the truck as silently as possible, but the rusty hinges of the old truck didn't do me any favors. We waited a moment to see if the sound attracted any attention from the property, but nothing stirred.

We could see partly down the driveway to the house, but the metal gate blocked the entrance for any vehicles to pass through. Deputy Todd motioned for us to climb over the gate and post up behind a large shrub about half-way down the muddy drive. As I lifted my leg over the "No Trespassing" sign on the gate, I saw the lock securing it in place had been cut through. The cut was clean and sharp—and very recent.

"Psst," I hissed. "Look at this." I pointed to the lock, and he too saw the severed metal.

"What do you think it means?" I whispered.

"Not sure yet, but let's keep moving. I don't want to stay out in the open." We shuffled silently to a secure spot behind the shrub.

"There." I pointed at the orange vehicle peeking under a tarp about thirty yards away. Other cars and trucks in various states of disrepair lined the side the property as well.

"A-yup. That looks like Vernon's all right. You said Harper was coming out here, but I don't see any sign of her."

Our eyes scanned around the property, but it was full of junk—rusted cars and bits of car parts filled most nooks and crannies. The house sat silent and dark, the porch in muted shadows. Two rickety rocking chairs moldered on the wooden decking beside dead potted plants, indistinguishable from the weeds growing up and into the railing, which gave the house a decrepit, spooky air. Bags of trash formed piles beside the house and an old bike lay on the ground, its wheels muddy. A single tree grew beside the path that led up to the house from the yard space, which Kenny kept clear of brush. Otherwise, enough thick shrubbery and vegetation grew in the surrounding space to provide sufficient cover and privacy.

My eyes scanned farther along the line of cars, and behind a large bush and out of sight from the main road, I spied the distinct outline of a mail truck. I sucked in my breath and tugged his jacket. "Look. It's her."

"Hmm, that doesn't bode well. You should stay here. We don't know what Kenny's capable of right now and he doesn't like visitors."

Kenny, I sneered. Kenny, who took my friend and held her against her will. Kenny, who trampled through town with his angry mug and sped his truck down Main Street without a care for others.

"Wait," I said in a low voice. "Where is Kenny's truck?"

"I don't see it."

"Neither do I. Do you think he parked it somewhere else?"

"I didn't see anything along the road."

"Something isn't adding up." I scanned the property again. Mail truck, Vernon's car, dark spooky house, muddy bike. "Muddy bike," I said slowly. "I recognize that bike."

"What bike?"

"There, by the house. I saw that bike at the Pie Parade yesterday and I've seen it before. I think it's Walter's bike."

"Why would Walter be—"

"Of course," I said, cursing my stupidity. "That's why Kenny's truck isn't here."

"What are you talking about?"

"It's not Kenny we're dealing with at all—it's Walter. Walter took Harper."

"You think Walter is behind this?" he asked, doubtful.

"I do now, yes. Harper and Angie and I have been digging around and when we found Vernon's car hidden here, we hatched a plan to have Harper investigate the property. We were so consumed by the idea of Kenny having killed Vernon that we didn't even consider Walter, his own brother. It's all starting to fit."

"I'm not following."

"I don't have it all put together yet, but I'm sure

that's Walter's bike, and Bea Trotter said Kenny would be gone all day—his truck isn't here. I think Walter left that note on the door. He has her here, somewhere, and we need to find her."

We scanned the property again, but nothing else hinted at where Harper could be hidden away. "Right," Deputy Todd said after a moment's pause and a deep breath. "I'm going to go around the back and peek inside the house."

"I'll come too."

He shot me a look with narrowed his eyes. "No, you will not. You will stay right here until I return. Understand?"

I frowned. "But—"

"Understand?" he repeated.

"Fine, but don't do anything that could put Harper into more danger."

"That's rich coming from you," he said before slinking away from our hiding spot toward the back of the house to our left.

Crouching behind the shrub, I couldn't help but fidget and continue scanning for any sign of movement along the property lines. Deputy Todd had been gone only a few minutes when I spotted something that seemed out of place. Something I hadn't noticed before. There was a large detached garage next to the house that Kenny probably used for vehicle repairs. On its side, in the faint light, I could barely make out two heavy metal doors laying open, slightly angled off the ground, leading to a space underground. A cellar.

I looked back to the house at the spot where Deputy Todd had disappeared around a corner. No sign of him. I looked back toward the entrance to the cellar.

Harper. I need to do something. Bolting from my hiding spot, I broke into an awkward sprint, hunched over, trying to remain hidden, and ran for the cellar. I stopped myself short as I came upon the entrance. A lock hung loosely from one side of the metal flap doors, cut cleanly through, just like the lock on the gate. A faint light sputtered from underground, illuminating the stairs leading into the earth. I took a deep breath and stepped cautiously into the viper's nest.

Twenty-seven

I REMAINED CLOSE to the wall and took each step slowly, keeping my eyes focused ahead of me, but the light from the single bulb cast a glare making it hard for me to see past the steps and into the room below. I stopped a moment at the foot of the stairs, with the bare bulb now behind me and let my eyes grow accustomed to the low light. The floor was hard and smooth, and an extensive structure of duct work and pipes piled high to my left. I could make out the aluminum and steel joints and tubes—probably support for the working mechanic's garage above. The rest of the room appeared empty, but my sight only stretched a few feet before the darkness took over.

"Harper?" I whispered.

"Don't come any closer." A figure stepped from the darkest corner, an outstretched arm wielding a gun broke the plane of flickering light.

I held my hands out before me. "Walter, don't."

"I'll do as I please," he replied, his voice shaking, unsteady, as though even he didn't believe the words.

"Did you bring the money?"

A muffled cry escaped from the far back corner of the underground room. Although shrouded in darkness, there was no mistaking that indignant tone. *Harper's here, probably gagged and tied up*, I thought. I searched around, but the stairs to the surface seemed to be the only way in or out and Walter had a clean shot if I made a move. How stupid was I, coming down here without a strategy to escape? I'd have to stall while I thought up a plan. "Tell me about Vernon," I asked. "How could you kill your own brother?"

"You don't know anything." In the faint light from the stairwell I saw the gun wobbling in Walter's hand as he shook in a rage—or fear. "He took everything from me. Everything! He knew I needed the money ever since the dealership closed. I've been struggling. I had to keep things going." Walter steadied the gun at me again.

I quickly shifted to my left, hiding behind the duct-work. "You don't have to do this. Put down the gun, Walter. I'm sure you're hurting. You've gotten yourself into this pit and you don't see a way out."

"You don't know anything about me," he shouted. "Vernon knew. He knew and he still kept things from me." He grew quiet and his tone changed, "I didn't mean to do it… I was just so mad."

I peered through a small opening in the ductwork. "I know, Walter. Vernon cut you out of his business, didn't he? But maybe he did it for your own good. He didn't want you getting into any trouble with the law, and he knew what he was doing was wrong. He was getting in too deep."

The gun sagged in Walters hand, and his sobs echoed

through the cellar. I thought I might have an opening to wrestle the gun from him, but I'd have to dart into the open room without any protection. He could very well shoot me before I got within fifteen feet.

I peeked around the corner, Walter had recovered and held the gun out in front of himself once more. An unexpected shot clanged against the pipe near my head. I dove to the floor. Another muffled cry arose from the corner—Harper was mad. The next shot ricocheted off the concrete flooring by my feet. I crawled along the ground, keeping the duct work between me and Walter, whose weary feet strafed with me, mirroring my movement to the other side of the room.

"I can't let you get away. You'll ruin me."

"Walter, please," I begged. I'd come to the corner of the room. If he came around the side, I'd be toast, like shooting fish in a barrel. Visions of Vernon's dead body filled my mind. I knew what Walter was capable of with a gun if he found me.

Movement caught my eye as Walter stepped into the light cast by the bare bulb at the base of the stairs. He squinted, trying to spot me through the glare. I scrambled quietly back the other way through the small space between the wall and the metal ductwork and piping. As I came to the end, I peered around the corner. Walter had moved closer to my last hiding spot. He was not five feet from where I had just been, staring through gaps in the metal, searching for me.

I needed to act fast. I looked around for something to throw, to create a distraction that would take Walter's attention away from discovering my whereabouts and possibly give me an opening. My hands searched in the darkness, slowly, so as not to disturb any loose items I came across, until my fingers touched something cold. I picked it up and felt it in my hands. A pipe, or something like a pipe. Whatever it was would work—I just needed it to be loud.

I kneeled in the dark corner and heaved the pipe across the room the opposite way, away from Harper and away from any light coming from the stairwell. As soon as the pipe clanged on the floor, Walter turned and fired a shot in the direction of the sound. The flash from the muzzle revealed the dark corner, proving it empty except for the pipe laying on the floor. Walter immediately turned around and squinted while retreating into the darkness, trying to work out my location.

"That's enough, Walter," came a stern voice from the stairwell. It was Deputy Todd, his thin frame casting an elongated shadow in the lamp light. He held his gun steady and outstretched, aimed into the darkness.

"Look out," I yelled as my eyes, now somewhat adapted to the low light, watched as Walter turned the gun toward Deputy Todd. Snarling, Walter pulled the trigger.

A small click emanated from the weapon. No flash. No loud bang. No shot fired.

"It won't work, Walter," the deputy said. "It's over."

Walter cocked his head at the gun, confused. Deputy Todd remained still, unmoving, his gun leveled at Walter. "Put the gun down. You have no bullets left."

Twenty-eight

I HELD HARPER close as we sat on the mossy porch of the Trotter house. Sheriff crews mulled about, lights flashing, but we remained still and silent. There weren't many words that came to mind, just a sense of relief. Relief that it was over, relief that we were safe and alive. No words could take the place of the safe return of a friend.

A pair of uniformed officers led Walter, head down, past us toward the waiting squad car. That it was Walter all along still stung. I'd felt sympathy for him, not knowing he was the killer and the whole affair seemed nothing more than the sad outcome of a brotherly rivalry gone too far.

Deputy Todd ambled up to the porch, weary lines on his face and boots covered in mud. "How are you holding up, Miss Tillman?"

Harper slumped against me under the warming blanket the EMTs had provided. They'd finished their inspection earlier and, other than being cold, she wasn't any worse for wear. "I'm doing okay," she managed. "I just want to get out of here."

"Understandable. You've given an initial statement, so why don't you head on home. I may come by later for a more detailed report, but at least Walter's in custody and he's not going anywhere."

"Angie's waiting down the road," I said. "Can we both go?"

"Yes. Same goes for you, Miss Lewis. I may come by for more questions later."

Harper and I shuffled down the driveway through the mud toward the road. Sheriff vehicles lined the drive and they'd swung the metal pipe gate wide open.

Walter's blank eyes followed us as we passed the squad car, no expression on his face, simply resigned to his fate.

Harper and I both hurried along the rest of the way to the road, eager to be out of his sight. Angie stood beside her car, behind the taped-off barrier farther down the road. She waved us down when she spotted us and we crawled quickly into the car and turned back down the road, leaving the Trotter property far behind us.

***

Angie made coffee in the morning and the three of us sat in silence on the porch, enjoying the cool salty air. We'd stayed together at the house that night and plunged into a weary, but restful, sleep. Mayor Dewey joined us not long after we arose, jumping into Harper's lap and curled up in a big ginger ball. He may have sensed her need for comfort, or possibly just sought out the warm blanket she had wrapped around herself.

"Walter…" Angie said, finally breaking the silence.

"Not what I was expecting. I suppose you never really know what's going on with your neighbors."

"Money does strange things to people."

"He ambushed me," Harper said.

"Oh, Harper." Angie lay a hand on her arm. "I'm so sorry this happened to you."

"Me too. It's all my fault. I never should have suggested the plan to spy on Kenny's property."

"It's not your fault. I was a willing participant. But I will say, in hindsight, we were pretty stupid."

"At least Walter is in custody and can't hurt anyone else."

"It's all so tragic," said Angie, shaking her head. "Look, here's Deputy Todd." Gravel shifted as the deputy's truck parked behind my Prius in the driveway. "Isn't it too early for questions?"

He took his time getting out of the truck and wandered slowly up the stairs, probably surprised to find us all there in a group. "Sorry to bother you ladies once again, but I wanted to make sure you were all right."

"Thanks, Deputy," I said. "We're doing okay. How are you doing? You were so calm last night—Walter could have shot you."

"I'm not a complete buffoon, Miss Lewis," he said, leaning against the porch railing, "despite what you might think. As you know, the gun Walter used was a Chief's Special—1952 to be precise—registered to Arthur Lewis, which *I* happen to know only houses five rounds. And, you'll remember, only a few bullets were missing from the box we found—five to be exact. One round for Vernon, and the other four I heard him shoot off one by one while you two do-si-doed in the cellar."

"But he could have bought more bullets."

Deputy Todd's face went blank. "Er, yes, I suppose he could have. But he didn't."

"How did Walter get the gun then?" I asked. "Did he steal it from this house?"

Deputy Todd shook his head. "Said he bought it off Bobby Teach. Walter thought he could get a mint for it at the pawn shop in Vista."

"Bobby…" My mind went back to everything I'd learned leading up to this moment. "I don't think Bobby's death was an accident."

Angie's eyes went wide. "You think Walter killed Bobby, too?"

I shook my head. "No, I don't think Walter killed him. Lovie said she saw Kenny's truck headed to the bluff the night Bobby died."

"So you think Kenny killed Bobby?" asked Deputy Todd.

I shook my head again. "But Kenny had rented his truck to Walter."

"But you said Walter didn't kill anyone…" Angie trailed off, confused.

I continued, "And Lovie said Walter was with her at the diner when they saw the truck. So, it wasn't Walter driving, and it wasn't Kenny driving."

"Who was it then?" asked Harper.

"Vernon."

"Vernon!" Angie gasped.

"Vernon?" Deputy Todd shook his head. "How do you figure?"

"The cause of Bobby's death was blunt force trauma, correct?"

Deputy Todd nodded. "According to the coroner, the wound was most likely caused by a metal tool, possibly a hammer or wrench or something."

"How about a mechanic's wrench?" I asked. "Of which there are many laying loose in the back of Kenny's truck."

"But why would Vernon have Kenny's truck?"

"Walter needed money, right? I think he offered to fix Vernon's car, for a price, of course, and promptly took it to Kenny to sub-contract the work. Walter took the opportunity to rent Kenny's truck, for a price, of course, which he promptly sub-rented to Vernon, for a profit, to use while his own car was being fixed by Kenny. They all did it for the money, nickel-and-diming each other dry."

"Okay, but *why* would Vernon kill Bobby?" asked Harper.

"Because of this house," I said.

The deputy eyed the three of us, confused. "I don't understand."

"We do." Harper exchanged a knowing glance with Angie. "They all wanted to steal something that was inside this house."

"Right. I suspect they would want anything of value, though. Bobby had a key he received from me, so he had easy access. That's how Bobby stole the gun without having to break in. And that's how Vernon found out Bobby had a key—from Walter. Walter shared everything with Vernon, remember? That's why he was so upset when Vernon started keeping secrets. At this point, Vernon and Kenny were already planning something—they had the blueprints."

"Blueprints?" Deputy Todd looked around at us for

an explanation.

I ignored him and continued, "Apparently, this whole town knows that Arthur's house is full of expensive stuff, or at least there were rumors. I think Vernon lured Bobby to the bluff to kill him—to stop him from discovering what was really in the house or from taking more of it. He needed to keep him quiet. And he wanted the key for himself."

"But then you showed up," said Angie.

"So, who was in the basement?" asked Harper.

"I suspect the set of prints we saw were Vernon's. He used the key to access the house while I spent that first night at your place, Angie. Kenny is probably the one who attacked me, but I can't prove it. Only he and Vernon knew about the secret room. And only Kenny was still alive at that point."

"Secret room?" asked Deputy Todd.

Harper held up a hand to shush him. "Long story."

"All this over money," said Angie. "I had no idea such dreadful behavior was going on in our little Starry Cove."

"I have to say, Miss Lewis, I'm not sure Walter would have ever crossed the Sheriff's radar if you hadn't puzzled it all out."

"It didn't all click together until I saw Walter's bike. He must have seen an opportunity once he found out I had money, and by then he'd already reached the point of desperation."

"I'm going to need you to come down later today and make a statement, Miss Lewis. I don't know if I'd be able to recount all this myself."

"Sure thing."

Deputy Todd tipped his hat and wished us well before driving away, leaving us seated on the porch to ruminate on what we'd learned.

"What are you going to do now, Poppy?" asked Angie. "The murder has been solved and your finances remain intact. Are you still going to work on the house?"

"Please tell me all this drama hasn't scared you off," said Harper.

I considered my friends—Harper curled up with Mayor Dewey, and sweet Angie sipping her coffee. Arthur had truly gifted me something priceless—a new life, a chance at friendship, along with the house—my house. And without knowing it, he'd given me an opportunity to heal old family wounds too. I thanked him silently for that, resting a hand on the railing, looking out onto the town.

"I'm staying," I said, turning back to my friends. "Besides, there are still too many unanswered questions. We haven't figured out what that notebook is yet. Something tells me it's important, and I mean to find out."

The End of Book 1

Lucinda Harrison is a writer and crafter who lives in northern California with her two mischievous cats. She is the author of the Poppy Lewis Mystery series.

Connect online at lucindaharrisonauthor.com

BOOKS BY LUCINDA HARRISON

Poppy Lewis Mystery Series
Murder in Starry Cove
Best Slayed Plans
A Foul Play

74738715R10142

Scotland
AN OUTLANDER TOUR

Ali Wood

TVTRAVELLER

Second edition published in Great Britain in 2020
by TVTraveller

ISBN 978-1-9162631-5-4

Copyright © Alison Wood 2020

Designed by Goldust Design

Covid-19 Notice: at the time of publication Scotland was emerging from
lockdown. Venue opening times and prices have been
updated where available. A few were still closed but anticipated
reopening by the time this guide was published. In such instances,
prices and opening hours have been left as previously published. Please
check websites before visiting as pre-booking may be required, visitor
details may have changed and not all facilities may be open.

For travel advice, consult the Scottish Government: www.gov.scot, and
VisitScotland: www.visitscotland.com websites before you visit.

Thanks to: *VisitScotland, Film Edinburgh, National Trust for Scotland,
Historic Environment Scotland, Fife Coast and Countryside Trust,
Pentland Hills Regional Park, The Scottish Railway Preservation
Society, Woodland Trust, Forestry and Land Scotland, Historic
Churches Scotland, Beecraigs Country Park, National Museums Scotland
and Glasgow and Edinburgh Universities, as well as the
many independent venues and organisations who helped with
research and photography*

Cover image: Culloden re-enactment, photo: National Trust for
Scotland Previous page: The dining room at Newhailes House, photo:
National Trust for Scotland

Contents

Chapter 1
INTRODUCTION

Scotland is one of the most cinematic countries in the world, and the locations chosen for Outlander will not disappoint. The Sony Starz production is a bodice-ripping, sword-swinging romp through the wilderness. Throw in some medieval castles, bloody battles and a 200-year-old love triangle, and you have a plot to singe the heads off the heather. Yet the romance between kilt-clad Jamie and his time-travelling 'Sassenach' plays second-fiddle to the real star of Outlander – Scotland. Never have the Highlands been so sexy... never have tourist bosses been so happy. After four seasons of the hit TV show, the 'Outlander effect' had more than doubled visitor numbers to the show's film locations, from Jamie's home near Edinburgh to the castle where he's imprisoned, and the battlefield at Culloden.

In 2020 – during the Coronavirus pandemic – tourism came to an abrupt halt, but at the time of going to press venues were opening once more. Be sure to check the websites before visiting.

There are over 90 sites to see in this three-week tour, including some fantastic new locations from Season 5 such as The Hermitage forest and Manderston House. Outlander fan or nay, these spectacular castles, lonely lochs, vast glens and soaring mountains are a must for any visitor to Scotland. The tour takes in some of the famous sites, such as Loch Ness and Glen Coe, as well some of the lesser known 17th century villages, churches and stately homes. A stopover in Skye gives

Glen Coe is featured in Outlander's opening credits

a glimpse of Hebridean life, whilst the start and (near) finish – in two of Britain's most vibrant cities – will satisfy the hungriest culture cravings.

If you're eager to get started, turn to chapter 3. Or if you need a recap on Outlander and its dazzling impact on tourism, read on.

OUTLANDER... HOW IT ALL BEGAN

Over a quarter of a century ago, computer professor Diana Gabaldon set out to write an historical novel. Her first book, Outlander, was just for practice.

'My goals were to learn what it took to write a novel, and to decide whether I wanted to do it for real,' she said. 'I wasn't going to tell anyone what I was doing, let alone ever try to publish it!' In 1990 the book (published in the UK as *Cross Stitch*) became a bestseller, and together with the seven that followed, sold 30 million copies worldwide.

'In essence, these novels are Big, Fat, Historical Fiction, à la James Clavell and James Michener,' explains Gabaldon, though pinpointing the content eludes her. 'Frankly, I've never been able to describe this book in 25 words or less, and neither has anyone else in the 20 years since it was first published.'

By the time movie director Ron D Moore read Outlander (having been recommended it by his wife) Gabaldon had written another seven in the series. Moore persuaded Sony to acquire the rights, and filming began in Scotland in October 2013. The show debuted on US cable network Starz in August 2014, and drew 3.7 million viewers.

In its first series, Sony Pictures distributed Outlander to 87 territories from China to the US, and Scotland has been

Fun fact

Diana Gabaldon's decision to set her 'practice book' in Scotland came to her in a 'weak-minded moment' when she was taken by a minor Dr Who character wearing a kilt. Coincidentally, the young Scotsman from 1745 was played by the actor Frazer Hines.

'Frazer has nothing to do with Jamie's last name – owing to the local PBS station cutting off the "Dr. Who" credits in order to run pledge appeals,' says Diana. 'I didn't know the actor's name until some years later, after the first book had been written. I did send a copy to Frazer then, though, thanking him for the kilt!'

welcoming a growing number of fans ever since.

Diana, who is consultant and co-producer on the show, even makes a cameo in S1 'The Gathering' where she appears as a wealthy merchant's wife.

THE OUTLANDER EFFECT

In a 2014 poll in USA Today, Scotland was voted the world's Best Cinematic Destination... and that was before the Outlander effect.

Some say Outlander is the new Braveheart; others claim it's Scotland's answer to Game of Thrones. Either way, the economic uplift from the Sony Starz show is undisputed.

According to VisitScotland, Outlander is now the most
mentioned screen inspiration for visitors, above Mel Gibson's
Oscar-winning epic Braveheart, Harry Potter and Highlander.

In 2016, spend on film and TV production in Scotland
reached £70m – the highest since records began. By 2017,
this was £95 million, thanks in no small part to Outlander.
Other contributors included T2 Trainspotting, starring Ewan
McGregor and Robert Carlyle, The Wife, starring Glenn Close
and Christian Slater, Avengers: Infinity War, and the Netflix
movie, Outlaw King. Eagled-eyed fans will spot Glasgow
University, Glasgow Cathedral, Linlithgow Palace and Doune
and Craigmillar Castles in the Robert the Bruce movie – all of
which appear in Outlander.

The biggest growth in visitors came from the US, according

photo: National Trust for Scotland

Memorial stone at Culloden

to Historic Scotland, followed by Spain, Germany, France and Italy, with Doune and Blackness castles being top of the list. Over a third of visitors cited film and TV as their reason to visit, with 57% saying they wanted to learn more about the history. It's not just visitor numbers that have soared. The gift stores are now dominated by Outlander-inspired jewellery, books and garments, with retail range sales rocketing from £32k in 2015 to £180k in 2019. If you see the gorgeous replica shawls and dresses on-sale at Doune, you'll understand why!

Rosie Ellison of Film Edinburgh points out that film tourism, or setjetting, is a global phenomenon that has boomed in recent years. 'It's remarkable to see that so many visitors are attracted to locations they have seen on the screen! It just takes a successful production!'

According to Jenni Steele, film and creative industries manager at VisitScotland, one in five visitors are inspired by the big and small screen.

'Film tourism is booming,' she says. 'Film and TV productions not only showcase the unique mix of stunning landscapes, rich heritage and fascinating stories, but can inspire set-jetting fans to visit.'

In 2018 the Association of Scottish Visitor Attractions (ASVA) saw visits rise for the fifth year running, with Outlander fans flocking to sites such as The Royal Burgh of Culross (+53%), Culloden Battlefield Visitor Centre (+11%), Aberdour Castle (+42%) and Glasgow Cathedral (+24%).

But it's not just the major tourist attractions that have benefitted. The small historical buildings – such as Tibbermore church, where the witch trials were filmed, and Wardlaw Mausoleum, where the Old Fox Lord Lovat was supposedly buried – have attracted much-needed funding.

Outlander fan groups have sprung up all over the world, with some – such as Inverness Outlanders – actively promoting their local area, creating maps, and liaising with the cast to get their landmarks on the tourist trail.

'It's just amazing what Outlander is doing for Scotland and for historic places of interest,' says The Inverness Outlanders. 'Without Outlander fans with their interest in real Scottish history, generous donations, and spreading the word we would be still be in the dark about some of these fascinating places. Tibbermore Church in Perthshire was struggling for money, but now with Outlander and its fans' help it will be standing for many more years.'

THE PLOT (JUST IN CASE YOU'RE A NEWBIE)

Based on the novels by Diana Gabaldon, the TV series Outlander is the story of English battlefield nurse Claire Randall, who travels back in time to the early 1700s and falls in love with Jacobite clan leader, Jamie Fraser. The only problem is, Claire's already married, and her husband Frank is stuck in the 1950s wondering where on earth his wife's gone.

Whilst Frank searches high and low, Claire and Jamie romp around the Scottish Highlands, collecting rents from villagers, dining with lairds in romantic castles, and pledging their allegiance to the exiled Bonnie Prince Charlie. When the Prince finally arrives in Scotland to reclaim the Stuart throne, fiction overlaps with history and his failed campaign, ending in his defeat at Culloden Moor, is the climax of S2. Pregnant with Jamie's child, Claire returns through the stones to long-suffering Frank, believing Jamie to have died at Culloden.

The early episodes of S3 sees the starcrossed lovers separated not only by the Atlantic but 200 years of history. Jamie is imprisoned, released, and has a secret son.

Dramatic Glen Coe appears in the show's opening credits

Meanwhile, Claire throws herself into motherhood and medicine. Everything's groovy in 1960s Boston until Frank dies, Brianna grows up and Claire discovers Jamie is STILL ALIVE.

Claire's back at those darned stones before you can say 'rabbit in a hole', and in one of the most memorable scenes ever, reappears in Jamie's print shop. He promptly faints.

After some lush Edinburgh scenes featuring colourful markets, brothels and wynds, Jamie and Claire return to Jamie's home in Lallybroch. Before they know it, they're on a boat to Jamaica in pursuit of Young Ian, who's been captured by pirates. Cue some grand balls, swooshing dresses and witty repartee, then they're back at sea, headed for the New World and the start of S4.

North Carolina has some surprises in store for Claire – as well as devoted Outlander fans, who learn the whole series was filmed in Scotland! When Brianna finds out her mother's going to perish in a fire, she hotfoots it to the 1700s, with boyfriend Roger in swift pursuit. She escapes loony Laoghaire, only to fall into the evil clutches of Stephen Bonnet, finding herself pregnant and fearful he's the father.

Meanwhile, Claire's having battles of her own with Mohawks, slavers and – most frightening of all – Jamie's Aunt Jocasta. Roger, useless as ever, gets himself captured by the Indians, resulting in some cracking episodes where the Fraser trio travel into the wilderness in search of the Mohawk village. Young Ian trades himself in for Roger, and they return to Aunt Jocasta's pad in River Run, where Brianna has given birth to Jeremiah.

Season 5 sees Roger, Brianna and Jemmy settle into domestic bliss, peasant-style (eg. pig-roasting, pleasant plucking, plagues of locusts, snake-bites and kidnappings), whilst Jamie's loyalty is put to the test when pitted against his godfather, Murtagh, a leader of the North Carolina Regulator Rebellion.

Claire's surgical skills reach new heights when she invents penicillin and brings Jamie back to life with an interesting alternative to CPR after he's bitten by a pit viper. Stephen Bonnet takes Brianna hostage then pays the price with a bullet in his skull (whilst tied to a stake in a rising tide). 'Was that mercy or was it to make sure he's dead?' Roger asks Bree.

In spite of some jolly weddings, babies and the return of Young Ian, the mood in the Colonies grows darker every day. In the final episode Claire is kidnapped, brutally attacked and rescued by Jamie and his men. The ending, on a stormy night, is full of foreboding. Jamie wraps his arms around Claire's bruised body and calls her a brave wee thing.

'How do you feel?' he asks. 'Safe,' she says. Cue a clap of thunder and the sound of hammering rain. Jamie frowns, the lights dim and we're left with the feeling they're anything but...

WHAT CAN WE EXPECT IN SEASON 6?

Outlander Season 6 will be loosely based on Diana Gabaldon's sixth book in the series, *A Breath of Snow and Ashes*. The series was commissioned at the same time as Series 5 and though the Coronavirus pandemic put a halt to shooting early in 2020, scriptwriters were still hard at work penning episodes. 'We have started... Ep 1!!! So excited,' Sam Heughan reassured a fan on Twitter in March. 'But you're going to love the rest of this season.'

Whilst it could be a long wait until the season airs, when it does, rest assured we'll be delving back into American history, the Regulator movement (the uprising in British America's Carolina colonies) and the story of the Frasers as they continue to settle in the New World.

Meanwhile, Diana Gabaldon is working long days to finish her ninth book in the Outlander series, *Go Tell the Bees that I'm Gone* – or *Bees,* for short. After *Bees,* she will write the tenth and last book in the Outlander series that focuses on Jamie and Claire. You can follow her progress – including background on the series, chapter titles and musings on the writing process – on her fun and hugely informative website, www.dianagabaldon.com

Fun fact

Fans of actor Sam Heughan call themselves Heughan's Heughligans. There are also Caitriots and Menziatics!

Chapter 2
PRACTICALITIES

HOW LONG IS THE OUTLANDER TOUR?

There are so many awe-inspiring locations to visit, that even three weeks might be a tad on the short-side. If you like to pack it in, great! If you prefer a bit of down-time, stretch it out to four. If you've less time, take a look at the shorter options.

22 days: an anti-clockwise loop from Edinburgh to Stirling, Inverness and Skye, returning via Glencoe and the Trossachs to Glasgow.
14 days: a linear route, south to north, taking in Edinburgh, Stirling and Inverness (finish at day 14)
12 days: a lowland loop from Edinburgh to Culross, Stirling and the Trossachs, finishing in Glasgow (skip days 9 to 18)
9 days: Edinburgh to Glasgow via Falkirk (skip days 7 to 19)
7 days: Edinburgh (days 1-4) and Glasgow (days 20-22)

A FEW THINGS TO BEAR IN MIND...

The Edinburgh Festivals take place throughout the whole of August. It's no exaggeration to say the city is one of the most exciting places to be in the world. The whole city's partying day and night, with live shows in hundreds of venues – many

The streets are alive with performers during the Edinburgh Fringe

of them free – and on the streets. But it's also crowded, there's no parking and accommodation is sky-high. Book early if you're visiting Scotland in August, and leave the car rental until you leave the city.

Take hiking boots and a decent set of waterproofs. Even in summer, the Highlands can get chilly. You'll need mossie repellent too for the midges.

Many of the Outlander venues from S1 and S2 are owned by national organisations so consider buying a saver pass (see below) otherwise multiple entries can be expensive.

The tourist board VisitScotland has some excellent suggestions for Outlander and other themed tours. Before you go, check out the website www.visitscotland.com and look out for the visitor centres in most towns and cities.

Travelling with kids? No problem. Scotland is a very relaxed, family-friendly country. You'll find baby-change facilities in all the toilets, high chairs and children's meals offered in the restaurants, and activities for kids in most of the attractions.

SAVER PASSES

Take a look at the Scene Spotter over the page to see which properties are run by which organisations. You may then find it cheaper to buy annual membership or a limited-time pass, rather than pay individual entrance fees. Prices and packages vary from year to year. The main options are available from the following sites:

Historic Scotland: *www.historicenvironment.scot*
National Trust for Scotland: *www.nts.org.uk*
Visit Britain: *www.visitbritainshop.com*

Tour options

ORKNEY

OUTER HEBRIDES

SCOTLAND

Portree
Nights 15 - 16

SKYE

Inverness
Night 14

Aviemore
Nights 12 - 13

Kinloch Rannoch
Night 11

Glencoe
Night 17

Stirling
Night 7

Falkland
Nights 9 -10

Trossachs
Nights 18 - 19

short-cut

Culross
Night 8

North Berwick
Night 3

Glasgow
Night 20

Falkirk
Night 5 - 6

Troon
Day 21

Queensferry *Night 4*

Edinburgh
Nights 1 -2

19

Scene spotter

Day	Visit	Overnight	
1	National Museum of Scotland	Edinburgh	
	Bakehouse Close		
	Museum of Edinburgh		
	World's End Pub		
	Tweedale Court		
	Signet Library		
	Summerhall		
	Lothian Chambers		
	Surgeon's Hall Museums		
	Georgian House		
2	Palace of Holyroodhouse	Edinburgh	
3	Flotterstone	Edinburgh/ North Berwick	
	Newhailes House (NTS)		
	Prestonpans		
	Preston Mill (NTS)		
	The Mart		
	Tyninghame Beach		
Detour	Glencorse Old Kirk		
	Gosford House		
	Arniston House		
	Manderston House		

Scenes
No scenes, but tells the history of Bonnie Prince Charlie
S3: Carfax Close, where Jamie has a print shop
S3: The building used for Jamie's print shop – see what's actually inside
Mentioned in the book Voyager
S3: Marketplace
S3: Setting for the Jamaica ball
S3: Lecture theatre where Claire meets Joe Abernathy
S2: Exterior of the National Archives
No scenes, but fascinating depiction of medicine in Claire's time
No scenes, but depicts life during the Georgian era when Outlander is set
Jacobite links but no Outlander scenes
S1: Where Jamie is ambushed by the Redcoats
S4: Where Jamie discusses land grants with Governor Tryon
S2: Real-life site of the battle of Prestonpans
S1: Mill at Lallybroch and court anteroom where Geillis and Claire attend witchcraft hearing
S5: Wilmington Fight Club
S5: Where Claire and Brianna are ambushed by Stephen Bonnet
S1: Where Jamie and Claire get married
S2: Stable building in the Palace of Versailles, S3: Helwater and Ellesmeere
S4: House in Wilmington where Claire operates on Edward Fanning
S5: Stables where Claire and Jamie fight and then make up

Day	Visit	Overnight	
4	Craigmillar Castle (HS)	Queensferry/ Edinburgh	
	Hopetoun House		
	Midhope Castle		
	Abercorn church		
5	Blackness Castle (HS)	Falkirk	
	Bo'ness and Kinneil Railway		
	Linlithgow Palace (HS)		
	Beecraigs Country Park		
	Muiravonside Country Park		
6	Kelpies	Falkirk	
	Callendar House		
	Gray Buchanan Park		
	Falkirk Wheel		
7	Dunmore Park House	Stirling	
	Doune Castle (HS)		
	Deanston Distillery		
	Stirling Castle (HS)		
DETOUR	Drummond Castle Gardens		
	Abercairny Estate (private)		
8	Culross Palace (NTS)	Culross/ Stirling	
	Royal Burgh of Culross		
9	Aberdour Castle (HS)	Falkland	
	Dysart Harbour		
	Balgonie Castle (private)		

Scenes
S3: Ardsmuir Prison where Jamie is imprisoned with other Jacobites
S1: Duke of Sandringham's Scottish home, duel scene, S2: Bedroom in Jamie and Claire's Parisian apartment, Parisian streets, Mary's bedroom, S3: Exterior stable scenes at Helwater, riding scenes with Geneva, scenes with Willie
S1: Lallybroch exterior, S2: Cave where Jamie hides, woods where Fergus is attacked, dovecote where boys find pistol
S4: Where Brianna visits Frank's grave
S1, S2: Fort William HQ of Black Jack Randall
S1: London station where Claire and Frank say a wartime goodbye
S1: Wentworth prison where Jamie is kept
S4: Where Claire gets lost after riding through the storm
S2: Backdrop to the Battle of Prestonpans, British encampment and English countryside
No Outlander scenes but iconic site en-route
S2: Kitchen at the Duke of Sandringham's home, Bellhurst Manor
S4: Graveyard where Jamie and Young Ian bury Hayes
No Outlander scenes but an iconic site en-route
S1: WWII hospital where Claire works
S1: Castle Leoch, including kitchen and grounds
S2: Wine warehouse in Le Havre belonging to Jamie's cousin
No Outlander scenes but Jacobite connections
S1: Orchard and park at Versailles
S4: Aunt Jocasta's North Carolina plantation
S1: Geillis's parlour, Jamie and Claire's bedroom whilst travelling, herb garden at Castle Leoch
S2: Jacobite encampment and makeshift hospital scenes, Geillis's house, street where she's carried away, village where boy has ear nailed to post
S2: Monastery where Jamie recovers after imprisonment
S2: Le Havre
S2: Eldridge Manor where Claire is rescued from the wolves

Day	Visit	Overnight	
Detour	Scottish Fisheries Museum		
10	Falkland	Falkland/ River Edge Lodges	
	Covenanter Hotel		
	The Bruce Fountain		
	Rotten Row & Sharps Close		
	Bruton Street		
	Falkland Palace (NTS)		
	River Edge Lodges		
11	Tibbermore Church	Kinloch Rannoch/ Rannoch Moor	
	Kinclaven Bluebell Wood		
	The Hermitage (NTS)		
	Faskally Wood		
	Kinloch Rannoch		
	Dunalastair Estate		
12	Adverikie Estate	Aviemore	
	Highland Folk Museum		
	Highland Wildlife Park		
13	Rothiemurchus Estate	Aviemore	
14	Highland Archive Centre	Inverness	
	Culloden battlefield (NTS)		
15	Beauly Priory (HS)	Skye	
	Reelig Glen		
	Mullardoch Dam		
	Corrimony Chambered Cairn		
	Wardlaw Mausoleum		
	Clava Cairns (HS)		
	Urquhart Castle (HS)		
	Loch Ness Centre		
	Skye crossing		

Scenes
S2: Home to The Reaper, the ship on which Jamie and Claire sail to France
S1: 1950s Inverness
S1: B&B where Frank and Claire spend their second honeymoon
S1: Where Jamie's ghost looks up at Claire's room
S2: Where Claire and Murtagh walk away from the boarding house
S2: Where Alex Randall is being cared for by Mary Hawkins
S2: The apothecary where Mary buys her supplies
S4: The Carolina Scottish Festival
S1: Cranesmuir Church, where Claire and Geillis are on trial for witchcraft
S4: Fraser's Ridge, including the location of the two Witness Trees
S5: Countryside scenes from episodes 11 and 12
S4: Mohawk village
S1: Where Claire and Frank enjoy their second honeymoon
S1, S4, S5: the site of the standing stones, Craig na Dun
S1: Where Claire is 'rescued' by the Redcoats
S1: Village where Dougal collects the rents
No Outlander scenes, but wildlife typical of 18th century Scotland
S1: Opening credits and woods where Claire first meets Jamie
No Outlander scenes, but visit if you're researching Scottish ancestry
S2: Culloden battlefield
S1: Claire meets the 'seer' Maisri
No Outlander scenes, but 'Fraser country'
No Outlander scenes, but 'Fraser country'
No Outlander scenes, but where Simon Fraser is buried in An Echo in the Bone
No Outlander scenes but the burial place of the Lovat Frasers
S1, S2, S3: Inspiration for the standing stones Craig na Dun
No Outlander scenes, but Jacobite links
Find out more about Nessie, which Claire calls 'the water horse'
Mentioned in opening theme-song

Day	Visit	Overnight	
16	Skye Museum of Island Life	Portree	
17	Glenfinnian monument	Glencoe	
	Glen Coe visitor centre (NTS)		
18	Ben Nevis	The Trossachs	
19	Loch Katrine	The Trossachs	
	Lodge Forest Visitor Centre		
20	Dowanhill Street		
	Glasgow Cathedral		
	George Square		
	St Andrews in the Square		
	University of Glasgow (HS)	Glasgow	
	Kelvingrove Park		
21	Pollok Country Park (NTS)	Troon/ Glasgow	
	Queen's Park		
	Calderglen Country Park		
	Dean Castle Country Park		
	Troon		
Detour	Thomas Coats Memorial Church		
22	Dunure	End of tour	

Key

NFS = National Trust for Scotland

HS = Historic Scotland

Scenes
No Outlander scenes but includes the story of Bonnie Prince Charlie and Flora MacDonald
No Outlander scenes, but where Bonnie Prince Charlie raised his standard
S1: The Study, opening credits looking to the Three Sisters mountains
No Outlander scenes but great views across Outlander country
S1: Roger Mackenzie takes Brianna for a drive
No Outlander scenes, but stunning forest trails
S3: The street where Claire and Frank Randall live in Boston, USA
S2: L'Hôpital des Anges in Paris, where Claire works alongside nuns
S1: Where Frank proposes to Claire in 1940s London
S4: Theatre where Jamie and Claire watch a play
S3: Harvard University, where Frank works as a professor
S3: Where Claire pushes baby Brianna in a buggy
S2: Outside Castle Leoch, French countryside between Le Havre and Paris
S5: 1960s park in Boston where Claire and Brianna meet
S4: Where Jamie and Willie go camping
S2: Beaufort Castle, where Claire and Jamie visit Lord Lovat
S1: Where Claire, Jamie and Murtagh board a ship for France
S5: Where Claire prays in 1960s Boston
S3 & S4: Departure port for the Colonies

Chapter 3
THE TOUR

DAY 1
EDINBURGH AND THE ROYAL MILE

Spend at least a couple of days in Edinburgh, where Claire and Jamie live in S3 – anything less and you'll feel short-changed. The Royal Mile, the beating heart of Edinburgh, is a maze of cobbled streets and pulsating alleyways, and features in several scenes from Outlander.

In 1765, over 60,000 people lined the Royal Mile to welcome Bonnie Prince Charlie to Edinburgh. It was here that he raised many a Jacobite sympathiser, especially women as noted by the French ambassador. 'In general all the young and pretty women are Jacobites and the most of them are only such since the arrival of the young prince.'

The historical Canongate and Holyrood sections of the Royal Mile are part of a UNESCO World Heritage Site. You can find out more about Scotland's history at the **National Museum of Scotland**, which contains over 20,000 artefacts.

In 2017 Diana was invited to the museum, where she was interviewed by fellow writer Lin Anderson about the story behind the books. Lin was impressed by Diana's depiction of Scotland, and was surprised to learn that the author had never been to Scotland when she wrote the first book.

'[This] impressed me even more,' says Lin. 'I knew then I

Edinburgh plays a prominent role in S3 of Outlander

had encountered a researcher; a writer that could combine fact and fiction seemingly effortlessly, yet as someone who attempts the same with forensic fact and fiction, I knew how tricky that can be to get right.'

Be sure to visit the Scottish History and Archaeology galleries and learn about the Stuart dynasty and the Jacobite rising – the real back story to Outlander – and the possessions and portraits associated with Bonnie Prince Charlie. In particular, don't miss the prince's travelling canteen (a cutlery set and two wine beakers) that may have been made for his 21st birthday. A replica was made for the Outlander TV series. *Open daily 10-5pm, free, Chambers Street, www.nms.ac.uk.*

After soaking in the bagpipes, street performers, quirky cafes and indie museums, it's time to seek out the key Outlander locations. In S3, **Bakehouse Close** doubles as Carfax Close, home to Jamie's print shop, and is one of the best-preserved examples of Old Edinburgh. Acheson House, opposite, is the exterior of the brothel where Jamie lives. Built in 1633, it has served a number of purposes – from the grand home of Sir Archibald Acheson, government minister for Charles I, to a dilapidated Victorian brothel known as the Cock and Trumpet. These days, it's the respectable headquarters of Edinburgh World Heritage. Adjoining the building – and spanning Bakehouse Close – is the fantastic **Museum of Edinburgh**. Here you can learn about the city's history and Jacobite past and chat to the staff about filming. Find out what's actually on the other side of the door to Jamie's print shop, and don't forget to visit the courtyard for an alternative view of Bakehouse Close. The entrance is at Huntly House, 142 Canongate. *Open daily 10-5pm, free, www. edinburghmuseums.org.uk*

On the High Street, **The World's End pub** – where Jamie comes to the rescue of an inebriated Mr Willoughby – features

photo: Ali Wood

Jamie's print shop on Bakehouse Close is actually the Museum of Edinburgh

in the book Voyager, though the on-screen version is actually a set.

Nearby, **Tweeddale Court** is another beautiful Edinburgh street, which appears as a market place. It's here that Fergus, now a grown man, spots Claire in S3 and hugs her. 'My lady,' he gasps. 'You've returned. It's a miracle.'

The lavish **Signet Library** on Parliament Square appears in S3 as the set for the Jamaica ball, and it doesn't look too different in real life. Downstairs, the Colonnades restaurant serves lunch and delicious afternoon teas whilst upstairs is a ballroom – which is used for a variety of events including weddings.

The arts venue, **Summerhall** used to be the University of Edinburgh's veterinary school. It's here in S3 that Claire meets Joe Abernathy in the anatomy lecture theatre. Edinburgh's vibrant arts scene is a must for any visitor, so why not

31

combine your Outlander tour with some cutting-edge theatre, a ceilidh or even a gig in the old Dissection Room?

It even has its own microbrewery and distillery! *Reception and box office open 9-6 daily, cafe and bar open 7 days, www. summerhall.co.uk.*

In S2, when Claire learns that Jamie survived Culloden, she visits the National Archives in Edinburgh with Roger and Brianna. On screen, the exterior is a building called **Lothian Chambers**, which was built in 1818 and based on the design of the Acropolis. It's now the French Embassy.

The real National Archives, renamed the National Register of Scotland (NRS), is a good starting point for those tracing their Scottish ancestry. After the Bonnie Prince fled Scotland, the Highland Clearances led to the eviction of thousands of Highlanders, many of whom settled in the lowlands, North America and Australasia. Might you be related to a Fraser?

photo: Museum of Edinburgh

The Museum of Edinburgh and Bakehouse Close

LITERARY EDINBURGH

In 2004 Edinburgh was designated the first UNESCO City of Literature. There are over 50 bookshops in the city, and in the Literature Quarter you'll find the Scottish Poetry Library, Scottish Storytelling Centre, Scottish Book Trust, Canongate Books, The Writers' Museum, Makars Court and the National Library of Scotland.

The birthplace of Sir Arthur Conan Doyle, Edinburgh provided inspiration for his detective Sherlock Holmes, who bounded onto the scene 125 years ago, bearing an uncanny (and controversial) resemblance to Conan Doyle's lecturer and friend Dr Joseph Bell. The city is also the setting for Ian Rankin's Detective Rebus, and several of Irvine Welsh's books, as well as the inspiration for JK Rowling. Harry Potter fans will spot some of the characters' names in the cemetery Greyfriars Kirkyard.

photo: Michaela Bodlovic Photography

University arts venue Summerhall, where Claire studies medicine

Not to be missed is the Scott Monument in Princes Street Gardens. Built after the death of Sir Walter Scott in 1832, it's the largest monument to a writer in the world!

EDINBURGH ON SCREEN

Edinburgh is a source of inspiration to over 350 filmmakers a year, so once you've exhausted the Outlander film locations, why not check out a few others?

Renton (Ewan McGregor) and Spud (Ewen Bremner) Choose Life on Princes street in *Trainspotting*, then nearly lose it again in front of a car on Calton Road. Not to be outdone, Houdini (Guy Pearce) takes Mary (Catherine Zeta Jones) and Benji (Saoirse Roman) up the Scott Monument at night in *Death Defying Acts*, whilst Robert (Tom Hanks) and Sophie (Audrey Tautou) act out the finale of the *Da Vinci Code* in Rossyln Chapel, which according to author Dan Brown is 'the most mysterious and magical chapel on earth'.

More recently, the 2018 film *Avengers: Infinity War* was filmed in Edinburgh's Old Town, the first time a blockbuster of this scale has been made in the city. The team spent seven weeks and £10 million, filming exclusively at night. Rosie Ellison, Film Commissioner at Film Edinburgh, explains: 'The filmmakers were looking for something unique, gothic and dramatic, and Edinburgh's Old Town with its medieval architecture fitted the bill.'

Fans of Julian Fellowes's 2020 drama *Belgravia* should head to Moray Place in the New Town, where the elegant Georgian houses were used to depict the London homes of the Trenchard and Brockenhurst families. For a taste of Georgian life, visit the nearby **Georgian House** at 7 Charlotte Square, *www.nts.org.uk*.

photo: Tom Bostock

Moray Place in Edinburgh's New Town was used for the set of Belgravia

THE HISTORY OF MEDICINE

With Claire being a doctor, medicine is a recurring theme throughout Outlander, and Edinburgh has always been a centre of excellence in this field. A visit to the **Surgeons' Hall Museums** casts light (and darkness) on the lives of the city's inhabitants, whose rickets-twisted skeletons, and TB-infected bodies dangle and float in oak cases dating to the 1700s. Open to the public since 1832, the museums contain one of the largest pathology collections in the UK, ranging from metastatic lungs to gangrenous toes. There's even the death mask of the executed criminal William Burke, still showing the noose marks on his neck! Burke, together with William Hare, preyed on the poor in the cheapest tenements, and sold their bodies to the medical profession. *Open daily 10-5pm, adults £8, children & conc £4.50, Nicolson Street, museum.rcsed.ac.uk.*

Overnight in Edinburgh

35

DAY 2
SAY HELLO TO THE QUEEN

When Bonnie Prince Charlie failed to capture Edinburgh Castle he briefly set up court at the other end of the Royal Mile in the **Palace of Holyroodhouse**, the official Scottish residence of Queen Elizabeth II. Take a multimedia tour of the grand palace and learn the history of British Royalty past and present. Note, as the palace is a royal residence it can be subject to closures at short notice so do check the website before arrival. *Open Nov to Mar: 930-430pm, Apr to Oct: 930-6pm, adults: £16.50, children 6-16: £9.50, family of 2 x adults, 3 x U17: £42.50, Canongate, rct.uk.*

Overnight in Edinburgh

Still a royal residence, the Palace of Holyroodhouse

photo: VisitScotland/ Kenny Lam

Fun fact

Did you spot the blooper? In S1 producers forgot to take down an owl nesting box at Flotterstone, which definitely wouldn't have been around in the 18th century

DAY 3

EDINBURGH OUTSKIRTS

One of the surprising things about Edinburgh is how close it is to the countryside. **Flotterstone**, one of the show's first locations, is near Penicuik in the Pentland Hills Regional Park. Described by producer Ron Moore as 'the perfect place for an ambush', it's here that Jamie is shot by the Redcoats. It's just three miles outside the city limits, and a great place to break-in that new pair of hiking boots (before the Cairngorms and Glen Coe later on!). There is an information point past the Flotterstone Inn, off the A702. Here, you can pick up leaflets about the Pentland Hills, and refuel at the Pentland Hills Café Express. The Glencorse View circular walk (marked by a heron on trail signs) starts here, and is a gentle 2.7 miles. This footpath leads you past the infamous ambush spot, located in a wooded area just before Glencorse Waterfall. See *www. pentlandhills.org for more information on the regional park.*

Next, head to **Newhailes House** in Musselburgh where Jamie sits down with Governor Tryon in S4 to discuss land grants. This elegant 17th century Palladian house played a key role in the Scottish Enlightenment, but is undergoing serious conservation right now due to an invasion of clothes moths! At the time of going to press, the house was

The dining room at Newhailes House

closed to the public but you can still visit the grounds and (hopefully by 2021) the Weehailes Playpark. Access by car is easy, but if you're saving the car rental for once you've left Edinburgh (Day 4 onwards), visit by bus (no. 30) to Newhailes Roundabout, or train from Edinburgh Waverley to Musselburgh. From here it's a 5-minute walk, *www.nts.org.uk.*

The first of two key battle sites on this tour (the other being Culloden), **Prestonpans** is famous both in Scottish history and Outlander. On 21 September 1745 it was here that Jacobite forces led by the exiled Bonnie Prince Charlie defeated the government army in less than 30 minutes. It was the first significant event of the Jacobite '45 rebellion and a dramatic Jacobite victory. Though filming took place in the studio and Muiravonside country park, the production unit very carefully recreated the skyline and topography.

'We're going to send the English to hell,' says Angus in episode 10. And they do, but not before he takes a fatal

Visit Scotland

Prestonpans, the site of a dramatic Jacobite victory

cannonblast wound to the chest.

You can walk around the battlefields – where there are information boards – and climb the viewing platform. *Battlefield Viewpoint, Prestonpans, EH33 1LZ.*

If the water wheel's turning at **Preston Mill** in East Linton, you're in luck! In 2018 it jammed, but thanks to a crowdfunding campaign (no doubt a few Outlander fans amongst them) work's started to get it turning again. Sadly, Jamie – although a dab hand at fixing Lallybroch's water wheel – has not been called in to help.

Remember the mill pond scene at Lallybroch where Jamie dives into the water to escape the Redcoats? Over 150 cast and crewmembers turned up for 10 days of filming in the summer of 2014. To convincingly transform the mill into part of an 18th century estate, they had to remove fencing, signage, and gates and draft in several trees and bushes to obscure the nearby roads and houses.

The mill also stars as the court anteroom where Geillis and Claire are questioned over witchcraft charges. Take a tour of the quirky meal mill, which was operational until 1959, then cross the river to Phantassie Doocot. Look out for otters and kingfishers en-route. The 16th century dovecote ('doocot' is Scots) held up to 500 pigeons.

Mill open May to Oct, Thu to Mon, 11-5pm. Guided tours only. Last tour at 415pm. Adult £6.50, 1-adult family £11.50, family £16.50, conc £5. EH40 3DS, www.nts.org.uk/Visit/Preston-Mill.

Whilst you're in East Linton, pop by **The Mart**, the hexagonal timber building which appears in Outlander S5 as Wilmington Fight Club. Fortunately the real-life entertainment's far less gory than two women beating the living daylights out of each other (and you're not likely to bump into Stephen Bonnet either) but the quirky 19th century space is used for events such as yoga, farmer's markets and art exhibitions. Check out the website to see what's going on. *The Mart, EH40 3DW, www.themart.co.uk.*

Preston Mill was used for the mill at Lallybroch

National Trust for Scotland

One of the happier moments in S5 – shortly before Stephen Bonnet appears on the scene – is where Claire and Brianna are splashing in the sea and watch whales breaching. The desolate windswept beach is **Tyninghame**, also known as Ravensheugh Sands. Just a 10-minute drive from Preston Mill, you need to search for Limetree Walk, Dunbar, and drive to the end of the lane. From here, wind your way through the woods to the beach.

Will you see whales? Probably not, but don't worry, Scotland remains one of the best places in the world for whale watching – you just need to head further north. Minke whales are commonly found off the Isle of Mull, Loch Gairloch, the Minche and the Moray Firth (where pilot, humpback and northern bottlenose whales have also been seen). Meanwhile killer whales can be seen in Shetland and – more commonly the Orkney Isles – where pods of up to 150 orcas are usually spotted several times a year.

Overnight in Edinburgh or North Berwick (15 mins away)

The Mart

The Mart is where the fight club scenes were filmed in S5

EXTRA TIME/ DETOUR

The following places take a bit of planning as tours need to be pre-booked or are only available on certain days. However, if the dates work, you should definitely tag these on to your Edinburgh stay.

Glencorse Old Kirk, in the grounds of Glencorse House, is where Claire and Jamie tie the knot. The house is a private family residence, open only for weddings and private functions. However, if you want to pre-arrange a private tour of the kirk (Scottish word for church), contact the owners at info@glencorsehouse.com (9 miles/30 mins, EH26 0NZ, www. glencorsehouse.co.uk).

Gosford House and estate featured in both S2 and S3. The grounds and backdrop of the house were used as the luxurious stable in Versailles in S2, and in S3 the house was used for the Helwater Estate, with the Robert Adam stables doubling as the stables where Jamie lived whilst working as a groom. The south wing's stunning Marble Hall was used as the interior of the Earl of Ellesmere's home.

This elegant neoclassical house is well worth a visit, though note that house and grounds tours take place on specific days only (1.5 hours), so check the website for details, call 01875 870808 or email caroline@gosfordhouse.co.uk. Private tours are also available (16 miles/ 35 mins, EH32 0PX, www. gosfordhouse.co.uk).

Arniston House doubles as the theatre in Wilmington where Claire's medical skills are called upon In S4, episode 8.

It's here that Governor Tryon introduces Claire and Jamie to high society, including his right-hand man Mr Fanning, and – much to Claire's delight – George and Martha Washington. Shortly after the dreadful play begins, Jamie 'accidentally' elbows Mr Fanning in the abdomen to create a diversion. Whilst Claire performs emergency surgery on Mr Fanning's hernia, Jamie nips away to warn Murtagh of the ambush.

The scene of the play itself was filmed at St Andrews in the Square, Glasgow. However, the horse and carriage approach, theatre lobby and surgery scenes – as well as the exchange between Jamie and the Washingtons – were filmed at Arniston House.

The present owner of Arniston, Althea Dundas-Bekker, inherited the home in 1970 at the age of 30, something she describes as 'bitter sweet'.

'Bitter because it involved the premature deaths of close members of my family,' she says. 'Sweet because of what Arniston is'.

A popular wedding venue with holiday cottages on site, Arniston also hosts events such as fireworks and Shakespeare performances. You can book a special Outlander location tour for groups of 10-20. The guided tour includes lunch, a short video and Q&A. Check out the website for more details. The grounds are free to explore on open days (12 miles/ 30-min drive, www.arnistonhouse.com).

Gosford House was used in the Versailles and Helwater scenes

Who can forget the sizzling stable scene in S5 where Claire and Jamie make-up after a row? Possibly the grandest horse lodgings you'll ever see, the stables were built in 1895 and belong to **Manderston House** in Duns, owned by Lord Palmer.

Manderston is a truly special house with a dazzling silver staircase, beautiful grounds and wonderfully creepy servant quarters in the basement. Though the main house doesn't appear in Outlander, it's starred in several other productions including Mrs Brown, Edwardian Country House and – most recently – the Julian Fellowes drama, Belgravia.

Guided tours are available in the summer (44 miles/1 hr from Edinburgh, TD11 3PP, www.manderston.co.uk).

*Distances are from Edinburgh

photo: Ali Wood

The stables at Manderston House appear in S5

DAY 4

GRAND HOMES AND SECRET LALLYBROCH

Edinburgh's 'Other castle', **Craigmillar Castle**, appears as Ardsmuir Prison where Jamie is imprisoned with Highland Jacobites. A mile outside the city walls, this medieval ruin once provided refuge for Mary Queen of Scots. *Open Apr to Sep, daily: 930-530pm, Oct to Mar 10-4pm, adults £6, children 5-15 £3.60, conc £4.80. EH16 4SY, www.historicenvironment. scot.*

From here, it's a 40-minute drive to **Hopetoun House**, the 17th century stately home that doubles as the home of the Duke of Sandringham. One of the finest examples of Scotland's grand architecture, it's so huge its clock towers had to be edited out for TV. As fans will know, it's pretty impressive on-screen, but in real life it's, well... flabbergasting. Upstairs you'll

Craigmillar Castle doubles as Ardsmuir Prison

photo: VisitScotland/Kenny Lam

find the spare room in Jamie and Claire's Parisian apartment, and downstairs the drawing room where the duke receives Claire. Volunteer guide, Ivor Mashford watched the scene being filmed.

'Simon Callow [who plays the duke] was chatty and talking to everyone. He said "do you think that bust looks like me?" And of course, we all said yes, but really it wasn't very well done as it was only meant to be seen from a distance.'

Outside, the cobbled streets around the Ranger's Room (great for kids) stand in for the Parisian streets where Claire and Mary are attacked. The lawn outside the west facade is where the duel was filmed between Jamie and the head of the McDonald clan, and the stables and grounds are also used for scenes at Helwater, where Jamie goes riding with Geneva and spends time with Willie.

Check the website to see when the house will be open again.

photo: Ali Wood

Magnificent Hopetoun House is the Duke of Sandringham's home

At present only the grounds are open for pre-booked tours. Adults £5.50, child £3.50, family (2+2) £15, pensioner/student £5, registered disabled £3.50, EH30 9RW, hopetoun.co.uk.

Don't leave Hopetoun without first buying a permit for **Midhope Castle** from the gift shop. The building provides the exterior for Jamie's family home Lallybroch. Be warned, it's not the jolly Fraser farm you find in Outlander, but a lonely ruin. It's atmospheric all the same, and two centuries ago housed 10 families of estate workers, including gamekeepers, foresters and carpenters. Opposite the car park are the woods where Jamie hides in S3. The mossy outcrop by the river was digitally remastered into his cave. *EH30 9SL, hopetoun.co.uk/access-midhope-castle, £4.*

On your way home, pop into **Abercorn church**, where Brianna is seen visiting Frank's grave in S4. Whilst sadly you won't be able to pay your respects to Frank, you can take a

The lonely ruin of Midhope Castle looks very different to Lallybroch

photo: Ali Wood

look at the fine collection of old gravestones. Many date back to the 1600s, before widespread literacy, so are illustrated with skulls and bones (emblems of mortality), and angels, cherubs or doves (immortality). The symbols also show the trade of the buried person, so for example, a horseshoe means a blacksmith, and a rolling pin a baker.

Overnight in Edinburgh or Queensferry

photo: VisitScotland/ Kenny Lam

Blackness Castle, where Jamie is flogged

DAY 5
BLEAK CASTLES AND ROMANTIC RAILS

Overlooking the Firth of Forth, forbidding **Blackness Castle** provides the setting for the Fort William HQ of Black Jack Randall in S1 and S2, where Jamie gets flogged. A garrison fortress and state prison, this heavily fortified 15th century castle is known as the 'ship that never sailed'. The producer, Ronald D. Moore, wanted it to feel more forbidding and bleak than Castle Leoch, and it was the interior courtyard that clinched the deal. 'It's cold and harsh and it just feels like a prison,' he says. 'You have this primordial, bleak, heavy fortress coming out of the ground. The wind comes off the water and it is cold. In every sense, it just goes right through you out there.' *Open daily Apr to Sep 930-530pm, Oct to Mar 10-4pm, adult £6, child £3.60, conc £4.80, www.historicenvironment.scot.*

A short hop away is **Bo'ness and Kinneil Railway**. Be sure to arrive before 330pm in order to catch the last steam train from the platform where Claire and Frank say their wartime goodbyes in S1. The trains, platform and even the cafe are kitted-out in period dress. Next door is the Museum of Scottish Railways. Breathe in the delicious smell of old leather and diesel in the lofty depot full of vintage trains, and admire the hand-painted signs for romantic-sounding destinations such as Corgi Junction and Plains. *Open daily Apr to Oct 11-430pm, EH51 9AQ, www.bkrailway.co.uk.*

Linlithgow Palace appears in Outlander as Wentworth prison where Jamie is kept, and finally overpowered, in the gut-wrenching scenes with Black Jack Randall. The birthplace of Mary Queen of Scots, this 15th century ruin was once favoured by Stewart kings and queens as a stopover between Edinburgh and Stirling Castles. *Open daily Apr to Sep 930-*

Bo'ness and Kinneil Railway features in S1

530pm, Oct to Mar 10-4pm, adult £9, child £5.40, conc £7.20, www.historicenvironment.scot.

Two miles away, set in the Bathgate Hills, **Beecraigs Country Park** was used for the forest scenes in The False Bride, S4, where Claire gets lost after riding through the storm. The 913 acres of managed mixed woodland is a popular attraction with a visitor centre, caravan and camping site, animals, walking routes and mountain bike trails.

With 170 acres of stunning woodland, **Muiravonside Country Park** was used for the backdrop to the Battle of Prestonpans in S2, and doubled as a British encampment, as well as English countryside. You could spend a whole day here as there's a mini demonstration farm, sculpture trail, children's play area and a café at the Visitor Hub courtyard. Download a map of trails at *www.falkirkcommunitytrust.org/venues/ muiravonside/images/large_map.jpg.*

Overnight in Falkirk

photo: Beecraigs Country Park

Beecraigs Country Park was used for forest scenes in S4

The Kelpies – not from Outlander, but definitely worth a visit

photo: VisitScotland/ Kenny Lam

DAY 6

ALL THE FUN OF FALKIRK

Now, **The Kelpies** most definitely DON'T feature in Outlander (you'll see why), but you can't visit Falkirk and not see these world famous equine sculptures. *The Helix Park, Falkirk, FK2 7ZT.*

Next, hop back in the car and head for **Callendar House**. This grand property dates back to the 14th century and has an authentic Georgian working kitchen, which appears in S2 of Outlander in the Duke of Sandringham's home, Bellhurst Manor. Don't go without a cuppa and a traybake from the newly refurbished tearoom. *Open daily except Tuesdays, 10-5pm, free, www.falkirkcommunitytrust.org/venues/callendar-house.*

From here, it's a 15-minute drive to **Gray Buchanan Park** on the west side of Polmont. In S4 a graveyard was erected in the middle of the park where Jamie and Young Ian bury Hayes.

photo: Falkirk Counci

Callendar House still has a working Georgian kitchen

In spite of the terrible weather, fans stayed out till midnight watching actors Sam Heughan and John Bell dig a grave, accompanied by dog Rollo. There are walks around the park, picnic benches and a play area. *Polmont, FK2 0XR.*

Stirling is a half an hour drive north, and your destination for the next couple of days. However, if you've time, take a short detour en-route to the magnificent **Falkirk Wheel**, which connects the Forth and Clyde Canal with the Union Canal. Again, not an Outlander destination, but this rotating boat lift is one of Scotland's finest feats of engineering and well worth a visit. One-hour *boat trips, including the lift cost £13.50 adults, £11.30 conc, child 5-15 £7.50, family from £37. A shorter 35-min Revolution Tour is also available. Open daily 10-530pm,www. scottishcanals.co.uk/falkirk-wheel.*

Overnight in Falkirk

DAY 7
DUNMORE, STIRLING AND DOUNE CASTLE

Start the day with a visit to **Dunmore Park House**, which was used in S1 as a WW2 hospital. It's a ruin, and rough underfoot, so best to photograph the exterior. To get there, you'll need to park at the Dunmore Pineapple, one of Scotland's most unique buildings, because it's... you guessed it – shaped like a pineapple! *Dunmore Park, FK2 8LU, free, www.nts.org.uk.*

Next on the itinerary is **Doune Castle** where visitor numbers have more than trebled since it starred as Castle Leoch, home to the MacKenzie clan. The castle pulled off a masterstroke by getting Sam Heughan, who plays Jamie Fraser, to narrate some behind-the-scenes gossip on the audioguide. But that's not its only claim to fame – Doune Castle is also where *Monty Python and the Holy Grail* was filmed! *Open daily 01 Apr to 30 Sep: 930-530pm, 01 Oct to 31 Mar: 10-4pm, adults £9, child 5-15*

photo: Ali Wood

Doune Castle in Stirling appears as Castle Leoch

£5.40, conc £7.20, FK16 6EA, www.historicenvironment.scot

Wash down your lunch with a wee dram (or coffee if you're designated driver) on a whisky tasting tour of **Deanston Distillery**, a former cotton mill at the entrance to Loch Lomond and The Trossachs National Park. In Outlander, the building appears as the wine warehouse in Le Havre, which belongs to Jamie's cousin. *Open daily, tasting tours £9-£25, 10-5pm, http://deanstonmalt.com.*

Alternatively, if you're not a whisky fan, head to **Stirling Castle**. Although this was passed over in Outlander, it still played a role in the Jacobite Rising when taken by Bonnie Prince Charlie in 1746. It's a magnificent castle – well worth an afternoon's visit – with many rooms, cafes and hands-on displays for the whole family. *Open daily, Apr to Sep: 930-6pm, Oct to Mar: 9-5pm, adult £14, child (5-15) £8.40, conc £11.20, FK8 1EJ, www.stirlingcastle.scot.*

photo: Ali Wood

The kitchen at Doune Castle was recreated on set

BEHIND THE SCENES

With its arched ceiling, the kitchen at Doune Castle looks uncannily like the one at Castle Leoch where Mrs Fitch boils up a brew to clean Jamie's wounds. In other Outlander scenes, we see cooks tending to open fires, pounding dough and preparing meat for the evening's meal. However, none of it was actually filmed here. An exact replica was made at the studio in Cumbernauld, which was so convincing not even the Doune castle staff could believe it was a fake!

An entire village was built at the front of Doune castle with houses, animal pens and canisters of smoke firing mist. Remember the scene where Claire and Jamie ride into the castle courtyard? Catriona Balfe, the actress who plays Claire, was shivering for real! Filming took place during the winter, and whilst the crew were kitted out in their thermals and coats, Catriona and co-star Sam had to repeat the scene several times over, her in a thin 1950s shift dress (which Mrs Fitch believes to be underwear) and him in a kilt!

DETOUR / EXTRA TIME

Take a breather at **Drummond Castle Gardens** in Crief and swoosh past peacocks and ancient yews like a lord or lady of Versailles. There's even a beech tree planted by Queen Victoria. The gardens double as the orchard and park at Versailles in S2 of *Outlander*, as well as having appeared in the film *Rob Roy. Open daily Easter to October: 1-6pm (11-6pm in June). Adult £10, child £3.50, family (2+3) £22, www. drummondcastlegardens.co.uk.*

Hidden in the Strathearn valley, 20 minutes further north, is **Abercairny**, home to the Moray family for over 700 years.

photo: VisitScotland/ Kenny Lam

The gardens at Drummond Castle were used for exterior Versailles

This doubles as Aunt Jocasta's North Carolina plantation, River Run from S4. In actual fact, that beautiful wooden house is a set – the lower front wall being the only one that actually exists, with a blue screen used for visual effects. The real house is, in fact, much grander and is open for events and weddings. It also has open days and Scotland's Garden events throughout the year so check the website to see what's going on, *www.abercairny.com, info@abercairny.com*

Overnight in Stirling

For a shorter tour, head straight to Day 19: Loch Katrine and the Trossachs.

DAY 8
CHARMING CULROSS

Time-travel (by car, not standing stones) to the **Royal Burgh of Culross** where every building in this cobbled village – including the palace, the pub and the electricity substation – dates to the 18th century or earlier. It's a filmmaker's dream, where Outlander fans can feast on flashbacks all day long – from Geillis's house in Cranesmuir to her parlour in the fairytale **Palace of Culross**. With its maze of warmly furnished rooms, low ceilings and wooden painted walls, the palace is strikingly different to grand and austere castles built elsewhere in the 1700s. If you have kids and you want them to behave, it's worth mentioning that the volunteer guide Brian plays the Outlander villager who nails the boy's ear to a post! *Palace open daily, Apr to Sep 10-5pm, Oct to Mar: Fri to Mon 10-4pm, adult £10.50, family £24.50, conc £7.50, KY12 8JH, www.nts.org.uk.*

Very little in Culross was altered for filming, though the buildings at Mercat Cross were painted brown to look more authentic. In the era that Outlander is set the streets would have been open sewers and the buildings suffered from, shall we say, splashbacks!

Lauren Jackson of the National Trust for Scotland was involved with the supervision and set up of the filming at Culross.

'It was amazing to see the properties transformed into 18th century locations,' she says. 'I'll never forget the amount of soil that was shipped in to fill the courtyard at Culross for a market scene, nor the time Diana Gabaldon shared her chocolate brownie with me in the rain whilst filming took place at Culross Palace!'

Overnight in Stirling or Culross

The courtyard at Culross Palace (above) and interior rooms appeared in a number of scenes

DAY 9
CASTLE-HOPPING IN FIFE

Given that there are over 2,000 castles in Scotland, it's no mean feat to be the oldest, as is the claim of Aberdour Castle. More importantly, of course, is its role in Outlander! This 12th century castle doubles as the monastery where Claire and Murtagh take Jamie to recover after his captivity in S2. *Open daily April to Sep: 930-530pm, Oct: 10-4pm, Nov to Mar 10-4pm, closed Thu & Fri, adult £6, child (5-15) £3.60, conc £4.80, KY3 0SL, historicenvironment.scot.*

Next, it's a 20-minute drive to **Dysart Harbour**. Here, the **Harbourmaster's House** and harbour appear as Le Havre in S2, where Jamie and Claire land in France. The harbour dates back to the mid 15th century, when it exported coal and salt to the Low Countries, expanding to the Baltic in the 16th and 17th centuries. Pop into the bistro at the Harbourmaster's House, a B-listed 19th century building, which is also the HQ of the Fife Coast and Countryside Trust. Here, you can find out more about the 117-mile Fife Coastal Path (well worth exploring) and interactive displays about the history of the region. During filming the interpretation centre and staffroom were used by cast as dressing rooms, and the staff were given a private tour of the set. One staffmember recalls watching from the office window as Jamie and Claire kissed – a scene they had to do many times over! *Open daily Mar to Oct: 930-430pm, Nov to Feb: 10-330pm, www.fifecoastalpath.co.uk.*

A 15-minute drive north of Fife is **Balgonie Castle**. This appears in Outlander S2 as Eldridge Manor where Claire is brought after being rescued from wolves. The 700-year-old castle is the home of the Laird of Balgonie and Edergoll. In January 1716 Rob Roy MacGregor paid Balgonie a visit with 200 clansmen and 20 Hanoverian prisoners. Other famous

photo: Fife Coast and Countryside Trust

Dysart Harbour doubles as the French port of Le Havre

visitors include Daniel Defoe, Dr Benjamin Rush (signatory of the American Declaration of Independence), James Boswell and Dr Johnson.

It's reputedly one of Scotland's most haunted castles, and Game of Thrones fans will be excited to know that the Great Hall was the inspiration for the bloodthirsty 'Red Wedding' scene!

Sadly the castle isn't currently open to the public but you can enjoy it from the outside.

EXTRA TIME/ DETOUR

The classic boat *Reaper* appears to be moored in Le Havre (actually Dysart harbour in Fife), but when not starring in blockbusters, she's kept at the **Scottish Fisheries Museum**, Anstruther, where she's lived for the past 40 years. Used for Jamie and Claire's escape to France, the *Reaper* is the last surviving Scottish herring lugger. The museum gives a fascinating insight not only into fishing but life in the coastal communities (21 miles/ 38 mins from Dysart, KY10 3AB, scotfishmuseum.org).

Overnight in Falkland

DAY 10
ROMANTIC FALKLAND

The pretty town of **Falkland**, nestled between the two Lomond Hills, doubles as Inverness. Described by Ron Moore as 'pretty much how you want a Scottish village to be in your mind's eye,' it's here that Claire and Frank stay on their second

photo: Scottish Fisheries Museum

The Reaper, which Claire and Jamie sail to France

The pretty village of Falkland was perfect for portraying Inverness

honeymoon, and meet the mysterious Mrs Baird, the owner of their B&B. In real life, this is the **Covenanter Hotel**, where you can eat dinner, and book the same room as Claire and Frank. **The Bruce Fountain** is memorable from the very first episode when the ghost of Jamie looks up at Claire's room.

Surprisingly good at spanning eras, Falkland also pulls off 18th century Inverness. In S2, **Rotten Row** and **Sharps Close** can be seen when Claire and Murtagh walk away from the boarding house, whilst **Brunton Street** is where sickly Alex Randall is being cared for by Mary Hawkins. Mary is buying her medical supplies at the apothecary when she meets Claire.

The apothecary scene was filmed at **Falkland Palace**, once the country residence of the Stewart kings and queens, and adored by Mary Queen of Scots. You can visit the apothecary (assembled post-Outlander) and learn about medieval cures. Follow in the footsteps of Mary Queen of Scots, explore the grand gardens and play chess on the giant outdoor board. Falkland also boasts the oldest tennis court in Britain... Game, set and match! At the time of going to press the palace and

63

gardens are closed but will hopefully re-open April 2021. Check the website for details, *www.nts.org.uk*.

Twenty minutes north of Falkland is **River Edge Lodges**, the idyllic setting for the Carolina Scottish Festival in S4 where Brianna and Roger have one of their many blow-ups. The entire resort was hired out to the show for two months during winter 2017. Most of the lodges were used by the Outlander film crew for costumes, catering, makeup, dressing rooms and a green room. However, there was also a 'hero lodge' which

photo: Mary McKay

photo: Mary McKay

Above: Lodge owner Mary McKay got to watch Outlander being filmed
Below: River Edge Lodges were used for the Carolina Scottish Festival

was completely redecorated in 1970s furniture for Brianna and Roger's cabin. Owner, Mary McKay, is a huge Outlander fan and explains how the lodge had a tent over it to simulate night time. Together with her daughter, Mary watched Roger (Richard Rankin) and Brianna (Sophie Skelton) kiss outside their own lodge, though sadly, the scene was eventually cut.

'They were so close to us that I could easily have reached out and touched them,' she says. 'They chatted a bit, gazing into each other's eyes and then... they kissed. Alannah and I turned to each other in a silent 'OH!' before turning our attention back to the filming.'

Find out more about Mary's experience in Chapter 4. *Lodges range from £380 to £801 per week, depending on the type of lodge and time of year. See www.riveredgelodges.com*

Overnight in Falkland or River House Lodges

DAY 11
MOHAWKS AND MOORS

A short drive north of River Edge Lodges is the pretty 17th century **Tibbermore Church** (PH1 1QJ), familiar to Outlander fans as Cranesmuir Church, where Claire and Geillis stand trial for witchcraft. It's here that the shocked women are seen sitting in the dock before Geillis is sent away to be burned and Claire escapes with Jamie. You'll need to arrange access to the church in advance. Contact the owners, Historic Churches Scotland, on 0131 563 5135 or 07780 682961, or by email at *contact@historicchurches.scot*

Now it's time to head for the Highlands. The roads start to narrow, the peaks rise and the traffic peters out. Be sure to dip your headlights for the mists that roll down the valleys, and slow for the cattle that wander across the roads.

If you're wondering why the countryside looks familiar, it's because you're heading into Outlander S4 & S5 territory. Not the North Carolina wilderness, as the producers would have you believe (with the help of some green-screen Blue Ridge Mountains), but Scottish woodland!

US fans were impressed with the authenticity of the North Carolina set. Vance and Kristie Brumbaugh, who visited Scotland in 2019, described it as 'spot on'.

'Fraser's Ridge is fictitious but is based on an area in Boone-Blowing Rock, North Carolina,' says Vance. 'Grandfather Mountain, mentioned by name, is real. If I hadn't known, I wouldn't have guessed Outlander wasn't filmed in North Carolina.'

Kinclaven Bluebell Wood near Perth was cleared of bramble, and redressed with moss, blue grasses, azaleas and ferns that would typically grow on a cliff-face. Throw in some 300 strawberry plants and bingo – you have Fraser's Ridge, where Jamie and Claire build a new life together in the

photo: National Trust for Scotland

Falkland Palace, adored by Mary Queen of Scots

Colonies. Four miles along a trail in the woods are the two large trees on the edge of Jamie's land, the 'witness trees', one of which Jamie marks with a carving of 'F.R.'

Since filming, Woodland Trust Scotland has diverted the path as there's a risk of branches or even whole trees coming down.

'Their decline is being managed naturally,' says George Anderson of the Trust. 'Many of these lovely old beech trees are now entering the final phase of their lives and will ultimately disintegrate where they stand. This brings great biodiversity benefits to the woodland as fungi and insects feast on the deadwood and in turn provide food for many birds and other wildlife.'

View them from afar, is the advice – don't step under the canopy – and, of course, NEVER carve trees (some fans are actually doing this and it's a real problem)! As well as spoiling the natural look of the tree, carving can allow pathogens to infect the tree, shortening its life span. The scene where Jamie carves initials 'F.R.' into the bark was made using an imitation

photo: Historic Churches Scotland

Tibbermore Church, where Claire and Geillis stand trial for witchcraft

silicon mould that was fixed to the tree and then removed.

'Woodland Trust Scotland understands that fans of Outlander are keen to visit filming locations,' says George. 'People are welcome to visit the wood and soak up the atmosphere of Fraser's Ridge. However we suggest people avoid the area under the canopy of these old beech trees. Anyone who does, must do so at their own risk.' *www. woodlandtrust.org.uk*

A 20-minute drive from **Kinclaven Bluebell Woods** is another magical location, the **Hermitage,** which appears in the final two episodes of S5. The lush Perthshire forest stands in for North Carolina, and is owned by the National Trust for Scotland. Designed as an 18th century pleasure ground for the Dukes of Atholl, it has a river and picturesque folly surrounded by towering Douglas firs. Look out for red squirrels and – if you're there in the autumn – salmon leaping up the falls as they head for their spawning ground upriver. Open year round. *The car park costs £3, free for NTS members, www.nts.org.uk.*

Faskally Wood, near the village of Pitlochry, is where the Mohawk Village was erected. Several different trees were used to make the wigwams, the counsel house and the jail where Young Ian is kept. The show's Art Production Designer, Gary Steel, describes how he loved building the jail.

'I like the idea that when you're inside and you look out it's like the rose window of a cathedral because of all the autumnal colours of the leaves. It's quite beautiful.'

The woodland is largely man-made, having been created in the 19th century as a Forestry Commission school. You can learn about the tree species in the Foresters' classroom, have lunch at the picnic spot and walk around the trails, including the Dunmore Trail with views over the lochside trees. Autumn is the best time of the year to visit, when the loch reflects every hue of red, gold and purple. Winner of the UK's Best Cultural Event, the Enchanted Forest music and light show takes place here nightly in October, and in 2021 will be celebrating its 20th anniversary. *PH16 5LB, forestryandland. gov.scot, www.enchantedforest.org.uk.*

It's less than 40 minutes (20 miles) to the pretty village of **Kinloch Rannoch**, where Claire and Frank enjoy their second honeymoon. Sited at the tip of a loch, this is a great base for walking, with 26 munros, as well as a 22-mile circular cycle route around the loch. Surrounding the village is Rannoch Moor, where Claire famously disappears through the stones in S1, and where Roger, Claire and Brianna watch Geilis disappear. Later, in S4, Brianna is seen at the stones, about to follow her mother into 17th century.

Whilst sadly the real 'Craigh na Dun' circle is made of Styrofoam and installed on location, everything else about the site will seem familiar. The countryside is part of the 17,000-

photo: VisitScotland/Kenny Lam

Kincloch Rannoch, where Claire and Frank go on honeymoon

SCOTLAND AN OUTLANDER TOUR

acre **Dunalastair Estate**, which leases holiday cottages and has been home to the Bunten/de Sales La Terrière family for 120 years. *www.dunalastair.com.*

Several clans were associated with this area, including the Menzies, Macdonald, Cameron and Duncan, and there's a Clan Trail around Loch Rannoch. If you're into wildlife you're in for a treat; keep an eye out for ospreys, red squirrels, pine marten, deer, buzzards and grouse.

Enjoy the breathtaking views of the loch or even take a walk through woodland to the dramatic peaks of the moor. Drive south of Dunalastair Reservoir to Tay Forest Park and look out for a turn-off towards the east side of the reservoir. Along here is the recognisable mound dotted with trees, which was used for Craigh na Dun.

Geographically speaking, the small community of Kinloch Rannoch is the centre of Scotland, but actually it's so far from anywhere, that its nearest railway station – 18 miles away on the moor – is the most remote in the British Isles. In fact, the train from here to Fort William crosses the same bridge that carried the Hogwarts Express in the Harry Potter films. The views are spectacular! The moor covers 150 square miles of uninhabitable peat bogs, lochans (small lakes), rocky crags and pinewood forest. If that sounds hostile, imagine it in the middle of 18th century Jacobite warfare!

To really get away from it all, catch the train north to Corrour (*Trainspotting* fans will recognise this as the station that Tommy visits with Renton, Spud and Sickboy) and walk the nine miles back to Rannoch station, or even overnight at the Scottish YHA hostel a mile away on the shores of Loch Ossian. There are three to four trains daily. *www.hostellingscotland.org.uk/hostels/loch-ossian.*

Overnight on Rannoch Moor or Kinloch Rannoch

DAY 12

CAIRNGORMS AND WOLVES

Drive an hour (40 miles) into the Cairngorms, the biggest national park in Britain and home to a quarter of Scotland's native woodland. By now, you're well and truly in munro-bagging territory (climbing mountains over 3,000ft) – a favourite pastime of Sam Heughan.

The Outlander cast spent a couple of weeks filming around Newtonmore. It's this footage – vast mountain ranges and wooded glens – that's emblematic of the show, and is probably the 'Outlander' you've come looking for! At the heart of this is the **Adverikie Estate**, which has an impressive Hollywood CV. *Mrs Brown*, the 1997 film about Queen Victoria and her servant John Brown, was filmed here, then later the estate doubled as Glenbogle in *Monarch of the Glen* (2000 to 2005). It played host to royalty again as Balmoral in S1 and S2 of *The Crown*, as well as Ewan McGregor in *Salmon Fishing in the Yemen* (2011). In 2018 it featured in Robert the Bruce biopic, *Outlaw King*.

In Outlander S1, Claire travels on horseback through the Adverikie Estate, having been 'rescued' by the Redcoats after pretending to be Dougal's hostage. There were 12 horses on set that day and the Redcoats were a team of re-enactors recruited for the show. Sam Heughan recalls that they worked like a real regiment on-screen and off, something he found amusing. 'It's quite funny when the sergeant of arms, a real drillmaster, makes them march to the tent to go have their lunch,' he told Conde Nast Traveler. 'They're a great bunch, very enthusiastic and very knowledgeable as well. We'd talk to them about the period and the weapons.'

The Victorian gothic Ardverikie House is a family home,

still owned by the descendants of its original founder. It was opened as a Highland sporting estate, and in 1847 hosted Queen Victoria and Prince Albert for three weeks. These days, forestry, deer management, hydroelectricity and farming are its main sources of income, plus weddings and tourism.

The estate is a supporter of the Scottish Outdoor Access Code so you can visit any time. No vehicles are allowed, though, so you'll need to park in the layby on the A86, a quarter of a mile west of Gatelodge, or access at Moy in a layby next to the concrete bridge. There are accommodation options on-site, too. *PH20 1BX, www.ardverikie.com.*

Half an hour further (17 miles) you'll come to the village of Newtonmore, home to the **Highland Folk Museum**. The cluster of 18th century croft houses mark the beginning of a mile-long stretch of homes dating from the 1700s to the 1930s, depicting Scottish rural life. Replicas of the turf-roofed Highland crofts were used for many period scenes in Outlander, including when Dougal collects the rents in S1. *Currently open Wed to Sun, 1030-4pm, pre-booking required but entrance is free (donations welcome), www. highlifehighland.com/highlandfolkmuseum.*

Just seven miles further on is the **Highland Wildlife Park** where you can see the wild animals that would once have been native to Scotland such as bears, wolves and bison. In the books by Diana Gabaldon, Claire ends up fending off a wolf after Jamie banishes her from Wentworth prison, though sadly this didn't make it to the TV series. *Open daily except 25 December, Apr to Oct & Nov to Mar: 10-4pm, Jul to Aug: 10-6pm, adults £18.50, children 3-15 £12.50, conc £15.50, PH21 1NL, www.highlandwildlifepark.org.uk.*

Overnight in Aviemore

photo: VisitScotland/ Cairngorms National Park

Lochan Mor (Lily Loch) in Rothiemurchus Forest

DAY 13
RAMBLE ACROSS ROTHIEMURCHUS

Aviemore, in the heart of the Cairngorms is an all-terrain playground for outdoorsy folk. In winter, it's a ski-resort, and in summer a hotspot for hikers, climbers and bikers. Full of pubs, outdoor shops and cafes, it's an energising place to be.

Covering the area between the River Spey near Aviemore and the top of the Cairngorm Mountains is the **Rothiemurchus Estate**. It's here, in a wooded area known as Tullochghru, that Claire first meets Jamie, whilst riding to Craigh na Dun after being rescued from Black Jack Randall. It's on the top of a hill about a mile south of the hamlet of Coylumbridge. Park on the main road near the Rothiemurchus Camp and Caravan Park and follow the trail southeast, which is marked on an OS map.

photo: VisitScotland/ Cairngorms National Park

Loch an Eilein Castle, hidden in the Rothiemurchus Estate

Rothiemurchus Estate has been owned by the Grant family for almost 500 years, and is open to the public. You can walk the trails, take a ranger-led tour, or go fishing, clay shooting, quad biking, archery and more.

Just southwest of Tullochghru is the castle ruin at Loch an Eilein (loch of the island), dating back to the 14th century. In 1690, the castle was briefly attacked by Jacobite survivors retreating from the Battle of Cromdale. The castle at the time was occupied by the women, children and old folk of Rothiemurchus. The Laird's wife, Grizel Mor (Big Grace), was said to have cast lead musket balls for the defenders and shouted abuse at the enemy. The ruin has long been a favourite of visitors to the estate, even bagging the impressive title of 'Britain's Favourite Picnic Spot' in a poll organised by Warburtons bakers in 2010. There's a trail right round the loch.

Overnight in Aviemore

Culloden, site of the last pitched battle on British soil

DAY 14: CHILLING CULLODEN

The compact city of **Inverness** sits at the mouth of the River Ness (which flows from Loch Ness) at the end of the Great Glen. It's here that Claire and Frank take their honeymoon, though on-screen, the village of Falkland stands in for Inverness. If, like Frank, you have Highland roots, head to the **Highland Archive Centre** to discover your family's Scottish heritage. The archive collections date from the 14th century to the present day covering the counties of Inverness, Nairn, Ross and Cromarty and Sutherland. The staff in the family history room are experts in Highland and Scottish genealogy; ask them anything, or email beforehand at genealogy@highlifehighland.com.

Nearby is **Culloden Battlefield**. At first glance, this lonely windswept plain seems to offer little to the visitor, but once inside the visitor centre, its importance is clear. Culloden is the site of the last pitched battle on British soil, and marks the end of the Jacobite Risings. In Outlander, it's where a big chunk of cast members meet their maker (and take home their last payslips!), vastly outnumbered and overpowered by the Redcoats. Though the battle was filmed elsewhere – Culloden is, after all, a war grave – it does appear in S2 when Claire lays a flower at the Fraser memorial stone.

Diana Gabaldon and various cast members have visited Culloden, including Richard Rankin (who plays Roger Mackenzie) whilst prepping for S2.

Open daily all year, Jan to Mar & Nov to Dec: 10-4pm, Apr to May & Sep to Oct: 9-530pm, Jun to Jul: 9-6pm, Aug: 9-7pm, £9.50 concession, £11 adult, £26 family, IV2 5EU, www.nts.org. uk/Visit/Culloden.

photo: VisitScotland/Kenny Lam

Clava Cairns, the Bronze Age burial stones that inspired Craig na Dun

Afterwards, connect with your inner-spirit at **Clava Cairns**, a group of Bronze Age burial cairns and standing stones that inspired Diana Gabaldon's fictional Craig na Dun. What remains of the 4,000-year-old cemetery would have once been part of a larger complex. The sites contain prehistoric burial monuments and the remains of a medieval chapel. There's even a 'split stone'. If you hear the stones start to buzz, stand well-clear! *Open daily year-round and free to visit, IV2 5EU, www.historicenvironment.scot.*

DETOUR: THE INVERNESS OUTLANDERS

This small group of fans from Inverness know everything there is about the city's connection with Outlander. In April 2016, on the 270th anniversary of Culloden, they visited the battlefield for a midnight service at the cairn. With the help of fans, they raised £430, which went towards a wreath and the Culloden Battlefield Centre. The group is active at all sorts of Outlander gatherings, and has produced a fantastic map for Outlander fans, not only listing TV locations but those associated with the books and Jacobite history.

The Inverness Outlanders are often asked what 'Outlandish' things people can visit besides Culloden Battlefield and Clava Cairns. Plenty, is the answer – and they're all related to Fraser country!

According to Diana Gabaldon, Jamie's character was inspired by an account she read in the book *Prince in the Heather*. The passage describes how 19 wounded Jacobites hid in a farmhouse after the battle. After two days they were executed under the Redcoats' command for No Quarter, 'except one man, a Fraser of the Master of Lovat's regiment, who survived the slaughter.'

As such, the countryside and places connected with the Fraser clan make a very enjoyable day out. As well as visiting Wardlaw Mausoleum (see Day 14), why not hike around **Reelig Glen** (*scotland.forestry.gov.uk/visit/reelig-glen*), drive along the beautiful roads to Mullardoch Dam and visit **Corrimony Chambered Cairn,** which features in book 7, An Echo in the Bone. It's here that Brigadier General Simon Fraser is buried after Jamie and Claire bring him back to Scotland. If you're spending a few days in Inverness, let the website and map be your first port of call. An audio version is available too. *https:// invernessOutlanders.wordpress.com*

Overnight in Inverness

photo: National Trust for Scotland

Culloden battlefield, where Bonnie Prince Charlie was defeated

A bit more about Culloden...

Culloden, near Inverness, is where Bonnie Prince Charlie's campaign to restore the Stuarts to the throne ended in tragedy. It was here, in 1746, that over 1,500 men were slain, two thirds of them Jacobites. Learn their harrowing story in a vivid 360-degree video recreation then take a minute to compose yourself on the lonely field, where the start positions of the armies are marked by blue (Jacobite) and red (Government) flags. In Outlander, Jamie manages to escape but in truth the Government army was told to 'give no quarter', meaning the wounded were to be bayoneted, and the fleeing shot by musket fire.

After the battle the moor was closed to prevent anyone tending to the wounded. It wasn't until three days later that the locals were invited to bury the dead. In the middle of the battlefield are memorial stones, some laid with sprigs of heather, others with wilting cellophane-wrapped carnations. There's 'Donald', 'Cameron' and 'Maclean' and over by the monument is the Fraser one, where Claire weeps for Jamie in S2. Don't be fooled by the clan names. In reality, each grave contains the remains of up to 200 men, and no-one knows who was actually buried where as the headstones were laid 135 years later. Curiously there's a stone for the English, too. It's a common misconception that Culloden was a battle between the Scottish and English, but actually two thirds of the Government army were from Scotland, a myth that Outlander does little to allay.

DAY 15
MAUSOLEUM MYSTERY AND
THE LOCH NESS MONSTER

Keeping history alive is the aim of the volunteers at the
Wardlaw Mausoleum in Kirkhill, eight miles outside of
Inverness. Built in 1634, this historic crypt was the burial place
for the Lovat Frasers, and was extended in 1722 by Lord Lovat,
the 'Old Fox' of the Jacobite Rebellion. The clan chief, who's
played by Clive Russell in Outlander S2, was amongst the
Highlanders defeated at the Battle of Culloden and convicted
of treason against the Crown. He was subsequently sentenced
to death and buried in the family crypt... or was he?

   The crypt was used by the Lovats until the early 19th
century, and fell into disrepair before being restored, thanks
to lottery funding and a grant from Historic Scotland. Diana
Gabaldon has visited the site, as has Richard Rankin (who plays
Roger MacKenzie) on the recommendation of the Inverness
Outlanders group. He enjoyed it so much he returned the
following week with co-star Sophie Skelton, who tweeted
pictures of 'Bree and Roger brushing up on their Fraser history'.

   With the Outlander connection, visitor numbers increased,
as did media interest. It was disputed whether the headless
corpse in the coffin actually was Lord Lovat, and the Scottish
press, Richard Rankin and even Diana Gabaldon were tweeting
updates. The matter was settled in October 2017 when world-
renowned forensics professor, Dame Sue Black, opened the
Old Fox's coffin and examined its contents. Over 500 people
gathered at the Kingmills Hotel in Inverness to listen to her
verdict. It was not, after all, the Old Fox, but the remains of a
25-35 year old mystery woman! The remains were re-interred
at the mausoleum, and the 16th Lord Lovat was there – along
with actor Clive Russell who plays the Old Fox on-screen – to

photo: Ali Wood

Urquhart Castle played a role in the Jacobite Risings

pay his respects. A commemorative plaque was made which reads: 'In this casket lie the remains of the 5 unknown people found in the coffin previously thought to contain those of Simon 'The Fox', 11th Lord Fraser of Lovat'.

Entry is free, though a donation helps keep the site running. Pre-booking is preferable but if you just turn up, knock on the door of Pilgrim Cottage (to the right of the gate) to get someone to give you a personal tour. Email *info@wardlawmausoleum.com,* 01463 831 742, wardlawmausoleum.com.

The three-hour drive from Inverness to Portree on Skye is unforgettable. But before you dip south to the glistening shores of Loch Ness, visit the tranquil ruins of **Beauly Priory**, founded in 1230 for an order of French monks from Dijon. It's here in Outlander that Claire meets Maisri, a 'Seer' in residence at Beaufort Castle. *Free, open Apr to Sep: 930-530pm, Oct to Mar, 10-4pm, www.historicenvironment.scot.*

Urquhart Castle, perched on a rocky peninsula on the edge of Loch Ness, is an iconic guidebook image. It was blown up by the last of the government troops garrisoned here during the Jacobite Risings. *Open daily: Apr to Sep 930-6pm, Jun to Aug: 930-8pm, Oct: 930-5pm, Nov to Mar: 930-430pm, adult £9.60, child 5-15 £5.80, conc £7.60, pre-booking essential, www.historicenvironment.scot.*

Don't forget to drop in at the **Loch Ness Centre and Exhibition**. OK, so Nessie doesn't really feature in the TV series Outlander, except for a passing reference as the 'water horse', but it's possibly the most famous monster in the world! In fact, Diana Gabaldon has visited Loch Ness and describes it as: 'Huge! Very, very deep and a dark blue colour in good weather – almost black in bad weather, under the clouds.'

Open daily from 10am. Last entry winter is 330pm, Easter-

Is Nessie an omen to Claire, or merely displaced in time?

Photo: Loch Ness Centre and Exhibition

Is Nessie real?

Here's what Diana Gabaldon thinks...

When asked by a school child if she thought Nessie was real, Diana replied:

'On purely scientific grounds, then probably not – at least, not if the monster is as big as it's been described; I've seen an analysis of the amount of biomass produced in the loch, and it isn't great enough to sustain a population of creatures of that size (see, there can't be just *one* monster, unless a) it's immortal, and we don't know of any immortal flesh-and-blood creatures, so you shouldn't assume that one exists, *a priori* (that means, "in advance of finding anything out"), or b) you have a situation in which the monster isn't confined to the loch. Unless that's the case, you have to have a population of a size to permit breeding; otherwise, they'd die out.'

However, Diana does share the fact that she believes time-travel is possible, so in this instance, all you need is a time-portal under Loch Ness, which would allow a prehistoric creature to pass through it. In her books there's a scene where Clare sees the Loch Ness monster at the lake. Later, she's talking to Roger and says she thinks it was a plesiosaur that may have travelled there through a portal like she did.

'I could see the poignancy of having this woman, thrown out of her own time, meeting a creature that might also be displaced – or might be an omen to her,' says Diana on her website, www.dianagabaldon.com.

Oct 5pm. Adult £8.45, senior & student £7.25, child 6-15 £4.95, family (2+2) £23.95.

Continue on to **Skye**, the largest of the Inner Hebrides, which is linked to the mainland by a bridge at Kyle of Lochalsh. This dramatic land of ice-sculpted peaks and volcanic plateaus, has appeared in dozens of films, including the *BFG* and *Prometheus*. Everywhere on the island is accessible in a day so it doesn't matter where you stay. However, the colourful harbour of Portree is well placed for a visit to the main sights such as the spiky Quiraing, and the basalt plateau: the Old Man or Storr.

Overnight on Skye

DAY 16
OVER THE SEA TO SKYE

Skye is just a short hop across the bridge these days but in 1746, after Culloden, Bonnie Prince Charlie would have made his escape by boat, hence the 'Skye Boat Song', whose melody is the title theme to Outlander. In Kilmuir, you can visit the grave of Flora MacDonald, the heroine who smuggled the prince to safety dressed as a lady's maid. Coincidentally, fashion designer Alexander McQueen is buried just 100m away.

Next door is the **Skye Museum of Island Life**, an atmospheric huddle of crofts with lit peat fires, wax figures and displays on rural life. James Boswell, on visiting Skye in 1773, noted: 'we had no rooms that we could command, for the good people here had no notion that a man could have any occasion but for a mere sleeping-place.' *Open Easter to Sep, Mon to Sat, 930-5pm, www.skyemuseum.co.uk.*

Overnight on Skye

Glen Coe also features in Braveheart, Rob Roy and Skyfall

DAY 17

MAGNIFICENT GLEN COE – FROM SKYFALL TO BRAVEHEART

It's a scenic three-and-a-half-hour drive to the village of **Glencoe**. Leave Skye via the car ferry from Armadale to Mallaig (35-min crossing, 63 per week) and take the A830, a famously picturesque route known as the Road to the Isles. After about two and a half hours you come to the **Glenfinnan monument**. It was here in 1745 that Bonnie Prince Charlie raised his standard and started the Jacobite Rising, without which there would be no Outlander (or battle of Culloden or Falkirk, or burning of Catholic meeting houses, banning of kilts and execution of Jacobites... but hey, let's not get side-tracked)!

Continue on to **Glen Coe**, the glen that features not only in the opening credits of Outlander (where we see Claire and

Jamie on horseback), but *Rob Roy*, *Braveheart* and the James Bond film *Skyfall*. With formidable knife-edged mountains, bruised skies and glacial valleys, it's easy to see why it appeals to film directors. The intimidating crags would have seen many clan battles during the 17th and 18th centuries, as well as the Glencoe Massacre in 1692. For 10 days the MacDonald clan entertained 130 government soldiers, only to be killed by them in a shocking breach of trust for being Jacobite supporters. *Find out more at the National Trust Visitor Centre. Open daily 10-4pm. No entrance fee but parking £4, www.nts.org.uk.*

Overnight in Glencoe

DAY 18
MIGHTY BEN NEVIS

Ben Nevis is Britain's highest summit (4,406ft). If you're fit, the weather's good and you want to climb it, the best place to start is the **Glen Nevis visitor centre**, a mile and a half southeast of Fort William. It's a constant uphill – no let-up – and at the top don't be surprised if there are icicles dripping from your hair! For views of Ben Nevis, but without the aching calves, travel to the **Aonach Mhor Nevis Range** and take the cable car up to the top of the mountain. The Gondola is also popular with winter climbers, paragliders and hang-gliders. *Usually open Wed to Sun, 930-430pm, but opening times vary due to maintenance. 1-day pass adult £19.50, family (2+2) £51, (2+3) £55, (2+4) £58. Winter season tickets available plus 2, 3 & 7 day passes. www.nevisrange.co.uk.*

Ben Nevis, Britain's highest mountain

Explore Loch Katrine on the steamship Sir Walter Scott

After a hike up Ben Nevis its time to rest your legs on the drive south to the Trossachs (2hrs 30 mins/ 90 miles).

Overnight in the Trossachs

DAY 19
LOCH KATRINE AND THE TROSSACHS

The rolling hills and glassy lochs of the Trossachs are as sedate as the Highlands are wild. Follow in the footsteps of the Victorians, regaling in stories of Rob Roy and Sir Walter Scott's famous poem The Lady of the Lake. No wonder Brianna is so taken with the area when Roger Mackenzie drives her around in S2! **Brenachoile Point**, on the northern shore of Loch Katrine, was where these scenes were filmed. For superb loch and mountain views, you can follow an easy 7km walk along the Art and Literature trail to Brenachoile View, and learn about the cultural history en-route. Download the map online at *https://forestryandland.gov.scot/visit/forest-*

parks/queen-elizabeth-forest-park/loch-katrine or pickup a
trail leaflet at **Lodge Forest Visitor Centre**.

Take the steamship **Sir Walter Scott** from Trossachs Pier,
sit back and enjoy the commentary about the legends of the
lake. The steamship was originally built on the River Clyde,
and had to be dismantled before being taken by barge to Loch
Lomond, then horse and cart to Stronachlachar. *Vessels depart
daily all year round from Trossachs Pier (45-min round-trip)
at 1030am and then every hour on the half hour until 330pm.
Adult £13, U16 £7.50, family (2+2) £33, conc £12, dog £2.
Download a timetable from www.lochkatrine.com.* Bike hire is
available at Trossachs Pier, *www.katrinewheelz.co.uk.*

Finish the afternoon at the Lodge Forest Visitor Centre at
Queen Elizabeth Forest Park in Aberfoyle. *FK8 3SX.* Take it
slowly, watching the young ospreys on the live web cam
before they migrate for Africa... or go quickly; very quickly – by
whizzing through the canopy on one of the longest zip-wires
in Britain! *https://goape.co.uk/days-out/aberfoyle.*

Overnight in the Trossachs

DAY 20
ARCHITECTURAL GEMS OF GLASGOW

From the Trossachs it's an hour-and-a-half drive (41 miles)
to the thriving, rejuvenated city of Glasgow, which plays
a starring role in the production (though not the plot) of
Outlander. As with Edinburgh, there's much to see in the
city aside from its film links, so allow an extra day or two to
explore the galleries, venues and world renowned 'Glasgow
style' architecture of Charles Rennie Mackintosh.

In Outlander S3 the setting changes dramatically when

Frank and Claire (now pregnant with Jamie's baby) move to Boston, USA. Actually, they don't go that far; their American home is on Glasgow's **Dowanhill Street**, a leafy, upmarket enclave in the West End. These traditional red sandstone townhouses were built at the turn of the last century by David Barclay, one of the architect brothers of the firm HD Barclay, who built many of the city's schools and public buildings.

In Outlander S2, Claire – now a Parisian lady of the manor – moonlights as a surgeon alongside the nuns at L'Hopital Des Anges. It's also here, in a heartbreaking scene, that Mother Hildegarde tells Claire her baby girl was stillborn. 'I am sorry Madame, she has joined the angels, she was born dead'.

The stirring scenes were filmed at the crypt at Glasgow Cathedral, a building renowned for its Gothic architecture and stained glass windows. Built in the 1100s and dedicated to St Kentigern, also known as St Mungo, it's the most complete

The crypt at Glasgow Cathedral is L'Hopital Des Anges

photo: VisitScotland/Kenny Lam

medieval cathedral on the Scottish mainland (having survived the Protestant Reformation intact), and it's here that Scotland's largest city first took shape. The crypt where Claire tends to the sick was built in the mid 1200s to house the tomb of St Kentigern, whilst the pulpitum, a richly carved stone screen between choir and nave, was added in the early 1400s.

Entry is free and a *new audioguide is available at £3 adults, £2 conc, £1 children. Open Apr to Sep: Mon to Sat 930-530pm, Sun 1-5pm, Oct to Mar: Mon to Sat 10-4pm, Sun 1-4pm, www. historicenvironment.scot.*

George Square is where Frank spontaneously proposes to Claire in 1940s London. Around the square are a series of important statues and monuments including those dedicated to Scottish heroes Robert Burns, James Watt, Sir Robert Peel and Sir Walter Scott. Grand, Victorian and imposing, the square, which houses the City Chambers, has played host to many films

photo: VisitScotland/Kenny Lam

George Square depicts London in the 1940s

91

over the years. It even doubled as Chicago in the Brad Pitt flick *World War Z*. Don't worry, the zombies have gone now.

Former church, **St Andrews in the Square**, appears in Outlander S4 as the theatre where Jamie and Claire are watching a play when they learn of Murtagh's planned ambush. The listed venue was built in the mid-1700s and briefly housed Bonnie Prince Charlie's army in 1745. After almost 240 years of continuous use as a church, the last service was held in June 1993. The building, described as one of the top six classical churches in the UK, was considered to be at risk and sold to the Glasgow Building Preservation Trust for £1. It was restored and reopened in 2000 as Glasgow's Centre for Scottish Culture, but sold again in January 2020. It's currently closed to the public. *1 St Andrew's Square, Glasgow, GL 5PP.*

The University of Glasgow doubles as Harvard where Frank works as a professor. Founded in 1451, it's one of the oldest

photo: VisitScotland

St Andrews in the Square doubles at the theatre where Claire and Jamie watch a play

universities in the world, and definitely worth a visit. Here you'll find the Hunterian gallery and museum, housing the fantastic Mackintosh House. Reassembled room-by-room, this striking space is furnished with Modernist art and furniture belonging to architect-designer Charles Rennie Mackintosh and his wife, the artist Margaret Macdonald.
It's a two-mile walk from the centre, or take the Underground to Hillhead, a train to Partick or Exhibition Centre (10-minute walk) or buses 4, 4, 4A, 15, x77. www.gla.ac.uk/hunterian.

Just across from the university is **Kelvingrove Park**, which briefly features in S3 when Claire is seen pushing baby Brianna in her buggy over a bridge, and a man is playing the bagpipes. The park is home to the beautiful **Kelvingrove Art Gallery and Museum**. Opened in 1901, there are 22 galleries to explore on everything from art to animals, Ancient Egypt and Charles Rennie Mackintosh. *Open Mon to Thu & Sat 10-5pm, Friday & Sun 11-5pm, www.glasgowlife.org.uk/museums.*

Overnight in Glasgow

DAY 21

FOUR COUNTRY PARKS

Whilst Outlander's Castle Leoch is filmed at Doune Castle, the grounds surrounding it are actually at **Pollok Country Park**, seven miles outside of Glasgow. The park also stands in for the French countryside between Le Havre and Paris. Well known for its trails, the 260-acre woodland is popular with walkers and runners, and makes a nice outing away from the bustling city. The centrepiece of the park is **Georgian Pollok House**. One of the grandest properties managed by the National Trust for Scotland, it was here in the cedar-panelled

photo: VisitScotland

Calderglen Country Park, where Jamie and Willie go camping

smoking room in 1931 that the trust was first conceived. The Maxwell family lived on the site for six centuries, though the main part of the house is mid-18th century. *Park open daily, year-round, free. Pollok House open daily 10-5pm. Adult £7.50, family £18.50, conc £5.50, 2060 Pollokshaws Rd, Glasgow G43 1AT, www.nts.org.uk.*

Just two miles away from Pollok Country Park is Queen's Park, which doubles as 1960s Boston (you can see the skyline added to the background). It's here in S5 that Claire meets Brianna and tells her about a patient who died from a penicillin allergy.

The 148-acre park was designed in 1857 by world renowned Sir Joseph Paxton and dedicated to the memory of Mary Queen of Scots (not Queen Victoria as commonly thought). Find out more about the park's history in a 1 hr 30 min heritage trail starting at the Glass House. Download a leaflet at https://glasgow.gov.uk/parks.

Another Outlander hotspot where you can stretch your legs is **Calderglen Country Park**. The park extends along the

Rotten Calder River, a tributary of the River Clyde, with the area around Horseshoe Falls providing the backdrop to Jamie and Willie's camping scenes. Say hi to the meerkats, monkeys and ringtailed coatis in the zoo, and if you've time, why not throw in a round of golf and picnic in front of the privately owned 17th century Torrance House? There's an adventure playground for kids. *Conservatory and zoo open year-round Mon to Sun 10-4pm, Strathaven Road, East Kilbride G75 0QZ.*

Half an hour south is **Dean Castle Country Park**. It's here that the 14th century castle stands in for Beaufort Castle, where Claire and Jamie persuade Lord Lovat to send men for the Jacobite cause. The 200-acre park has woodland walks, an adventure playground, urban farm and tearooms. Inside the castle you can see collections of historic weapons, armour and musical instruments. *Note – the castle is closed for refurbishment until June 2021.*

Finish the afternoon with a deep breath of sea air. It's a 20-minute drive to the coastal town of **Troon** in Ayrshire, which overlooks the Isle of Arran and Ailsa Craig. Walk along

photo: VisitScotland/Paul Tomkins

Troon, where Claire, Jamie and Murtagh board a ship for France

95

the esplanade or the sandy beach where Claire, Jamie and Murtagh arrive at the end of S1 to board a ship for France. Whilst you're unlikely to see a 300-year-old ship, Troon is a yachting haven, as well as a golf hotspot (home to seven courses including Royal Troon, which regularly hosts the Open Championship). Imagine Jamie and Claire as they set sail, their homeland becoming a smudge on the horizon.

Overnight in Glasgow or Troon

EXTRA TIME/ DETOUR

Thomas Coates Memorial church in Paisley has recently undergone transformation into a state-of-the-art events space. The enchanting Gothic Revival church appears in the very first scene of S5, episode 5, where Claire is seen praying in the 1960s. Though currently reserved for private events, it's worth checking the website in case tours become available at a later date (12 miles/22 mins from Glasgow, PA1 2BA, www. coatspaisley.com).

DAY 22
PEACEFUL DUNURE

Tiny **Dunure Harbour** stands in for Ayr Harbour, the port where Jamie and Claire board the Artemis in S3, and where Brianna and Roger start their voyage to the colonies in S4. Remember when Young Ian swims out to Silkies Island? It's in fact not an island, but the ruins of **Dunure Castle** dating back to the 13th century. Sitting precariously on the beach, it's been a ruin for 300 years, but was once the stronghold of the powerful Kennedy family, today associated with Culzean Castle four miles away. It even hosted Mary Queen of Scots for three days (where didn't the lady go!) as the guest of Gilbert Kennedy, the 4th Earl of Cassilis.

Sadly this is the end of your Outlander adventure, but hopefully not your love affair with Scotland! Prestwick Airport is half an hour away, Glasgow Central Station and airport just over an hour, and Edinburgh two hours. Safe journey.

And finally...

The location you'll (probably) never visit

Unless you score a role as an extra on Outlander, you're unlikely to ever set foot in Craigh na Dun. The standing stones, along with the interiors of Lallybroch, Castle Leoch, and dozens of other locations, live within the vast Wardpark Studio in Cumbernauld, North Lanarkshire. For many years, this was the Isola Werke UK factory, employing around 550 people to make circuit boards. It was closed down for eight years after the recession hit, falling into disrepair until entrepreneur Terry Thomson bought the site in 2013. Though the chairman of an engineering company, Thomson's vision was in another direction entirely. He transformed the 130,000 square feet of buildings and warehouses into a professional film studio, and pitched for his first big contract – Outlander! Unfortunately for fans, the studio's off-limits, so you'll have to make-do with rolling glens, medieval castles and grand stately homes instead.

Chapter 4

INSIDER STORIES

"IT LOOKED LIKE ALIENS HAD LANDED"

Mary McKay, owner of River Edge Lodges explains how her home became an Outlander set

In September 2017 I received a phone call from Beverley on the Outlander film locations team. She'd been scouting and thought our lodges may be suitable for the show. 'Had I heard of Outlander?' she asked. Had I heard of it? I'd only read ALL the books some years ago after my Dutch friends introduced me to Cross Stitch. I always thought, as I was reading the books, that the story would transfer perfectly to film... all those opportunities for atmospheric shots of the Scottish landscape and with a bit of history thrown in.

After various meetings with the film location team about 20 people turned up in sleek black vehicles, wearing black puffa jackets and black shades. It was like a scene from *Men in Black*. They spent ages looking inside and outside the lodges.

We were presented with a document several pages long of what the team wanted to do to the lodges. The attention to detail was impressive, including covering the kitchen units with period tiles and painting the walls, replacing curtains and blinds, covering up light switches, etc.

The hero lodge decked out in 1960s furniture

Two of the lodges were called the 'hero lodges'. One was used as the green room for the actors. The other was used for filming outside and then later, inside. Other lodges were used for some of the crew, catering, female changing and male changing.

Outlander took over the park for the month of November and into December. First came the Art Department, then the props company and 24-hour security to monitor everything and keep the set top-secret. The team got to work with painting the inside and outside of the lodges, taking our furniture out and putting their furniture in.

Tim, the locations manager lived pretty much on-site in one of the lodges, overseeing everything. My husband, John is a builder (carpenter by trade) and he was involved in fixing up lights and other jobs around the site. Again I was amazed at the attention to the tiniest detail, for example a certain type of outside light that was around in the 1960s was sourced and several of them brought in to dot around the park.

Filming begins

On the day of filming, a huge truck arrived, bearing the mammoth light that was to be used to illuminate the set. This was fixed to a 16-tonne scissor lift, and a large generator was rigged outside our office, far enough not to be heard when filming. Traffic lights were set up on either side of the bridge into our village so that the traffic could be stopped at intervals when shooting was taking place.

Things all started to hot-up as large numbers of other vehicles and film crew appeared. My daughter, Alannah was studying for exams and every so often she'd have to go out for a walk along the river to clear her head. I went with her sometimes. On this day, it was late afternoon starting to get dark and we wandered down our usual route by the river, which would take us past the hero lodges (oops!). There was a fair crowd gathered there who must've had a heads up about the filming (not from me!). We couldn't see much so we went under the bridge and up onto the road to see the traffic control working well (although people had no idea why the traffic was being stopped!). As we got up on top of the bridge looking down at the lodges we suddenly noticed the humongous scissor lift with a very bright light on top. It looked like aliens had landed. Many of the villagers were looking and pointing and wondering what the big light was all about. However, the best-kept secret in Bridge of Earn had worked as by the time people were aware that Outlander was filming, it was all over.

As Alannah and I wandered back home the security guy at the gates jumped out (again) and asked us who we were and what was our business there. We explained that we lived here and he reluctantly let us past. I thought he was going to ask for a strip search! We managed to get through the huddle of media folk and made it back home unscathed.

Watching the takes

Tim came up to the office for a chat. The crew were taking a break and he asked if I would like to come up and watch the filming when it re-started. Would I? Is the Pope Catholic? I grabbed Alannah from her neuroscience studies and Tim met us outside. He guided us amongst all the vehicles and wires and cables and crew. We all had to stop dead still after a signal from someone with a walkie-talkie. All traffic had stopped again and nobody moved a muscle until the signal to stand down again. Traffic moved and we were able to continue across the park towards the cameras.

It was a cold night and we were well wrapped up. We walked past some of the actors who were waiting to be called.

They were stamping their feet trying to keep warm. Alannah asked me who they were. I replied that they were probably extras. They waved and said hello and we continued following Tim until we were right behind the cameras. We mingled with the crew and Tim showed us which camera to look into to see exactly what was being filmed.

Then it was a call for silence again and the camera rolled. Who should come walking up to OUR lodge towards the cameras, but Roger and Bree! Not extras then. They were so close to us that I could easily have reached out and touched them. They chatted a bit, gazing into each others eyes and then... they kissed. Alannah and I turned to each other in a silent 'OH!' before turning our attention back to the filming. They did this several times over and it was filmed from different angles, before moving on to the next bit.

The scenes inside the lodge took place within a 'closed set'. The whole lodge had a huge tent over it to simulate night-time. There was a minimal crew and not so many vehicles and people milling around. Filming lasted all day, again taking shot after shot from different angles. Poor Sophie and Richard must have been shattered.

And then it was all over and it took another few weeks to restore the park and the lodges. And it all seemed to have been a dream. Except that I found a call sheet from the filming at Ballathie Woods [now Kinclaven Bluebell Woods], near Perth, where Fraser's Ridge is filmed.

"HOLY COW, DID THIS REALLY HAPPEN?"

Kimberly Shaw-Walker recalls the time Sam and Catriona turned up for filming at Arniston House

I grew up in Michigan and read the Outlander books back in '95. I was taking a flight from Alaska to Detroit and needed something to read. The girl in the bookstore recommended Outlander, so I gave it a go. I must admit, it took me four attempts to get past the first 38 pages. Finally, I forced myself and realised it was a real page-turner. I inhaled it after that! Little did I know that two decades later, I'd be going into work each day to watch Outlander being filmed on our doorstep!

The summer I started working at Arniston House, we had a visit from the Outlander location scout. We spent six hours showing him around. It wasn't a lot of time considering this is a 6,000-acre estate. We missed bits, of course, so took some drone footage to show him afterwards. The location scouts don't get to see the script, so their guess is as good as ours as to which scenes they're scouting out. They just work to a brief. We spent hours going through the books trying to guess which ones they might be!

We did know they were considering us for River Run, but by September, when we hadn't heard from them, we figured we didn't get it. But then, in late October, the production team got in touch querying some other outdoor scenes, which we later learned were Brianna on foot after coming through the stones, and Jamie trying to reach Murtagh. As it turned out, neither of these were filmed at Arniston, but instead we got season 4, episode 8, Wilmington!

The cast and production crew arrived in March 2018. It was by far the biggest crew we've ever seen, despite having had *Churchill* filmed here.

There was so much to do – it was kind of crazy. An incredible amount of work was required in the lead-up to filming. It took eight days to build the set for just three days of filming. When we found out it was to be a Jamie and Claire scene we were ecstatic. But the challenge was on – with such a high-profile scene, we had to keep a really tight lid on things.

I conferred with all the staff: 'I know where you live!' I said. 'If I see something on Facebook or a Twitter feed...'

Had word got out, they could have pulled the plug on us anytime. Even after filming we couldn't disclose our involvement – not until Sony had aired those scenes. Fortunately for us, Wilmington was on the trailer, so that was it – 'We're in!' Man, did we get flack afterwards for keeping it quiet!

Sam and Catriona were really nice, and we also met the actors who play Governor Tryon and his wife, and George and Martha Washington. They used two bedrooms and the lounge for the green rooms where the cast could relax between takes. The dining room was the prosthetics suite! Though Sam's green room was indoors, to be fair, he did go outside a lot. Every time I saw him, he was carrying a latte. The Outlander team have, hands-down, the best coffee vans I've ever come across!

The location manager was really helpful, and explained how we could make the property more attractive for filming. For example, we've since increased the size of the car park and expanded the plumbing.

When the crew left, they were like a tornado in a trailer park. It was unreal; it took less than an hour to pack up all the electrics – the cables, padding, etc – and break-down the draperies. The funny thing was, they'd had to kill the power to put the wax candles in for filming. On the last day, when they left, the house was pitch black. My colleague Henrietta and I just stood there and looked at each other, thinking: Holy cow, did this really happen?

Soon after appearing in Outlander, we took enquiries from new tour groups. I've met Diana Gabaldon a few times – she's great, and really enthusiastic – so I asked her to recommend a couple we could work with.

Henrietta and I oversee the film-group tours. We've got the Outlander call sheets – the schedule issued to cast and crew – and run a Q & A session. Sony let us use the clips where Arniston's featured, so we've strung them together and air them as part of the tour. We also took some video footage of our pre-filming set-up. Arniston is still a private house, and as it was only the ground floor used for filming, this is what we show people in the tour.

photo: Film Edinburgh

The grand hallway of Arniston House

"MANY OF THE ACTORS HAD NEVER EVEN RIDDEN A HORSE!"

Olivia Ancell looks at the funny side of when Outlander filmed at Preston Mill

Over 10 days in June 2014, 150 cast and crewmembers from Outlander set up camp at Preston Mill and Phantassie Doocot to film some of the first season's most pivotal scenes. But before the cameras could roll, several aspects of the mill had to be altered to make it fit the 18th century Lallybroch estate. All signs of 21st century life were removed – from modern fences and trees to signage and gates. Conversely, some 18th century implements were added, including a specially built animal pen. When Preston Mill was operational, it's said that the miller kept three pigs; the producers certainly did their research. For extra authenticity, a wooden cart was added and burlap sacks were piled high.

The crew then undertook a little horticultural work and kindly trimmed the nettles surrounding the mill pond so that the unclothed Jamie wouldn't get stung on his way in and out of the water!

As a final touch, set designers covered the interior of the mill with flour to make it appear like just another day-in-the-life at an authentic working mill. In reality, Preston Mill stopped its commercial activity back in 1959.

Undoubtedly one of the most demanding alterations involved artificially raising the water table on the mill race (pond) – from less than 20 inches to 5 feet – in order that it be deep enough for the heroic Jamie to plunge into. This task was skilfully achieved through a combination of man-made dams and controlled flooding. Luckily for actor Sam Heughan, the filming took place in June. However, as we Scots know all too well, it can't have been easy to act out a whole scene in what would have still been close to freezing water!

After a few labour-intensive days of set dressing, the mill was ready for its close-up... but not without an inevitable hitch seconds before the cameras started rolling. Once Jamie had jumped into the water, the director gave the command for the English Army to gallop onto the set for the episode's critical ambush scene. However, this posed a somewhat unforeseen problem – many of the actors had never even ridden a horse before! Needless to say, the filming was halted; a period of intensive riding lessons ensued for the Redcoats to get up to standard before filming could resume. Eventually, after much practice, a few of the Redcoats managed to approach the mill at a respectable 'trot'. Unbeknownst to the viewers at home, the horses' grooms were positioned just out of sight, ready to rush in and help many of the actors halt their horses when the camera wasn't looking!

They say "beauty is pain"... and well, for the sake of art and capturing this next shot, it would appear that all notions of health and safety were cast aside to shoot the brave young Jamie inside the workings of the mill, attempting to repair the damage using a hammer. For this shot, the cameraman was wedged into a tight space between the fanner and the gears, with his head just a few inches away from the moving parts of machinery! The situation could have potentially become disastrous, but thankfully the experienced crewmember held steady and emerged without a scratch, while the director was able to shout, 'that's a wrap'!

Flour faux pas

During the filming period, the property was closed to the general public, but with the production complete, Preston Mill's dedicated conservation team set about restoring the site

Work had to be done to transform Preston Mill into an 18th century mill

back to its original appearance. Wheel blades were replaced, the flooded mill pond was drained, and all gates, signs, and fences were carefully put back in place in preparation for everyday visitors and National Trust for Scotland (NTS) members to once more enjoy Preston Mill and Phantassie Doocot!

During the re-setting of the property, the NTS conservation team decided that the flour, which had been dusted around the interior of the mill, provided a nice addition. As such, they decided to leave the set designer's work alone. However, before long the flour turned black and mouldy, attracting some very unwelcome visitors – not Redcoats this time, but rats! The flour swiftly becoming cement-like in its consistency; luckily, the conservation team were able to expertly remove all traces of the flour without damaging any of the mill's original 17th-century materials.

In April 2015, the scenes filmed at Preston Mill appeared on screens across the world, and visitor numbers soared.

"JAMIE JUST WALKED UP AND DOWN!"

Rosie Ellison explains the Bakehouse Close conundrum

I run Film Edinburgh, the film office for Edinburgh, East Lothians and the Scottish Borders. We work with producers and location managers right from the beginning when they're casting their nets to find the ideal location for their next programme. Once they've decided to film here we'll make it happen for them. We work with local businesses and the council to get roads closed, take down street furniture, turn clocks to different times... whatever they need to make their vision a reality

We've got such a historic city centre that it's often only small things we change for period dramas – for example, we might

photo: Ali Wood

Edinburgh Museum (Jamie's print shop) as seen from the courtyard of Edinburgh World Heritage (the brothel) cover up the yellow parking bays, remove planters and the city bikes.

A lot of filming goes on in Edinburgh and we're happy for people to mill around and watch it – though we do close off particular streets so they don't wander onto the set. Takes are short, though, and people can move on again quickly. We don't want to stop them getting to their destination.

Outlander is a large creature! Nowadays they tend to film in enclosed areas, and visitor attractions at night when they're closed to the public. When they filmed S3 in Edinburgh we had vehicles parked at West Parliament Square for easy access to the Signet Library, which was used for the Jamaica ball. Bakehouse Close – which stands in for Carfax Close, where Jamie has his print shop – was also closed to the public.

The funny thing about the Edinburgh scenes is that other than the market – which was filmed on Tweedale Court –

photo: Ali Wood

Bakehouse Close (Carfax Close) as seen from the steps of Edinburgh Museum (Jamie's print shop)

they all take place in this tiny close. They didn't film on the Royal Mile at all; it's all Bakehouse Close. They built an arch at the back end, and when Jamie comes out of the brothel (actually Edinburgh World Heritage) he walks up and down, up and down, but actually the building used for the printers is right opposite!

It was great that Outlander filmed in Edinburgh – a lot of the actors are Scottish and live and work in the city, so you see them around from time to time. There are also many locations just outside of the city you can visit too such as Craigmillar Castle and Hopetoun House. Outlander seems to have filmed everywhere now!

"WHO IS THIS JAMIE FRASER?"

Author Ali Wood recalls the trip that sparked the idea for this book

It was whilst on a *T2 Trainspotting* tour of Edinburgh that I first heard of Outlander. I got talking to a publicist at Sony Starz: 'Outlander's going to be massive,' he told me. 'It's already got a huge following in the US.' His companions agreed. Rosie Ellison of Film Edinburgh had been involved with the production team, sourcing film locations, and Erin Hickey of VisitScotland was fielding press enquiries daily about the locations. Even the tour-guide, in between discussing the iconic Trainspotting chase scene, digressed to Sam Heughan's kilt.

'Who is this Jamie Fraser?' I wondered. 'Why is everyone talking about him?' I returned home, binge-watched Outlander seasons 1 and 2, and got straight back on the phone to Erin. 'I HAVE to come back to Scotland,' I told her. 'Tell me where all these stunning locations are!'

Two months later, with VisitScotland's A3 map in hand, I drove across Scotland with my husband and three young kids (aged 1, 3 and 6). We couldn't see every Outlander location, but we had a pretty good go. We played football in the grounds of medieval castles, cards in the tea-rooms, and coaxed tired legs across vast glens with pockets full of boiled sweets.

Since then, with the help of over 90 venues and volunteer staff, I've been updating my list of locations. Three seasons later (and after a few more visits to Scotland) this is the result.

Radio Times billed me as a 'Superfan' (I was flattered, but I bow down to those of you who really are) and I found myself live on BBC Radio Scotland, talking 'set-jetting' with host Kaye Adams. Telling Scottish people which Outlander sites to visit in their own country felt very bizarre!

Over the page is the story, first published in 2017, that gave me the idea for this book.

photo: Ali Wood

Edinburgh – beautiful in rain or shine (or both)

FOLLOW IN THE FOOTSTEPS OF OUTLANDER

The TV series might be for adults, but its Scottish locations make a great family holiday as Ali Wood discovers on a tour from Edinburgh to Inverness

I'm racing up a narrow spiral staircase. 'Give me five minutes,' I call over my shoulder. 'Sure,' says my husband, a question mark in his voice. He's baffled by my new interest in Scottish history – this is our fourth castle in half as many days – but he obliges and takes the kids to the gift shop. Breathlessly, I cross the turret to a quiet spot by the window. I smile, close my eyes and on my audioguide, key in 19. Again.

The minute Sam Heughan speaks, Doune Castle explodes into life. I no longer see the car park full of tour-buses, but a village of thatched croft houses and animal pens. The American and European accents converge into broad Scots, and I breathe in the smell of wood smoke.

'The front of the castle is where the Outlander team built an entire village,' says the actor who plays Jamie Fraser in the hit TV series. 'Canisters of smoke created some good old Scottish mist... but when Jamie and Claire rode through the village into the castle courtyard, they didn't need to make it 18th century. That ride up to the castle was absolutely magnificent.'

I open my eyes just a little, and imagine Jamie and Claire (played by Catriona Balfe) as they ride up the driveway to Castle Leoch, him in a kilt – her in a pale shift dress.

But just as Sam starts to speak Gaelic, I hear little footsteps on stone steps, and the discordant whine of 'I'm huuungry'. My secret liaison with Jamie is over, but it won't be the last Outlander fix I've planned for our family holiday in Scotland.

Rewind two days, and we're at the Bonnie Prince Charlie

photo: Ali Wood

Buy a wardrobe like Claire's in the Doune Castle gift shop!

exhibition at the National Museum in Edinburgh, a great place to start a tour. Whilst the kids explore the lifesize mammals suspended from the ceiling, I hum along to The Skye Boat Song, the title theme to Outlander, and read about the exiled prince who plays a central role in the series.

During his campaign the Bonnie Prince set up court for six weeks at the Palace of Holyroodhouse, the Queen's official residence in Scotland, which we visit afterwards. As my daughter's fast asleep in the buggy, we can't take the stairs. However, a staff-member kindly takes us up in the Queen's own lift. 'Prince Charles and William were here yesterday for the Edinburgh Tattoo,' she tells us. 'Kate and the children flew ahead to Balmoral.'

Whilst my six-year-old quizzes her about their helicopter, my three-year-old slips behind and presses the alarm button. A siren goes off. I've never seen anyone so fast on the walkie-talkie! 'Cancel that,' she says, then turns to us with a nervous laugh: 'This is the Queen's lift, remember! We might just have raised the British Army.'

After the palace, we wander back to our apartment via the cobbled streets of the Royal Mile, pausing at boutiques selling cable-knit sweaters and Harris Tweed. A souvenir shop blasts out a bagpipe rendition of Radio Gaga and whilst the kids disappear into a fudge shop I nip next door to jeweller Hamilton & Young to admire their new Outlander range of brooches, rings and necklaces. They even let me take a selfie with their cardboard cut-out of Jamie Fraser. Sadly, this is as close as I'm going to get to the show's hero.

After leaving the capital, we drive towards Hopetoun House, a lavish 17th century stately home near South Queensferry. The property is so big that parts of it had to be digitally removed for its appearance as the home of the Duke of

photo: Ali Wood

There's plenty to see at the vast Hopetoun House

Sandringham. Upstairs is a bedroom that appears in Jamie and Claire's Parisian apartment. The film crew used the same bed but changed the hangings. Downstairs is the drawing room where the duke receives Claire.

When the kids have finished exploring the house, I leave them at the Ranger's Room with the hands-on activities (a real bonus for families) whilst I peek at the cobbled lanes which stand in for the Parisian streets where Claire and Mary are attacked. Afterwards we head to the lawn outside the west facade. I'm sprinting after my son, who's about to pick the biggest mushroom I've ever seen, when a distant shot makes me jump. I'm not the only one; a startled deer bolts right in front of us towards the woods. This is where the duel was filmed between Jamie and the head of the McDonald clan, and I half-expect to see them emerge from behind the trees.

Later, when I mention the incident to the lady in the gift

photo: Ali Wood

The bedroom from James and Claire's Parisian apartment Hopetoun

photo: Ali Wood

Gloomy Midhope Castle — not at all like Lallybroch!

shop, she tells me they practise clay pigeon shooting nearby. She notices I'm holding an Outlander map and gives me directions to another location that's not actually on it: Lallybroch, or Midhope Castle to be precise. Though the building is derelict, it belongs to the estate and a £5 visitor fee applies.

By the time we arrive at the 15th century castle which doubles as the exterior of Jamie's family home, the kids are asleep. My husband stays in the car, and I walk along a nettle-fringed track to the house that two centuries ago housed 10 families of estate workers, including gamekeepers, foresters and carpenters.

The doorways are tacked with 'Danger keep out' signs, and the windows covered in Perspex. As I creep past they reflect the movement of the trees, and I feel like I'm being watched. I peer through the slats on a doorway, and can

photo: Ali Wood

The 'cave' where Jamie hides is just outside Midhope Castle

just about make out a pile of rubble and a gnarled tree stump growing through the floor. All that remains of the upper storeys are a few wooden joists. It's nothing like the jolly Fraser farm in Outlander full of tapestries and fruit bowls.

As I turn to leave a crow caws, the sky darkens and I feel a heavy drop of rain on the back of my neck. It's as though I've stumbled into an Alfred Hitchcock set, not Jamie's beloved home (which was actually created at the studios in Cumbernauld).

On returning to the car I'm cheered by the sight of six pheasants waddling past, only to learn from the car-park attendant they've been released from pens for the hunt that takes place tomorrow. Though what he tells me next makes me smile:

'Are you an Outlander fan?'

I shrug, unsure as to the correct answer.

photo: Ali Wood

The playground at Culross was a great hit with the kids

'You know, they filmed season 3 here.'

'Oh?'

'But I don't want to ruin it for you...'

'Ruin away', I say, after all I've just seen the real Lallybroch.

He leans forward, as though the pheasants might be bugged, and nods towards the woods.

'Over there, next to a stream, is a ledge where the film crew hung a black blanket. In the books, Jamie hides in a cave, but there aren't any caves for miles around so I reckon they made one right here.'

I take a closer look and can see how with the help of CGI the mossy ledge could easily be made to look like a cave.

'But that's just my theory,' he admits, adding that he hasn't actually seen Outlander nor read any of the books.

The kids sleep all the way to Stirling, which is where we base ourselves for the next couple of days. There are a dozen

Outlander locations around here, but we start with a visit to Bo'ness and Kinneil Railway, which was transformed into the wartime London station where Claire and Frank say their goodbyes. Unfortunately we miss the last steam train, but the kids spend a good hour exploring the museum, a lofty depot full of vintage trains that smell of old leather and diesel. The boys play on the Royal Mail train whilst I try to imagine the destinations behind the beautiful hand-painted signs.

The next day we travel further back in time to the Royal Burgh of Culross, where all the buildings date to the 18th century or earlier. In Outlander this stunning village doubles as Cranesmuir, where Geillis lives, and where the young lad has his ear nailed to a post. The 'nailer', I'm told on good authority, is actually one of the volunteers at Culross Palace. I mention this to the boys with the hope they'll be better behaved this time. At least there are no lifts.

Culross Palace is enchanting. It's easy to see why the Withdrawing Room was chosen for Geillis's parlour. The garden also makes an appearance as Claire's herb garden at Castle Leoch.

Very little in Culross was altered for filming, I learn from one of the guides (who sadly is not 'Brian the nailer'). The only thing that changed was the Mercat Cross area. Here, the buildings were painted a dull brown. I must look confused, so he explains that in the 18th Century the streets were open sewers. The kids explore the palace rooms with delight, stopping to dress up as lairds and make flowers in the craft room. Though they've never seen Outlander they're fast becoming its youngest fans. In fact, as I stand in the Kings room, which makes an appearance as one of Jamie and Claire's bedrooms, I make a mental note to add a pin to our Amazon account.

One of the few modern additions to the village of Culross

photo: Ali Wood

Yet another one of Jamie and Claire's bedrooms!

is the lovely children's park, which is where I deposit my husband and kids whilst I pop into the gallery to see the Outlander photography exhibition. On the way back I ask a man for directions to Geillis's house, without even thinking to explain who she is.

'Right there behind you,' he says from his garden.

I spin around to see that it's covered in scaffolding and undergoing restoration.

'That's where the nasty folk carried her away when she was accused of witchcraft,' he adds. 'In fact, it was quite funny because in one of the scenes they were trying to create mist. Just as they did so my neighbour was testing out his new chimneys and the entire lane was filled with thick smoke. The director was saying "Cut! Cut! I didn't ask for that much!"'

After Culross, my family plead for a day without castles, so we head for the picture-book hills and lochs of the Trossachs

Every street in Culross was a delight to explore!

where Roger Mackenzie takes Brianna for a spin. We take
the steamer across Loch Katrine, sipping hot chocolate
and listening to stories of Rob Roy and Sir Walter Scott,
then we stop at the Lodge Forest Visitor on the way back.
Unfortunately the kids are too young for the zipwire (one
of the longest in the country), but we do have plenty of fun
damning the stream on the Waterfall Trail.

In just under a week we've seen eight locations linked to
Outlander and Bonnie Prince Charlie, but the most important
– on both counts – is yet to come. Just outside Inverness is
Culloden, where the prince's campaign to restore the Stuarts
to the throne ended in tragedy.

The story is told in the visitor centre, which has a harrowing
video recreation, but a great cafe where we seek comfort
afterwards in the way of coffee and shortbread. Once
fortified, we step back out onto the moor where the start

positions of the armies are marked by blue (Jacobite) and red (Government) flags. I tag on to a tour group halfway through, at the point when the battle is lost and Bonnie Prince Charlie is escorted from the battlefield.

The guide waves her hand towards the road. 'Many of the men fled in that direction, but the Government army gave the order to "give no quarter", which meant the wounded were bayoneted and those fleeing shot by musket fire.'

We continue towards the memorial stones, where the hum of distant traffic mingles with American and Scandinavian accents. I've yet to hear a Scottish one.

'The battlefield was closed for three days to prevent anyone tending to the wounded,' the guide continues. 'Then the locals were invited to bury the dead, but by now they've been stripped and looted and no-one knows who they are.'

Everyone is silent.

As we reach the memorial stones, the sun pierces the dark sky, turning the grass a luminous green and casting a brief spotlight on the gravestones. There's 'Donald', 'Cameron' and 'Maclean'; some have cellophane wrappers full of wilting carnations; others are laid with sprigs of heather. Some stones simply say 'mixed clans'. Over by the monument is the Fraser one. I recognise it instantly as the spot where Claire weeps for Jamie, believing him to have died at Culloden.

Each of these graves contains up to 200 men, I hear the guide say, but the headstones were laid 135 years after the battle, so no-one knows who was actually buried where. There's a stone for the 'English', too, but there's a problem with that, she says.

'A third of the Government army were from Scotland. This was a civil war; to decide which king should be on the throne. It's a common misconception that it was a battle between the Scottish and the English but that's just not true.'

For a while after we leave Culloden I'm still mulling over what the guide said. I think back to evil Black Jack Randall and noble Jamie Fraser – the English Redcoat and the avenging Scots warrior – and I'm not sure Outlander has done much to quell that misconception. Still, one thing I can't accuse the show of is being dull. As we drive through the Highlands to Skye, past heather-cloaked mountains and pinewood forests, I'm grateful to the series that introduced us to this beautiful country. It's sparked a new family interest in castles, and left me (and countless fans all over the world) with a fondness for curly haired men in kilts!

photo: Ali Wood

Culloden Battlefield was a sobering experience

125

"THERE ARE SO MANY LOCATIONS THAT I LOVE"

Jenni Steele, Film and Creative Industries Manager for VisitScotland, talks about her Outlander experience

Working in cultural tourism in Scotland is a pretty exciting job. It creates so many opportunities for us to work with a range of sectors, including film and TV, literature, arts, crafts and music.

Developing partnerships between tourism and the creative industries not only provides inspiration for our visitors, but helps business growth in Scotland. In short, it's about telling the stories of Scotland through a range of outlets, giving our businesses the opportunity to capture the imagination of our customers – whether they are viewers, readers or visitors.

Film and TV tourism has been a steadily growing trend over the last few years, and we know that one in five people now come to Scotland as a result of having seen the locations in a film or on television programmes. One particular show has had a hugely positive impact on tourism in Scotland, and that's Outlander.

When it debuted in 2014 we knew it would be popular – with its storyline featuring our history and heritage and the many Scottish film locations – but the TV series and the books have created many more opportunities for tourism than we had first imagined. It's wonderful to see how fans have fallen in love with Scotland as well as the story and its characters.

By 2018, some attractions were seeing a considerable increase in visitor numbers – some as much as 120% on previous years. Fans want to visit the locations they see on-screen, but they also want more. They want to delve below the storyline – to discover our history, find out about the music, language, fashion and food and drink of the time. Some want to trace their ancestors and find their own connections to Scotland. It's an opportunity for people to really immerse themselves in the land that inspired Outlander.

Throughout the seasons the locations differ because the storyline moves between the Forties, the Sixties and the 1700s. You see a lot of castles in the first series, and in the second – when the plot moves to France – you see locations such as Drummond Castle Gardens, which doubles as the gardens of the Palace of Versailles. In S3 Edinburgh's old town features a lot, then in S4 and S5 you have the forests, rivers and scenic landscapes that double as North Carolina.

There are so many locations that I love from this series, and one of my favourites has to be Culross in Fife. It's so enchanting with its narrow streets and cobbled wynds. It's brilliant for filmmakers and visitors alike – you really feel you've gone back in time.

We hope you enjoy reading about all the fascinating locations, and discovering your own special places in Scotland which create fond memories and a place to come back to in years to come.

Happy travelling!

ABOUT THE AUTHOR

Ali Wood is a British magazine journalist. She lives in Dorset with her husband and three young children. Her work has appeared in a number of publications, including *Radio Times*, *Voyage*, *BBC Countryfile*, *BBC Wildlife* and *Country Life*. She's also a Features Editor on a leading yachting magazine. Find out more at *www.tvtraveller.co.uk*.